To Kim,

TWO DOWN

The Inconvenient Truth

SUZETTA PERKINS

Thank you for being the jewel that you are. I appreciate you. Blessings, Suzetta

TWO DOWN © 2017 by Suzetta Perkins

ISBN: 978-1548485108 (Print)

ACKNOWLEDGMENTS

To my Father above from whom all my blessings flow, thank You for wrapping me in your love. Without You, nothing is possible.

To my family, I appreciate the love and support you've shown me over the years, especially my son, Gerald (JR), who's been my rock in all of my endeavors—domestic and on the road. To my granddaughters Samayya and Maliah, keep making Grammy proud.

Book clubs continue to be my heart. So many of you have blessed me beyond measure. Words with Friends—Simone, Montina, Angela, Traci, Sonya, Letetia, Myra; you blessed me by reading all of my books in a nine month period and I never got tired of riding to Goldsboro with my road dawg, Mary Farmer. The discussions, the wonderful meals, the camaraderie, and the beautiful Pandora bracelet you presented me at the end of our tour was priceless. The Divas Read Retreat in Charleston headed by Jennifer Jennings was an amazing time. I met some wonderful people and new friends that weekend. To my girl, Deborah Miller, from Charlotte, you've blessed me time and time again, and I thank you. I'll never forget that you purchased a copy of *Hollywood Skye* for several members of your family and then invited me to the most luxurious afternoon of fun to discuss the book. And the added icing on the cake was being treated to the Charlotte Bobcats game. To Vedas Neal, who's a member of the Board of Trustees at Fayetteville State University, who threw me the most Hollywood style party on a Friday evening with a bounty of AKA friends and family to celebrate *Hollywood Skye,* I thank and celebrate you. I felt so special to be surrounded by a wonderful group of women and to discuss my book, as if the characters were in the room. And Vedas, you were *Hot, Hollywood Style!*

Black Pearls Book Club, I love you. Carmen, Althea, Jan, Tanya, Jamie, and Theresa--your love and support is what endears authors to you. The wonderful luncheon at Fitzgerald's Seafood in Raleigh with all the wonderful props that showcased my work humbled me. The discussion was vibrant and your wonderful gift made me smile. And to Thal Morris and the Girlfriends of the Carolinas, thank you for always thinking of me and providing access to your world of books. And to Sandy Keys in Arlington, Texas and the Cosmo ladies, thanks for making Hollywood Skye your monthly read.

There are so many other people who have contributed to my literary well-being. I can't name them all but I want to give a big shout out to Kim "Gotbooks" Knight, who blessed me with a signing at her wonderful store, Between the Lines Book Store in Baton Rouge, Louisiana. Kim is so giving of herself, and I appreciate her hospitality and for taking care of a sister. I'd also like to acknowledge my friend, Diane Rembert. We met for the first time in 2016 at the National Book Club Conference, however, it seemed that I knew her a lifetime. She'd always bought my books for her mother when I'd come to Columbia, S.C., and so it was wild when we met on a humbug in a room toasting another author. Thank you, Diane, for featuring me on your show, Diamond's Literary World.

To my sisters and brothers of New Visions Writers Group— Jacquie, Casandra, Sandy, Monique, Pam, and Titus—thank you for your consistent love, trust, and faith that we share amongst us. While I already had a dedication page, I want to also dedicate this book to our fallen sister-friend, Karen Brown, who we lost a few weeks ago, but was a literary guru in her own right, although she never got to publish her book. Rest in peace, my friend. You'll always be in my heart.

DEDICATION

To my dad, sister, brothers, son-in-law and countless other family members who served in the United States military, covering all branches of service. I, the country owe you a debt of gratitude, as you put yourselves on the line during the Korean conflict, Vietnam, the cold war, the Persian Gulf Wars that include Iraq. I feel safer because of you.

❦ I ❧

The flash was blinding, but no one took notice, especially the targets of the intended bootleg photo shoot. Stooping behind a well-trimmed bush that separated a parking lot from the hotel, she snapped photo after photo, but kept her position.

The rain came down in torrents and her tears along with it. This wasn't the first time nor would it be the last that Persenia Charleston would acquire evidence that her husband, Reginald, was cheating on her. He was a well-decorated Colonel in Uncle Sam's army with nineteen years of service, on target to become a Brigadier General in a matter of days. He maintained that he was going to be a career lifer—a synonym for thirty to forty years of military service or until the military had no more use for him. But if he wasn't careful, Persenia could bring his house of cards tumbling down any minute with one phone call. She didn't and wouldn't; it would have an adverse effect on her too.

Drenched and soaking wet from head to toe, with teeth grinding on top of each other, Persenia stood up and glared at the hotel where her husband and one of his female soldiers had entered. She held back the urge to run after them...to shout obscenities or hit one or both in the head with her umbrella that lay on the muddy ground. She was too sophisticated for that, so she willed her tears to cease; but they wouldn't. So, she retreated with her clothes stuck to her like glue, got in her car, and drove home.

Persenia peeled off her wet clothes in the large, pristine-white bathroom and left them lying in the middle of the tiled floor. Her body temperature was as cold as the Washington State weather and the tile she stood on, and she shivered, her mind wandering to the image of her husband with his mistress.

Washington State was a sometimes-dreary place with its constant rain, fog, and cold. Even though it was spring, it felt like it was the dead of winter. For those who loved to wear coats and boots, this was the place to be, since the natives wore them almost year-round.

Persenia gravitated to the weather and certainly loved her coats and boots. In fact, she needed a separate closet to house the thirty coats and ninety-nine pairs of boots she owned. Persenia pushed the picture in a file in a protective part of her brain and entered the shower.

Water cascaded down her face, washing away the sweat and elements of her rendezvous with justice. As much as she willed the images of Reggie and his whore to stay at bay, they kept coming, tempting her to get even and make the bastard pay. And then the fat angel in all of her glory, who resembled her mother, spread her wings of protection around her, offering peace and solace. And for a moment, Persenia let the hurtful memory go.

Retreating from the shower, she toweled off and sat her naked body in the vanity chair that faced the oriental mirror with its splashes of gold leaf tossed about the perimeter of its white frame. Persenia took a long look at herself in the mirror—her large, brown eyes with the half-inch thick black lashes nestled in her nut-brown, blemish-free skin. Her beauty and complexion belied her age—she was creeping up on another decade. She was still attractive and would look good on any man's arm, that's if she wanted to be someone else's ornament. But by any stretch of the imagination that wasn't even conceivable in her book of etiquette.

For a brief moment, Persenia thought about calling her one friend...her best friend, Carlitta Morgan, but then thought better of it.

They were buddies from the time they'd walked into Miss Pepper's class at Castlemont High School in Oakland, followed each other to U. C. Berkeley and became cheerleaders, to being each other's Maid of Honor at the other one's wedding.

On the low, Persenia was jealous of Carlitta; she and her husband were a team and they seem to love each other hard. Carlitta bore three children for her husband and had fun, often taking exotic trips to Cancun, France, the French Riviera, as well as the usual trips you take with kids that include Disney World. But Persenia's troubles weren't for Carlitta's ears. Time and time again, she's listened to the gossip girls as she called them on *The View*, who admonished naïve women who were going through bad episodes with their spouse or significant other to keep whatever was rumbling in their head off their tongue and out of the ears of their sister girlfriends.

Another minute passed and Persenia pulled her wet, shoulder-length hair behind her ears and continued to stare at the reflection in the mirror. A second or two later, she brushed her face with her hand and began to speak out loud, sounding like a well-rehearsed anti-aging ad made for television.

"You'll never be rid of me, Negro," Persenia said, pointing her finger at the mirror. "I'm going to be the recipient of everything Uncle Sam affords his soldiers and their families. If you think I'm going to suffer behind your infidelity and mental abuse, guess again. Well, that may be a lie; however, I'm not going to allow your freelance, booty-call service to destroy me. I choose to be happy. And when the time comes, and it will come, I'll have all the ammunition I need to make you see the error of your ways. And if you don't, I will strip you of every military stripe and medal you've ever earned."

❦ 2 ❦

IN THE BEGINNING

Almost eighteen years had passed since the Charlestons' said their vows and promised to love and cherish each other forever—until death they did part. It was 1997, and it had been a beautiful, sunny day for a wedding that took place at The Westin St. Francis San Francisco at Union Square. Three hundred friends and family attended the lavish affair.

The "Grand Dame," as the St. Francis had been dubbed, first opened its doors in 1904. After a forty-million-dollar transformation in 2009, it was still a prestigious landmark, close to all the upscale shopping, dining, Chinatown and the Theatre District.

Reggie Charleston graduated undergrad from U. C. Berkeley. He'd gone to Berkeley on a football scholarship and had hoped to make the pros; however, he was sidelined more than he played due to one minor injury after another. In his senior year, Reggie met Persenia Drake, who made the cheerleading squad in her sophomore year at Berkeley. Although Reggie wasn't the star on the U. C. Berkeley Bear's football team, his charm and good looks caught Persenia's attention. It didn't take long before they became a couple.

The newly formed duo was both from the Bay Area—Reggie from San Francisco and Persenia from Oakland. Being surrounded by family and friends and not having to go away during fall or spring breaks, they were attached at the hip night and day, that is until Reggie graduated, couldn't find a job, and announced that he was going into the military as an Army officer. Soon after, he headed to Officer Candidate School and from there he went to Fort Bragg, North Carolina. It wasn't too long afterwards that Reggie asked Persenia to be his wife.

Twelve blissful years they enjoyed, and even now Persenia wondered if some of those years were a lie, since the last six were pure hell. For eighteen years they remained childless, although they wanted them, however adoption wasn't an option that they would consider. And it was the underlying belief in their circle that Persenia's inability to have a child fractured their marriage.

Late nights were nothing new to Persenia. She understood that her husband was immersed in long talks—planning and strategizing about how they were going to defeat the enemy in the complex wars that stretched from Iraq to Afghanistan. There were times that he stumbled home smelling like stale cigarettes and booze, although he claimed he indulged in neither. But the distinct smell of a woman's scent lay on his body one too many times, and while Persenia may have been the last to know, it didn't take her weeks, months, years or a public scandal to clue her in on what was going on under her nose.

She confronted him; he denied it. She confronted him again; and he denied it yet again. Reggie didn't understand why Persenia didn't understand that the essence of his daily tasks placed him with men and women every day...and some in close proximity. However, the more Reggie denied that he was involved with other women, the keener Persenia's instincts became.

But she had more shopping to do in Europe or perhaps Dubai. She'd heard Reggie mention Dubai one too many times in the last couple of months. If he was making a trip there, Persenia planned to be on the same plane with him.

☙ 3 ❧

FAKING THE FUNK

He had an answer for everything. Persenia couldn't believe her ears when Reggie volunteered his whereabouts the night before like it was no big thing. They hadn't spoken a word to each other after he finally came home at three in the morning. And he was out of the house before she was able to bat an eye and get her morning going.

Entering the house at the end of a full work day, Reggie dumped his gear in the family room as he usually did and found Persenia on the deck, sitting on a patio chair reading an *Essence* magazine.

"Hey, babe," he said, walking up behind her, placing a kiss on top of Persenia's head.

It might have been nice if a bouquet of flowers had accompanied the kiss, but in truth Persenia would've rather had a new Michael Kors bag instead.

Persenia twisted her head to get a better look at her husband. Her face was vacant—no warmth or smile anywhere in sight. Her eyes roved over his six feet, five-inch body frame that was clad in green and brown camouflage army fatigues. His hair was peppered with specs of

6

silver—the silver becoming more dominate every day. Reggie's rich-chocolate good looks were relaxed and tension-free. And then she looked at his twisted smile and the lips that had serviced someone else other than herself less than twenty-four hours before.

"Hi," she said and cast her eyes back to the story she was reading.

"Wow that was an icy greeting." Reggie reached down and cupped Persenia's chin and turned her head in his direction. "You won't believe who I was with last night."

The last statement made Persenia take interest and ignore the magazine for a moment. She removed her chin from her husband's grasp and rolled her eyes for effect. "I haven't a clue."

Reggie sat in the seat across from Persenia. "The War Chiefs, as I call them, had a special called meeting last night, and I was given the task of escorting Major General Kaleah Neal to the meeting. I'm sure you remember her. She couldn't stop talking about the party you hosted several years ago; in fact, she asked about you.

"Anyway, she joined our task force meeting last night to talk about reduction in force and how it will impact the wars that are still raging in the Middle East. She was in town for something else that was classified."

Some of the ice around her heart thawed. Persenia wanted to be mad as hell after getting all drenched and muddied while trying to catch her husband in what she purported to be a liaison with one of his lecherous subordinates. But the question remained, why were they meeting at a hotel? She started to ask, but then realized she couldn't let Reggie know she was spying on him. "She's a good leader. You need a woman to keep you straight."

"I agree. I'd like to invite her over for dinner tomorrow night."

Persenia stared at Reggie. For some damn reason, he seemed too easy-going and carefree in his approach and announcement—like he was concocting a plan for a bigger adventure that she wasn't to be a part of. Or was it her insecurity talking trash to her? She let down her guard. "That will be nice. I'd love to see Kaleah again," she sneered.

Reggie leaned over and kissed her on her cheek. "I'm not sure why you become so suspicious whenever I talk about another woman."

"Who's acting suspicious?"

"Your body language is talking a mile-a-minute. Remember, I'm trained to detect the enemy, and I'm getting some terrible vibes from you."

"You're exaggerating, Reggie. Maybe, I am a little miffed about you coming home late without calling me."

"I called home several times, but you didn't answer. Kaleah is my job, Persenia, and you're the only woman who has my heart. Now go and put on some clothes; I'm going to take you out to dinner. You've been stuffed in this house all day. You really need to get a hobby."

"I have one, honey. It's called being the wife of an army officer."

❦ 4 ❧

DINNER AT SIX

When Persenia and Reggie arrived at Joint Base Lewis-McChord on this tour of duty, they were blessed to move into a brand, spanking new military house that was complete with all of the up-to-date stainless-steel appliances. Their ultra-modern furniture in colors of beige, persimmon, a touch of brown and yellows that Persenia was so fond of made the place look fabulous. The house boasted three bedrooms, one which Reggie used as a study. All of his many plaques and awards were plastered on the wall like a mini-military museum.

Wanting the evening to be special with little effort of her own, Persenia brought in a caterer to prepare dinner. Filet mignon and lobster tails were the entrees for the evening—only the best for her Colonel and the Major General. A scrumptious grapefruit salad, scalloped potatoes, baby carrots, and string beans seasoned with tarragon completed the main menu. For dessert, they would have a choice of key lime pie and pineapple-coconut cake, and for their liquid palate, a red or white wine or ice tea, if preferred, would be served.

Persenia looked at the large crystal, wall clock that adorned one of the walls in the foyer, with its twelve equal arms that looked like crystal starbursts jutting from its center, each representing one hour on the clock. Pleased that she still had ample time before her guest arrived, she retreated to her bedroom to get dressed.

A red-and-silver silk chemise hung on a pink, silk hanger. Persenia peeled the dress from the hanger and slid it over her body. It covered her like a smooth, satin glove, accentuating her curves on command. Persenia still had the body of a model and every inch of it rocked the dress. On her feet, she slipped on a silver pair of Louboutins with its red soles to complete the look.

Her silky, jet-black hair was blown dried and left to hang straight. Parted in the middle, Persenia's hair fell to her shoulders. She looked like a black goddess that couldn't be denied. If nothing else, Reggie would be looking in her direction all night, salivating and feasting on her beauty, while Major General Kaleah Neal would be left wondering why she was invited to dinner in the first place.

࿐

Reggie reached the house thirty minutes before dinner was to be served. He quickly ran to the bedroom and jumped into the shower, shaved, splashed on some after shave lotion, and then dressed in a pair of black slacks and a red Polo shirt. He hadn't seen Persenia yet, only announcing his arrival with a series of shouts before entering his room and taking a shower. But his lip dropped to the floor when he saw her as they both raced to the front door to open it.

The doorbell rang again, and Reggie reached out and turned the knob.

On the other side of the door was Major General Kaleah Neal, covered up by a heavy, wool coat to protect her from the nasty weather outside. The earlier part of the day gave hope that the evening would be equally gentle, but what Washingtonians could vouch for was that the weather in the Pacific Northwest was unpredictable and rain was almost always in the forecast.

Persenia smiled. Major General Neal wouldn't be getting all of her husband's attention tonight.

"Kaleah, come in," Reggie said, ushering her into the house. "And while you don't need any introduction, I'll give it anyway. This is my wife, Persenia."

Persenia smiled at Kaleah and shook her hand. "Welcome. Come in and make yourself at home."

"Thank you." Kaleah walked in and scanned her surroundings.

"Let me take your coat," Reggie said. Kaleah turned her back to him and Reggie slid the coat from around her. "You can never be unprepared for the weather."

Persenia's jaw dropped when Reggie peeled Kaleah's coat from her body. She was dressed in a winter-white pantsuit and a winter-white cashmere turtleneck sweater that captured her flawless complexion against her hazelnut-brown skin. Her breasts jutted out from underneath the jacket like the nose of a B-52 bomber, the sweater accentuating the curves. She wore a healthy gold cross on her chest that held several diamond stones. And on her feet, she wore a pair of three-inch, off-white calf-skin boots.

Persenia couldn't stop looking at the woman's chest and apparently neither could Reggie. In a moment of awkward silence, Reggie offered to get drinks for the ladies—a Pinot Gregio for Kaleah and Lambrusco for his wife. Returning with the wine, Reggie moved the group to the dining room with the table set with Persenia's best china and Waterford Crystal stemware. They took their seats—Reggie and Persenia sitting across from each other at the long end of the table and Kaleah taking a seat on the empty side. Quieting her fears, Persenia instructed the caterer to serve dinner.

Kaleah took control right away. "Colonel, I like the way you handled yourself last night."

Already, Persenia didn't like the tone of the conversation. She sat back without making a sound and listened for clues.

"Well, I wanted to be heard. I believe the others were satisfied with my strategy on how we're to move forward with this offensive. I agree that President Obama is in between a rock and a hard place on bringing our soldiers home; however, this is what we signed up for when we gave the oath to defend our country."

"You said it, Colonel. When we go before the Joint Chiefs of Staff next week, we'll be on one accord."

Reggie is going to Washington, D. C. next week and he's yet to say anything to me about it, Persenia thought. And she hated how casual Kaleah was with her husband, calling him Colonel instead of addressing him as Colonel Charleston, although she out-ranked Reggie. She sighed.

"Are we boring you, honey?" Reggie asked sarcastically.

"Military comes before home; I understand. Anyway, I'm used to it."

Kaleah smiled at Persenia for the first time that evening. "So, what are you doing these days, Persenia, besides keeping that handsome husband of yours in shape?"

Persenia gritted her teeth silently and managed a smile, although she noticed that Reggie had a wide grin on his face. "Besides being my wonderful husband's assistant, I'm forming a foundation for women and children who're abused."

Reggie's eyebrow arched, but he kept his mouth shut.

"You failed to mention this to me, Reggie. I'm always interested in supporting a well-deserved foundation, especially one that has been set up by dear friends and makes sense to me."

Dammit, she thought she was having this conversation with Kaleah. Persenia was seething again. How did everything always go back to Reggie?

"This is all Persenia's idea. I wasn't even aware that she was passionate about any...this cause."

"You didn't ask, dear."

With a nod of her head, Kaleah took a sip of wine. "It's a wonderful idea, Persenia. Is there any particular reason why you choose that platform?"

Persenia watched Kaleah carefully. How dare she question the reason for her platform? It was true that she'd come up with the idea in the last three seconds, hadn't written one thing on paper as to forming a foundation, let alone even to stop and consider the nuts and bolts of making one happen. Regardless, it wasn't Kaleah's business.

"It's a subject I've always been passionate about," Persenia heard herself say. "In my travels over the years, I've come across many military spouses who've been physically and emotionally abused at the hands of their husbands, even more so since the wars in Iraq and Afghanistan."

Kaleah sat her glass of wine down on the dining room table. She glanced in Reggie's direction but turned back to face Persenia. "I agree; it's become a big problem."

The wine certainly helped to soothe her inner nervousness. Feeling more confident and in control of the conversation, Persenia continued. "In my talks with lots of women, I find that they are seeking solace outside of the home..."

"In what way?"

"They're cheating on their spouses. They're looking for someone who isn't judgmental and cares what they think." Persenia thought she saw a nervous twitch on Reggie's face. "The war has taken a toll, and for those women or men whose military spouse is taking drugs for PTSD, they are enduring the abuse double time. There are already online counseling websites for women who have PTSD, but I'd like to do more...possible build a place of refuge.

"One of the spouses I spoke to just last week told me she caught her husband coming out of a hotel with another soldier. When the soldier looked up and saw his wife observing him, he confronted her, cursed her, and then beat her terribly when he arrived home, as if she was the one in the wrong. He was an arrogant bastard, and although his wife realized that the war had made him crazy, she didn't deserve the kind of treatment he was giving her. It's a damn shame. We have to find a way to help spouses, especially the women, protect themselves from this kind of abuse; we've got to find a way to bring an end to the war."

Both Reggie and Kaleah sat in silence. Persenia wasn't sure what to make of it, as she was caught up in her own fictionalized story. She was still struggling with the events on last evening, and now she was satisfied that she'd place a hint of what was eating her in their laps. There was no way for them to know why she was saying what she did, but if they were innocent, there was no need to worry.

Any pending conversation was held for later as the caterer entered the room.

"Filet mignon or lobster?"

"Umm," Kaleah said. "I'm famished. I'll have the lobster."

"So, will I," Reggie added, looking across at Persenia.

Persenia smiled at the caterer, a tall, medium built brother who wore a white chef's hat and a white apron bearing the name of his catering company. "I'll have the filet mignon."

"Any more wine, ladies?" Reggie asked.

"Yes, I'll have another glass of Pinot."

Persenia said nothing. She continued to watch Reggie and Kaleah, trying not to be so transparent in her feelings. She was disgusted at the way Kaleah kept looking at Reggie, as if they shared some secret. They were acting too familiar—like Reggie was Kaleah's husband instead of the other way around.

As the caterer placed the plates on the table, Persenia caught Kaleah off guard. "I'm surprised you haven't found someone permanent to share your life. It has to be hard with the rigorous schedule that you keep to date, but I'm sure you've come across what could be a suitable mate."

Kaleah rung her hands together and began to speak when Reggie cut her off.

"Persenia, that's a terrible question to ask. Her personal life is off limits."

Persenia stared at Reggie, who had begun to pull meat from the lobster tail. "It was a simple question, Reggie. I can't talk about military strategies, as that's not my life. I was only being conversational."

Taking another sip of her wine, Kaleah waved her hand. "It was a simple question, which I'll answer." Kaleah looked at Persenia. "Yes, I've met someone who I'd like to be with, but as you alluded, our schedules are such that it doesn't leave much time to date. In fact, he lives in another state and our present dating habits tend to be quick phone calls when we get a chance. But I do hope to settle down one day...and maybe have a child, if it isn't too late."

Persenia looked away. She cut into her steak without saying anything in return. And then she heard Reggie offer his two cents when no one had asked for it.

"We've tried to conceive, but we haven't been fortunate to get pregnant."

"I'm sorry," Kaleah said, butter knife in her hand. "If I wasn't so career oriented, I'd probably have two or three. But it would be selfish to have a child suffer because I couldn't be with them all the time, given my schedule."

"We've discussed adopting, but Persenia has always been adamant about being the one to birth any children we brought into the world. We've given up on the idea of having children now."

The nerve of Reggie to share their shortcomings with this woman Persenia considered a stranger. If her life was personal, so was theirs. She was tired of Reggie and his self-serving ways. Maybe she'd have to get a side piece—someone who was going to make her happy.

$$ \text{❦} \quad 5 \quad \text{❦} $$

EVERYBODY HAS SECRETS

Persenia flipped through the pictures on her digital camera that she took last week, analyzing each shot like a forensic scientist. She wasn't ready to give a verdict as to whether Reggie was or wasn't screwing Major General Kaleah Neal behind her back—at least not yet. She wouldn't put it past Reggie, though, to engage in such unscrupulous behavior, even with someone who out-ranked him. He'd used his rank and persuasive nature many times before on other women, although they didn't need any prodding. The evidence always came back—a pair of panties in a suitcase, photos that he thought he'd hidden away from her prying eyes, and the mere scent of a woman on his body after a long night out that was disguised as a business meeting. It wasn't her imagination; she knew the deal and heard the rumors like everyone else. Persenia was well aware that the women in her wives' club had called her a ton of fools under their breaths, but truth be told, many of them were subject to the same ridicule.

She shut the camera off and placed it in her lingerie drawer. The pictures weren't suggestive other than the fact that Reggie and Kaleah entered the hotel together. Regardless of what they claimed to have been doing on that evening, she'd let the sleeping dog lie—for now. Sooner or later what happened in the dark would come to the light.

On Friday, Reggie was on a plane...on his way to D. C. to meet with the Joint Chiefs to discuss troop drawdown and the growing crisis with the Islamic State of Iraq and Syria better known as ISIS. And, of course, Kaleah would be there. For sure, they would all share a lunch and perhaps a couple of dinner meals together. However, the questions remained in Persenia's head. How would Reggie spend the hours beyond dinner and with whom? Trust was a bitch.

"Later for this," Persenia said out loud. She grabbed a jacket and headed outside. Waving to her neighbor next door, she quickly opened the door to her black BMW X-3 Sports Wagon and drove off.

Persenia jumped on Interstate 5 and headed north to Seattle to see an old friend from high school. Kimiko Avery was Carlitta's cousin, and although Persenia and Carlitta were thick as thieves, they often included Kimiko in on their escapades.

The drive was pleasant. Mount Rainer stood statuesque far off in the distance snow still visible on its cap. It was an imposing figure but had such a calming effect, especially on a half decent looking day. She turned on the radio and began to smile as Pharrell Williams was banging out his song *Happy*.

Happy was the operative word, but Persenia wasn't sure why she was happy. Maybe it was that Reggie's three-day stint in Washington, D. C. gave her alone time to do and be what she wanted to be. When Reggie was away—out-of-sight, out-of-mind—she didn't care what he was doing until the rumors began to float. Whatever the reason, Persenia felt happy, and she sang right along with Pharrell, her voice louder as the song progressed.

She'd finally arrived in Seattle and was happy to see the metropolitan city laid out before her. Seattle was home to the Space Needle, the remaining physical evidence of the Seattle World's Fair that was held in the state of Washington in 1962. It was also home to the largest airplane and space missile system company—*Boeing*—and the largest employer of Seattle's King County and surrounding communities.

Persenia left the interstate and headed south. She navigated her way like an old pro and was pleased when she rolled onto Kimiko's driveway. The house was small—a yellow stucco number, with a one-car garage and a chain-link fence surrounding the perimeter. Grabbing her purse, Persenia jumped out of her car and proceeded to Kimiko's front door.

Before she had barely stepped onto the porch, the door opened. Kimiko was on the other side welcoming her with a smile and an air kiss. Persenia reciprocated with a hug and received a much needed one in return.

"Girl, you look good, with that curly afro all over the place. And you haven't gained an ounce since I last saw you."

"Persenia, I accept all of your compliments. It's a lot of hard work for a girl to keep this fab body, especially since I'm a few years from hitting the forty mark."

"I hear you, Kimiko. You, Carlitta, and I will be celebrating the big four-o."

"Come on in and have a seat. I have a surprise for you."

A surprised look crossed Persenia's face. "A surprise? What kind of surprise?"

"Hold your horses. You'll see in a minute."

Contrary to how the outside of the house looked, Kimiko had the house hooked up. Her taste in clothes, art, and household décor was off the charts. Everything was done in white this and white that and it was pretty evident that there weren't any children in the vicinity. Her mother, who was Japanese, had a flare for the arts and her Afro-American father, who was also Carlitta's mother's brother, was an accomplished guitarist and played a lot of the clubs in San Francisco back in the day, especially in the Fillmore District.

Persenia followed Kimiko down a long hallway with one of Charles Bibb's paintings adorning the wall. At the end of the hallway, light flooded the area. Turing right, there were three or four steps that led down into a more open, spacious room—a family room—and Persenia stopped in her tracks when she saw Jacoby Morgan, Carlitta's husband, sitting there.

Jacoby got up from his seat and went to where Persenia was standing. He hugged and squeezed her tight, before finally placing a light kiss on her cheek.

As if in shock, Persenia hit her chest lightly with her hand. She cocked her head a little to the left for affect. "So, what are you doing here? How are Carlitta and the kids?"

"They're doing fine. Carlitta decided to go back to school and get her Master's. We live in Santa Clara."

"So, you're a Silicon Valley kid now."

"Yeah, I'm still in software and making that long change. What I love the most about where I live is that it's close to Levi Stadium, the new home of the San Francisco '49ers."

"I guess you're in seventh heaven; poor Carlitta."

"She and I are season ticket holders. You did hear the "s" at the end of the word holders. Carlitta loves football as much as I do. Remember, you were both cheerleaders at Berkeley rooting for me and Reggie."

"Bragging as usual; I'm not mad. Good, long money will get you just about anything."

Kimiko laughed.

"So how is Reggie?" Jacoby asked.

"He's fine. Now what are you doing in Seattle?" Persenia pressed, changing the subject.

"I'm in Seattle on business, and while trying to save a dollar, Kimiko let me stay with her. There's nothing like having family located in strategic places."

"With all of the money you make, mister, and by your own confession, you're being cheap!"

Everyone fell out laughing. "You're cheap," Persenia repeated. "Kimiko, make sure he pays you for his hotel stay."

Kimiko continued laughing. "Would you like something to drink, Persenia?"

"Why don't I take you ladies out to lunch? One of my homeboys, Remy Westbrook, who used to play for the Seattle Seahawks, is also in town. Actually, he lives on one of the islands not far from Seattle. Let me call and see if he's available to join us."

"Is that okay with you, Persenia?" Kimiko asked.

"Well, I was hoping that we would have some girl time—do a little shopping and whatever else, but I guess that'll be okay."

"I won't tell Reggie if you don't," Jacoby said.

Persenia stared at Jacoby. "What is that supposed to mean?"

"Nothing, Persenia. Girl, you're too serious. I was only messing with you."

"Well, I hope not. I get that you're taking us to lunch and you're inviting a friend. I'll call Reggie and tell him that's what I'm doing. I have nothing to hide. Do you?"

"Let's go," Kimiko said, without allowing Jacoby an opportunity to answer the question. "You've got my girl all riled up about nothing. I want to have a few drinks, eat, relax, and talk."

"But…"

"Don't make me change my mind, Jacoby. I can have as much fun shopping with Persenia."

"Look, ladies, I'm sorry. I got out of my lane for no reason. Persenia only has eyes for Reggie and I was trying to insinuate that if she was in the presence of another man, she might be uncomfortable."

Persenia looked from Jacoby to Kimiko. What was really going on that had Jacoby saying stupid things? He wasn't making any kind of sense to her. Only someone who was trying to hide something would give themselves away by acting stupid. "I'm ready."

Jacoby and Persenia went out of the front door while Kimiko went into the garage from inside the house to pull out her car. Jacoby had flown in and had yet to get a rental. How was he going to get back and forth to the place he was doing business? Red flag for sure.

The garage door inched up and Kimiko backed the car out. To Persenia's surprise, Kimiko was sporting a silver, 2-door, 2013 Jaguar XF. It seemed that everyone was doing well for themselves. Jacoby rushed to and held the front passenger door open for Persenia, and when she was settled, he jumped into the back seat.

For a moment, all was quiet as Kimiko navigated from her home toward West Seattle. After about fifteen minutes of silence, Kimiko and Jacoby began to chatter about people they knew from home. Persenia pretended to listen while scanning Facebook messages on her phone. She had yet to hear from Reggie. She was sure he made it to

D.C. and that she would've heard something by now. Maybe he was already tied up in a meeting. In any event, he was an inconsiderate bastard and Persenia wasn't going to waste time worrying about him.

"Remy is going to meet us at Jak's Grill," Persenia heard Jacoby say. "His text says that he'll be there in fifteen minutes."

"I love their porterhouse steak," Kimiko said, making a quick right. "It's been voted the best steakhouse in Seattle two years in a row."

"I'm ready to grub with you two beautiful ladies."

Persenia still had yet to say anything.

Twenty-five minutes later they pulled up at Jak's grill. Standing out front was a muscular, cocoa-brown brother, with short, curly black hair. He stood about six feet and had to weigh at least a good two-hundred and seventy-five pounds. Persenia licked her lips.

"There's Remy," Jacoby hollered from the back seat.

☙ 6 ❧

SEATTLE BREEZE

K imiko parked the car and the three tumbled out. Jacoby led
the charge, anxious to meet up with Remy. It had been a
number of years since they last saw each other, and it was
quite evident when they came face to face.

"Remy, my man," Jacoby said with enthusiasm, elated upon seeing
his friend. They bumped chests and gave each other the brotherly
hand sign while the ladies stood back and watched.

"Jacoby, the wide receiver," Remy finally said after all of the formal-
ities and rituals of meeting up were performed. "Brother, you look
good." And then he whispered out of earshot of the ladies. "And who
are those fine specimens you rolling with?"

Jacoby leaned over and whispered in Remy's ear. "The lady with the
curly 'fro is Carlitta's cousin and the other chick is her friend. She's
married to a guy in the military, who also happens to be one of my best
friends."

"Damn, they both are fine, but I was especially looking at the
chocolate sister with the shoulder-length hair. I'd love to have her for
dessert."

Jacoby chuckled and called the ladies over. Reluctantly, Persenia followed Kimiko to where the men stood.

"Ladies, this is my homeboy, Remy Westbrook. We grew up in San Francisco's Mission District, did the whole school thing—from kindergarten through high school—but he left me after that and headed to UCLA to play football. And Remy, this is Kimiko Avery, Carlitta's cousin," and pointing, "this is Persenia Charleston."

"Nice to meet you." Remy stared at Persenia much longer than he did Kimiko.

Introductions complete, the group went inside and were seated. The conversation began at a slow pace, although after a minute or two, Jacoby picked it up and ran with it. The ladies were bored, as the entire conversation was about football.

Thankful for small diversions, Persenia smiled at the waitress, who came to take their drink orders. "I'll have water with lemon."

Everyone looked in her direction.

"No libations?" Jacoby asked Persenia, glancing sideways at his homeboy.

"No, I'm a responsible driver, and I will be getting on the road when we finish lunch."

"There's no reason to rush off, is there?"

"No more than I need to get home to take care of some business later."

"Oh, I'm sorry for prying. I figured since we have a party of four and we're out having fun that we turn this afternoon into an evening out."

Persenia looked at Jacoby. He certainly wasn't acting like a married man. She understood having some freedom, but he seemed too carefree for her.

Persenia raised up her hands in surrender, although she had no thoughts of being caught up for the night with her best friend's husband. Even Kimiko acted nonchalant about the whole thing. "While I thank you for the offer, I'm going to eat lunch and bid you people farewell."

There was silence after the waitress took the drink orders and sauntered off. Jacoby flashed a look at Remy and he raised his eyebrows. Whatever the signals meant, Persenia wasn't thinking about them. Just then, her cell phone rang.

"Excuse me; I need to take this call."

Persenia hit the TALK button, left the table, and went to the lobby. "Hi, babe."

"Hey, babe, I made it to D. C. last night...checked in at the Gaylord at the National Harbor. When I arrived yesterday, I had to go straight to a meeting. I was exhausted when I finally got to the hotel and fell asleep on the bed. We're on a fifteen-minute break."

"Glad you called. How is Kaleah doing?"

"I haven't spoken to her yet; she wasn't present at yesterday's meeting. I'll give her your regards."

"Please do that."

"Well, I've got to run. I wanted to let you know that all was well... no plane mishaps or lost baggage. I hope you aren't having too much fun without me."

"Reggie, please. You're never here; the little time we are together, you're talking politics and military tactics."

"That's not fair, Persenia. It's all been for us. Now, I've got to run. Love you."

"Love you, too," Persenia said with little feeling. And the line was dead.

⚜

THE CONVERSATION SEEMED LIVELY WHEN PERSENIA RETURNED TO the table. "You all are having too much fun." She noticed how extra friendly Jacoby was with Kimiko. Again, it was probably her imagination running wild. Conversations with Reggie did that to her. He really didn't give a damn how she was feeling or what she was doing.

"So where are you all going to hang out this evening," Persenia heard herself say.

"We're going to a club downtown," Remy responded, staring Persenia down. "Did you have a change of heart?"

"Change of heart? No, but I might have changed my mind about running home so soon." Persenia saw Jacoby and Remy share glances.

"We'd love to have you." A faint smiled crossed Remy's face.

"And I can't hold these two brothers down by myself," Kimiko added. "I need my girl with me."

"Well, said like that, I might go for a little while. But I do have to go back to Tacoma tonight; so, I won't be staying long."

Jacoby pounded his fist in his hand. "Sounds like a party to me. I'm ready to eat and get my drink on. Persenia, you are now the designated driver."

"I got you until I'm ready to leave. What you do after that is on you."

"We'll get a cab," Kimiko said, slurping down the last of her Tequila.

The waitress came back and took their food orders and another round of drinks. Even Persenia loosened up and joined in the spirit of things.

"You're beautiful," Remy said into her ear.

Persenia sat up straight and turned slightly toward him. "Thank you." She took a sip of water. Persenia felt his eyes burning a hole through her soul. No matter how ratchet Reggie was in their marriage, he was still her husband and she was going to honor her vows.

More drinks came followed by dinner. Everyone was in a jovial mood. They ate and drank, although, Persenia was the only one with water.

And then it hit Persenia in the head like a coconut falling from a tree. Jacoby and Kimiko were sharing more than a room for a few nights; they were kissing cousins. All the touching, feeling, and pretending that they were drunk didn't fool a soul, and when Jacoby suggested that she and Remy go off on their own, it didn't take a rocket scientist to figure it out.

She was mad as hell. How could Jacoby and Kimiko betray Carlitta? Carlitta was family down to the cuticles on her nails. She loved Jacoby and their kids and had given up all that learning and a degree in nursing to nurse Jacoby's career. With all of the lying and deceit swirling about her, Jacoby was probably lying about Carlitta going back to school. Persenia would've been better off staying home, although she'd probably would've spent the whole day wondering who Reggie was with.

Biting her tongue, she followed Remy out of the restaurant. Jacoby and Kimiko had yet to come out, but when Persenia left the table, not one goodbye did she utter. She and Remy stood for another five minutes when he finally said that he'd get the car.

Just as they began to pull away from in front of the restaurant, Jacoby and Kimiko surfaced. Persenia turned her head and looked straight ahead.

"You still feel like going to the club?" Remy asked. "It's awfully early."

"No, I'd like to ride around Seattle for a while, if you don't mind."

"They have a monorail that goes downtown. We can catch it and go to some of the shops in the area. There's also the Space Needle if you want to venture there."

Persenia liked that Remy was not only cool, but he was a gentleman with class. He seemed to have a good head on his shoulders. "The monorail sounds like fun. Let's do that."

Remy smiled. "Your wish is my command."

7

SEATTLE

The day was turning out to be better than Persenia expected. She didn't need Kimiko around to have a good time, and she was rather enjoying Remy's presence. That made her no better than Kimiko or Jacoby, but she hadn't done anything except spend some time with a man who wasn't her husband. Ummm.

Persenia began to think about all of Reggie's whoremongering, at least those affairs she was aware of, and began to have second thoughts about what she was doing. As they reached the Pike Place Market, Persenia shoved her negative thoughts to the back of her head. People were buying fish and the fish merchants were throwing them to the customers to catch. This was exciting. A crowd was gathered around, chilling out and enjoying the goings-on.

Before Persenia realized what she was doing, she threaded her arm through Remy's and held on tight. All the things she thought she was going to do with Kimiko, she was enjoying them with the company of a man. She even found a nice pair of black leather boots that Remy insisted on paying for.

"No strings attached," Remy said.

"No, I'm going to pay for my own boots."

"My treat; end of conversation."

Persenia blushed and conceded.

"I'm going to take you to one of my favorite watering holes, and then I'd like to take you back to my place for some conversation. I'm sure that you've guessed by now that whatever you thought about your best friend's husband has turned out to be a lie. I hadn't met Kimiko until today, but I was well aware that Jacoby was having an affair with her. This isn't the first time he's been to Seattle."

Persenia wasn't sure she wanted to comment, especially since her being with Remy left her little room to judge. But she was intrigued as to why Remy would share that with her. "So why tell me? You sold your brother out faster than I could say... I wasn't born yesterday. The clues have been there all day, and Kimiko was unusually quiet. Usually we're in high gear, but she was being extremely careful around me. I wouldn't have the heart to tell Carlitta, but she'll find out and throw both of their asses out on the street."

"And what about you?"

"What about me?"

"Jacoby told me you were married."

"And you want to know why I'm here with you."

"Precisely."

"If you were made aware that I was married, why did you suggest taking me out? Buying boots for me—since you're judging?"

"I'm not judging; I only wanted to understand the person behind Persenia since you feel a certain way about Jacoby cheating on his wife."

"It's not only that, but he's having an affair with his wife's cousin. The whole thing is wrong as two left shoes—out-of-order. Although Kimiko and Carlitta are cousins, they are as close as sisters. Kimiko has not only betrayed their trust, she has severed their friendship, although she doesn't know it yet."

"Enough about them; what is your position before we proceed?"

Persenia looked long and hard at Remy. She shook her head. "This isn't a good look for me either."

"Again, why are we here?"

"All right, Remy, you are much an enabler as I'm in the wrong. However, to answer your question, I...I was looking for validation and you may have possibly given it to me. My husband has been unfaithful for a long time. It was him that called while we were at the table."

"I thought it might be your husband. You seemed guarded."

"He holds a high position in the Army. He has so much at his disposal, including female subordinates as well as those who are his equal. Reggie, that's his name, can get whatever he wants. He says he loves me, but he really doesn't give a cotton-pickin' damn about me— only when he's home and tired from all of his whoring that he gives me a sideways glance."

"Something is wrong with that guy. I can't understand a man who needs to run off and be with someone else when they've been blessed with a woman like you. From the short time that I've been pleased to be in your company, I find that you have intellect, charm and beauty."

"It's the thrill of the hunt for Reggie. He uses and abuses women like Tina Marie used to sing about."

"How do you know? On second thought, the question should be... why are you still with him?"

Persenia was closed mouth for a moment. She couldn't believe that Remy was so perceptive, analyzing everything she put before him. "To answer your first question, I have proof of some of Reggie's doings; I won't go into the details. Truth is I love my husband. We vowed to be together until the end. Even sitting here in your car at this moment feels like I've broken my wedding vows."

"Why do you feel that way?"

"Jeez, you ask a lot of questions."

"An inquiring mind wants to know."

Persenia laughed then sighed heavily. "Look two wrongs don't make a right. I have to admit that being with you made me feel like someone cared—the validation. Sure, I'm using you as a scapegoat, but the moment presented itself, and I went for it."

Remy touched Persenia on the arm. "I'm glad you were honest with me. Instead of going to my favorite spot, I'll take you to get your car. I respect your feelings and wouldn't want to be the brother who'd take advantage of you. I've enjoyed our brief time together..."

"Remy, stop."

Remy turned the ignition on in the car. "What's up?"

"I don't want to go to my car; I'm not ready to go home. Why don't we go to your place and continue our conversation? I'm enjoying your company."

There was a moment hesitation and then dead silence. The car idled as Remy seemed to collect his thoughts. "Are you sure you want to do this in light of everything you said? I'd love to continue the conversation, but I can't promise you that I won't try and steal a kiss or two. Consider yourself forewarned."

"I'll take my chances." Persenia buckled her seatbelt and turned in her seat and looked forward.

They drove along talking about everything from sports to politics. Persenia relaxed and enjoyed the view, verbalizing how beautiful Washington State was with all of its evergreen trees and bodies of water. They'd been driving for some time, when Remy headed for the harbor, which placed a puzzled look on Persenia's face.

"I'm confused. I thought we were going to your house. We are in Fauntleroy?"

"We're taking the ferry to get there. I live on Vashon Island."

Persenia sat up straight in her seat. A ferry ride and no telling how far away from the heart of Seattle she would be. As much as she was enjoying Remy's company, getting on a ferry and floating miles away from the mainland was like having one foot on a banana peel. She could slip and fall down and not be able to get to safety that easily.

When Persenia didn't respond, Remy pulled over to the side and stopped the car. "Are you having second thoughts about going to my home?"

"It's not that, Remy. This may not make sense, but I feel safer being on this side of Vashon Island. What if we get stranded? What if something happens to the ferry and I can't get back to Seattle to pick up my car? Furthermore, why do you live there?"

"There's nothing to fear. I enjoy the peacefulness of this place; I'm more of a loner than I advertise. The ferry has yet to let me down, and I think you're going to enjoy the experience." Remy smiled and tickled Persenia under her chin.

What little sun they had was fading fast. Persenia sat with her arms folded, contemplating what she should do. Thoughts of Reggie crossed her mind but were quickly dismissed. "Okay," she finally said, "as long as I can get back at a decent hour. I still have to pick up my car and drive an hour to Tacoma."

A frown formed on Remy's face. "I've got to be honest with you. There isn't a ferry after seven."

"That means I will be stranded there until tomorrow and I didn't plan to stay overnight."

Remy started up the car. "Let's go back."

Persenia closed her eyes and sighed. Opening them she turned to Remy. "I'll probably regret this in the morning; I'll go. I'm not sure why I should trust you since you weren't forthcoming about the ferry, but maybe I'd just like to see what Vashon Island has to offer."

Remy smiled, put the car in gear and headed for the ferry terminal.

❦ 8 ❦

WASHINGTON, D. C.

T he day's affairs went quite well, in fact, too well in Col. Reginald Charleston's estimation. His meeting with the Joint Chiefs went beyond expectation, as they seemed to be locked into a solid plan to take care of ISIS. But the good news was that as soon as he returned to Washington State, he would be promoted to Brigadier General with orders to report to the Pentagon. For as long as Reggie was in the Army, at least a one star was his goal.

He took a taxi from the Pentagon to his hotel. The Gaylord National Resort and Convention Center sat high, overlooking the National Harbor. The four-star hotel with its luxury rooms and too numerous amenities to mention was the first-choice for many top-notched events held in D. C. and the surrounding Maryland area.

Waterfront Street and the hotel came into view. The taxi pulled to the front of the hotel and let Reggie out. He was a handsome specimen of a man, even in his Army camouflage uniform and combat boots. There were the usual stares from admiring females, but Reggie kept on walking.

He entered his room and straightway abandoned his military clothing. The coolness of the room made him shiver. Not wasting another minute, Reggie went into the bathroom, stared at himself in the mirror and pounded his chest. For a man who was about to lean on forty-two, his body was still in relatively good shape.

Reggie showered, shaved and threw on his favorite after-shave cologne. Steam filled the bathroom and he took a towel and wiped the condensation from the mirror. Now able to view himself, he pulled a comb through his salt-and-pepper hair, which was cut short and tapered around the ears, essential for serving in the military.

He heaved a sigh of relief, left the bathroom, and headed for the closet to retrieve his attire for the evening. He pulled out a pair of black slacks, a black shirt, and a sky-blue blazer and laid them on the bed.

For a moment, his mind seemed to wander. He went to the nightstand where he dropped his cell phone and picked it up. He cruised through several applications, as if looking for something specific, and after a couple of minutes, he laid the phone back down and got dressed.

Pleased at how he looked, Reggie picked up the phone again. He touched the phone icon and after a second or two, made a selection with his stylus. He hit the speaker button and waited. After the second ring, he heard her voice.

"Hey, soon to be Brigadier General."

"How about that?"

"I say well deserved."

"Well, I thank you, Major General Kaleah Neal." They laughed. "Look, instead of you coming into D. C., why don't I meet you on your turf?"

"I was hoping to take you to some quaint restaurant where we wouldn't be noticed and could enjoy ourselves without having to look over our shoulders."

"You can also be too careful. But if it's your desire to show me a good time, I'm ready."

"Your words have been taken under advisement, however; I'm looking forward to receiving my one star next week. I don't have to remind you that General Petraeus thought he was going to get away with his misdeed."

"He almost did. When no one is thinking about you and you think you've got it made in the shade is when people get careless, Reggie. We won't let that happen, although I did admit to your wife that I was in love with someone I was having a long-distance affair."

"Certainly, you weren't talking about me." They both laughed. "Persenia fell for the line I gave her about meeting with the Joint Chiefs last week. She has no clue that the likelihood of the Joint Chiefs meeting at Joint Base Lewis-McCord was nil to none."

"Women are intuitive. Don't for one moment underestimate that wife of yours. Women have a sixth sense about them, and I wouldn't put it past Persenia to be plotting her own game plan. I caught the lie about the foundation. Something is smoldering underneath her exterior. We do need to be extra careful where she is concerned."

"As much as I hate to say it, you're right again. Right now, I don't want to talk about Persenia. I want to have a nice dinner with the real woman in my life and then bring her back to this fabulous hotel I'm staying at and make sweet, lip-smacking, passionate love to her. My body is all in knots thinking about what I'm going to do to you."

"If I wasn't hungry, I'd say skip dinner. But I definitely want what's on the dessert menu. Col. Reggie Charleston, I'm going to work your body until you call out my name and beg me to quit."

"I look forward to the conquest."

"You're on. Where are we going to meet? I'm famished."

Reggie gave Kaleah the address to the restaurant, ended the call and left the room.

$$ 🪷 \quad 9 \quad 🪷 $$

WHAT'S DONE IN THE DARK

The sun had set and only the lights that lit up the Seattle skyline were visible. The cool breeze coming off of the Puget Sound caused Persenia to cuddle closer to Remy. She hadn't planned it; it was more out of necessity. Small murmurs of conversation came from the other passengers, but Persenia kept quiet, relishing the moment of silence between her and Remy, although her mind was flooded with *what ifs* and *what am I doing here*."

Remy was quiet, his chin resting on the top of Persenia's head and his arms wrapped around her waist. Persenia could hear him breathing, a sign that his warm flesh was ready for what lie ahead.

After thirty to forty minutes, the captain called out on the bullhorn, "Vashon Island."

Remy squeezed her, kissed the top of her head, and squeezed her again. "Are you ready?"

Persenia sighed. "I guess as ready as I'm going to be." She untangled herself from Remy and prepared to disembark, her mind racing a mile a minute.

As soon as the boat was moored to the ramp where they were to get off, Remy grabbed her hand and headed for his car. They got in and waited for the cars ahead of him to disembark. As soon as they were free to move, Remy pulled forward and drove off the ferry.

Remy squeezed Persenia's hand. She wanted to resist but she didn't. Instead, she clasped his hands and intertwined her fingers with his.

Vashon Island seemed so peaceful. There were a lot of shops and eateries that she'd like to indulge in at another time. Persenia took in all that the darkness allowed her to see and was at peace.

Driving for more than ten minutes, Remy made a series of lefts and rights and pulled up a small incline. Looking off to the side, Persenia could see the Sound in the distance. And then Remy pulled into the driveway of a huge, modern structure that reminded Persenia of a concrete mausoleum that someone made into their architectural dream. It would've had a cold exterior if it weren't for the beautiful pencil-tall evergreens that outlined the perimeter and the colorful spotlights that highlighted the real beauty of the place.

"You're staring," Remy said. "A penny for your thoughts."

"So peaceful," Persenia heard herself say.

"Would you like to get out?"

Persenia smiled and tapped his hand. "Why not, it seems safe enough."

Remy jumped out of the driver's seat and rushed around to open the door for Persenia. He offered his hand and she took it.

"Do you act this way with all the women you bring to your castle? Or is it the butter you put on popcorn before you sink your teeth in?"

"I'm offended, Persenia. My intentions are pure. If we should take it further than a glass of wine and a bit of conversation, I'm in for the ride. But please know that I'm not here to coerce you into doing anything you don't want to do."

"It's hard to get off the island."

"You're safe with me."

"Okay."

Persenia took Remy's hand and followed him into his home. The interior looked like something out of *House Beautiful*. Remy had exquisite taste, and it was hard to imagine a single, ex-baller in a gorgeous place away from everyone. Ballers like him seemed to enjoy show-boating what they had—most of them growing up in a single-family home with below middle-class incomes. But Remy wasn't boastful. His eighteen-room hideaway included a movie theatre with a stand-alone popcorn popper and stand; a library that you entered through double-mahogany doors that contained books of Shakespearean plays, Sherlock Holmes mysteries by Sir Arthur Conan Doyle, history, and, of course, a large collection of African-American authors; a large study; five bedrooms not including the master; and an indoor swimming pool inset in the middle of the floor plan with a glass ceiling that hovered overhead.

"This is beautiful, Remy." Persenia clutched her chest as she continued to move from room to room—the rooms painted in creamy eggshell, accented in yellow and gold.

"I made all of the purchases myself."

"You have exquisite taste."

Remy smiled. "There's one room I've yet to show you."

Persenia stopped in her tracks and turned to look at Remy. "Look, I'm not into domination, so if that's the kind of room you're taking me to, we can change our course right now."

"I'm no Christian Grey, and I'd never want to have you that way. To calm your fears, it isn't that kind of room. Are you ready?"

Taking his hand, Persenia proceeded on without saying another word. And then she blurted out, "If anything is out-of-order, I want to leave immediately."

"Trust me."

Remy opened another set of double doors that opened into a studio of sorts that had a picturesque view of the Sound, with sailboats moored along the shoreline. The floor of the studio was adorned with black and white marble tiles, but the beauty in the room was a black, grand piano that sat amidst a set of tall palm trees. Two sides of the room were sheer glass that went floor to ceiling. A remote-controlled apparatus enclosed the room with wall-to-wall drapes, but the scenery was too nice to shut out what was beyond the glass walls. Besides the four black-and-white, brocade, high-back chairs, two long, white leather couches adorned the remaining walls that were decorated with the art of Charles Bibbs and Pancho. Persenia didn't recognize the artist of the other works.

⚜

WHILE PERSENIA ENJOYED THE VIEW, REMY SLIPPED FROM THE room. Less than ten minutes later, he returned with a silver tray that contained two wine glasses and a chilled bottle of Pinot Gregio. He sat it down on a silver server that sat in the room and poured them each a glass.

Persenia took the glass when offered and sipped. "Good." She smiled.

"Sit," Remy said, as he held his glass and ushered Persenia to one of the brocade chairs. She followed where Remy indicated and sat down.

They sipped and enjoyed the moonlight. They sipped and let the silence talk for them. They sipped until Persenia felt Remy's mouth on hers.

Unapologetically, she kissed him back without any reservations. She stood up so Remy didn't have to bend down and accepted his mouth...his sweet tongue that he gingerly gave. And then it was as if the heat was turned up full throttle and the desire for each other increased two-fold.

Remy was a talented kisser. His lips were soft and tender and the taste of the Pinot was on his tongue.

Persenia's body trembled from his touch. It seemed that her soul was on fire, and the tingle that became a violent throbbing between her legs was total confirmation. Persenia's mother's words ran rampant through her brain, *don't let your body rule your head,* and she tried to make sense of it all. But her body was winning and she wanted the forbidden fruit that the lust in her heart so desired.

Pulling back from Remy's tight embrace, Persenia picked up her glass of Pinot and took another sip. She sat the glass down and looked into Remy's eyes, noticing the sparkle in them. Hesitating for a moment, she laid her hands on his chest. "I want you to make love to me."

Amused, Remy took a sip of his drink, put it down, and lifted Persenia's hands from his chest. "So much for wine and conversation."

Persenia smiled. "I like you; I like your style. You're smooth in the way that Sade sings about the "Smooth Operator." Persenia reached up and held Remy's cocoa-brown face in her hands. She placed a well-deserved kiss on his small lips and rubbed her hand through his short, curly, black hair.

He grabbed Persenia around the waist and tightened his fingers together across her back. His lips gave her what she desired, finally thrusting his tongue within the cavern of her mouth. Remy allowed his hands to slip to the smooth humps of her buttocks, squeezing them like he was exercising each hand for a twenty-count workout. She felt the hardness of his penis as their bodies melded together...the excitement of it all sending Persenia into oblivion. She hadn't felt this way in a long time.

It was at that moment she let her thoughts roam to Reggie, her beloved husband. If he wasn't making her feel the way Remy had, who was on the receiving end of his male prowess? Reggie was an aggressive lover. He'd been that way on the football gridiron and he was in bed. He was possessive and took control...something that Persenia had loved about their lovemaking. There was passion and love all rolled together, but somewhere on the road to nowhere, both went in another direction. "I'm ready, Remy."

❧ 10 ❧

TOO CLOSE FOR COMFORT

The taxi ride into the heart of Washington, D. C. in the evening was a much calmer experience than it was earlier in the day. Anticipating seeing Kaleah again, Reggie brushed his hands over his clothes, licked his lips and stole a glance in the taxi's rearview mirror. The taxi arrived at Dukem Ethiopian Restaurant in thirty minutes.

Reggie paid the fair and got out of the cab. He stretched his limbs and then looked up and down the street for Kaleah. Not seeing her, Reggie went inside.

The noise and friendly banter that came from the happy patrons were welcoming. And then his face lit up like a lighted Christmas tree upon seeing Kaleah sitting off to the right.

Kaleah was dressed in a black-fitted knit dress that broke bad just above the knees and hugged her breasts like it was nobody's business. It was obvious a push-up bra was wrapped around her twin girls, as her cleavage spewed out from behind the plunging neckline at the delight of many male diners, who were seen salivating.

Reggie sat down next to Kaleah. "Hello, beautiful. You're wearing that dress."

"Thank you; I'm glad you approve."

"I do indeed. What's the wait?"

"Approximately twenty-five minutes. I wasn't aware that you like Ethiopian food."

"Love it. Of course, I had the real thing when I was in Ethiopia for a short stint. I love spicy food, and when I discovered this town had some of the best Ethiopian cuisine, I make it my business every time I come to town to stop by. Dukem is my favorite."

"I've been here a few times, and I can say it agrees with me. The food is great, the atmosphere is pleasant, and it isn't so off the beaten path."

"For all of those reasons, I wanted to come here. And, I don't believe many of our co-workers were thinking of venturing here tonight."

"Did you take a poll?"

"You can say I did on the sly. I'm in intelligence, and I must be smart in the areas of war and play."

Kaleah giggled. "I like that about you."

Reggie stared at Kaleah for some time. His eyes roved over her body, especially her breasts that begged for him to lay his head. It took some years to discover that she was the right woman for him. He loved Persenia but not in the way he'd come to love Kaleah.

For more nights than he could count, he toiled over telling Persenia that he wanted a divorce. She'd been a good wife to him, and he had no real complaints. Persenia was a loyal, stand-by-your-man woman, and Reggie knew that she loved him unconditionally.

It was terrible that Persenia continued to believe that her inability to give him a child was why he'd become distant and unloving. Quite the contrary; he'd been searching for something he'd been missing in his marriage—that one spice...maybe two that made the whole thing sizzle. Persenia hadn't delivered and neither had the countless other women he'd bedded while married. He wasn't attracted to them, but why keep throwing out apples if they keep landing at your feet?

"A penny for your thought."

"Oh," Reggie said, opening his eyes wide as if he was coming out of a stupor. "My mind had slipped into preparing for my permanent duty station at the Pentagon."

"Well, you can think about that later. I want all of your attention."

"You've got it."

৩৫৩

THEY DINED AND ENJOYED EACH OTHER'S COMPANY. KALEAH mimicked the meal that Reggie had chosen—cubed lamb fried with onion, rosemary, and jalapeno pepper. A spicy Awazie sauce was poured over it. They also had a nice serving of Dukem's specialty salad.

Every now and then, Reggie would stop and put his fork down when he'd catch Kaleah staring at him. She batted her eyes and blew seductive kisses his way. Reggie smiled but didn't want it to appear they were on a romantic interlude.

Meals completed, Reggie paid the bill and stood up. Like the gentleman he was, he went around to where Kaleah sat and pulled her chair out for her."

"Hey, Colonel Charleston and Major General Neal," Reggie heard the voice say behind him.

Reggie turned around and stared into the eyes of Major General Michael Forbes. His blonde hair and icy-blue eyes made him look much younger than the recorded date on his birth certificate. "Major General Forbes, fancy meeting you here. Kaleah and I were going over..."

"Still going over the strategic plan we discussed earlier today?" Maj. General Forbes asked, interrupting Reggie's train of thought and attempt to gloss over why he was there.

"Not at all, General. Since this is Major General Neal's town, I accepted her invitation to get a bite to eat before turning in to prepare for tomorrow's session." Out of the corner of his eye, Reggie saw Kaleah turn up her nose behind Major General Forbes' back and roll her eyes. He did everything he could to keep from laughing.

Major General Neal turned and acknowledged Kaleah again. "Nice of you to show the Colonel around. After next week, he'll be one of us."

"Right you are, Michael. It was good seeing you again. It's past my bedtime, so I'll be running along."

"Don't rush off on my account."

"We were leaving," Reggie said, ready to get the hell out.

"Are you here by yourself?" Kaleah asked Michael. "Maybe we can catch a cab together."

"Well...a...no."

Both Reggie and Kaleah jerked their necks back and stared at Michael. "So where is she," Kaleah asked, pushing her index finger into Michael's chest. She moved around the men and pretended to look high and low.

A short, red-head balancing on four-inch black pumps sauntered up to Michael. Reggie recognized her right away and faintly remembered having a conversation with her. He remained quiet as Kaleah began to talk.

"Oh, Miss Secretary," Kaleah said, throwing out her hands before letting out a small giggle. "I guess I'll have to take a cab by myself." She winked at Michael.

"This is Rebecca Dickerson my secretary; I'm sure you remember her from earlier today. I thought it would be prudent to take her out for dinner after all she's done for us today in setting up the meeting and all of the other logistics. In fact, Reggie, I can call you Reggie since we're off-duty, can't I?"

Reggie wasn't amused. "Sure, why not?"

"As I was trying to say, I have you to thank for us ending up at this wonderful restaurant. Ms. Dickerson mentioned to me that you were thinking of coming here."

Reggie saw the smile that crossed Kaleah's face and her mouthing the word *intelligence*. "I'm glad you enjoyed the food, General. It was a good choice. Now I must run; so we can do this all over tomorrow. I'll make sure you get your cab, Major General Neal, before I head back to my hotel."

"Thank you. I'd appreciate that."

"We could ride together; we may be going in the same general direction," Michael called out. "What hotel are you at Reggie?"

"I'd prefer to catch a cab by myself. I need to make several phone calls. I'll see you tomorrow."

"Okay then," Michael said. And Major General Forbes and Ms. Dickerson walked out ahead of them.

Kaleah turned to Reggie and smiled. "That was a close one."

"Too close for comfort. Meet me at my hotel in an hour."

"It's done."

🌿 11 🌿

THE SECRET IS IN THE PUDDING

Reggie was annoyed at having been seen by a higher up. All of his careful planning had been for nothing. He'd underestimated a few simple words with a secretary, who he'd given little thought to, long after their chance conversation.

"Damn, I've got to be more careful."

He took out his cell and dialed Persenia's number. Speaking with her would cause his sin or guilt to be diminished—at least that's how he felt. It didn't matter that he was wrong as two left shoes—a two-timing male whore who wore his credentials on his chest as if he was God's gift to the United States Army.

The phone rang and rang. Puzzled, Reggie hit the END button and redialed but with the same result. Maybe she wasn't speaking to him, since he didn't exactly bestow her with kisses upon his departure. He was too in a hurry to see Kaleah.

After two more tries, Reggie put his cell away and looked out the window. For a few moments, he wondered where Persenia might be. All was forgotten as soon as the cab drove up in front of the hotel.

ॐ

ALTHOUGH SOMEWHAT TIRED, REGGIE PREPARED FOR HIS rendezvous with Kaleah. He got comfortable; replacing his street clothes with a pair of burgundy silk shorts and a smoking jacket of the same color and fabric, with the lapels of the jacket done in black. He allowed his chest to breathe, exposing an ample amount of think black hair that was sprinkled with strands of silver.

Moving to the restroom, Reggie brushed his teeth, rinsed his mouth with mouthwash, and splashed on some after-shave lotion. Pleased with what he saw in the mirror, he waited for his guest to arrive.

Ten, fifteen, thirty minutes passed without a peep from Kaleah. Sitting on the side of the bed, Reggie picked up his phone from the nightstand to see if he'd received a text, but there was nothing. Maybe she was tied up in traffic, but he'd been in the room going on an hour. Why hadn't Kaleah called?

His temperament now changed, Reggie grabbed his cell phone and called Kaleah. It went straight to voice mail. He didn't believe it. Reggie called again, and the call went immediately to voice mail. The phone went airborne and hit the carpet.

"Damn all these bitches," he said out loud.

Reggie got up and went to the refrigerator and plucked a beer from inside. He retrieved the can opener from its resting place and released the lid from the bottle. A small amount of foam settled on top and he lifted it to his lips and drank the contents almost in two gulps. Unsatisfied, he tossed the bottle in the trash can and went and lay down on the bed.

No sooner than his head hit the pillow, Reggie heard a knock at the door. He sat up and listened to see if there would be a second. Thirty seconds later, there was a rat-a-tat-tat on the door.

He got up from the bed, tied his jacket at the waist, and went to answer the door.

"Who is it?"

"Were you expecting someone else?" the seductive voice asked.

Reggie opened the door, his mood lukewarm. "Where have you been? I thought you were right behind me."

"I took a small detour. I stopped at a convenience store to pick up a couple of personal items and before I made it inside, I ran into an old buddy of mine. Gregory Pate and I go way back, and we had a little catching up to do."

"And you kept me waiting?"

Kaleah came inside and pushed Reggie playfully on the chest, deciding to let her hand nest there. "Jealousy doesn't become the soon to be brigadier general. Like you, I've been around a long time. People walk in and out of your life all the time, but I swear there are six degrees of separation when it comes to the folks I've had a chance meeting with, especially those who are memorable."

Reggie dismissed Kaleah, not wanting to hear anymore of her meeting with this Gregory Pate individual. She seemed as if she was riding on a cloud, even when she spoke his name, leaving Reggie to wonder whether Kaleah was playing him for a fool.

Before Reggie spoke another word, Kaleah was out of her tweed skirt and white, long-sleeve blouse. She kicked off her heels and watched them land in the middle of the room. And without warning, the feisty Kaleah peeled the robe from Reggie's shoulders and began to place kisses on his body—first on the mouth, his chin, moving down to his neck, and then his chest until only moans of appreciation oozed from his mouth.

Now under her spell, Reggie fell back onto the bed and let Kaleah take control. She crawled...dragged her body across his like he was a hot bed of coals. To someone standing on the outside looking in, Kaleah looked like a crocodile moving stealthily through the water, stalking its prey, waiting for just the right moment to devour him. And then she went into an animalistic frenzy, tasting her man like a greedy troll...his body succulent to the taste and she adding the spice.

The bed seemed to levitate, knocking against the wall and back down to the floor again. The heat from their bodies clouded the atmosphere, steaming up the windows that were hidden behind drapes that blocked out the outside world.

And as if a button had been pushed, Reggie sat up and rolled

Kaleah over, consuming her with his tongue and giving her all of his attention and loving. Kaleah liked it rough; Reggie gave her rough. He conquered every part of her body like a savage beast, and they both screamed together when the heat of their passion couldn't withstand any more.

Feeling full and satisfied, if only for the moment, Reggie rolled off of Kaleah, caught his breath, and gave out a sigh. He rolled onto his side and raked his fingers through her short hair.

"You're beautiful and I want to be with you forever." He kissed her nose and hugged her to his chest.

"Those are the words I've waited to hear."

"I choose to be happy, and that'll only happen when I'm finally with you."

❧ 12 ❧

DO WE HAVE A FUTURE?

Remy noticed a slight hesitation when he took Persenia's hand. This woman was beautiful, feminine, and vulnerable all rolled into one. He could easily take advantage of her. But it wasn't in his DNA, although his buddies would think him crazy with Persenia being this close in proximity to him—in his bedroom. Whatever magical thing that was unfolding between them, he wanted it to come naturally and without any pressure. If it meant that he had to tame the naughty stallion that was ready to ride the gorgeous princess, then it had to be.

"How are you feeling?"

"Besides a little giddy, I've actually mellowed out."

Instead of sitting in one of the two chairs that sat next to the fireplace, Remy sat on the side of the bed. Persenia scanned the room and seemed pleased with what she saw, and a few seconds later joined Remy. And he wasn't ready for what came next.

Persenia reached over and held Remy's head with both hands. Her lips reached out and touched his, lightly placing on him the most seductive kiss he'd ever had. At least that's how he felt at that moment.

And then she got up and sat on his lap so that she was facing him and pushed him down on the bed with her on top.

Closing his eyes, Remy accepted her seduction readily. Still dressed in their clothes, Remy couldn't deny the intensity of the passion that flowed through his veins and other parts of his body. Her hungry lips sought his and devoured him without taking a breath. And then he felt her body move slowly on top of him, no doubt the heat of passion arousing her as much as it did him.

Without saying a word, Remy rolled her from on top of him until she fell onto her side. He continued to kiss her, stroking the fires of desire as they swallowed each other. Before he could change his mind, his hand left her face and touched her leg, rubbing it up and down.

"Why don't we get comfortable?" Remy asked, his hand now glued to the swell of her buttocks.

"Okay," Persenia said softly, sitting up. She lifted her arm and began to pull her sweater off.

"Let me help you with your clothes. Just give me another one of those slow, juicy kisses before you do."

Persenia kissed him nearly mulling him to death. Remy was baffled. He wondered if it had been awhile since she'd been with a man, although she did say she was married. He pushed the thought out of his head and kissed her back, now wanting her even more.

Pulling her close to him, Remy helped Persenia out of her sweater. His eyes captured her breasts that were held up by a simple, black, push-up bra. He noticed what appeared to be a birthmark up above the nipple of her right breast. "You're beautiful." Persenia blushed. "Cashmere." He held her sweater to his nose and sniffed. "Smells like you. Nice and powdery."

Persenia smiled.

"Lie down." Persenia obeyed. Remy unzipped her jeans and slowly pulled them off. A pair of black-satin bikini panties hid her crown jewels. "Don't be afraid; I want to look at you when I take them off."

Persenia closed her eyes when she felt Remy's hand grab her

waistband. He had stoked her embers and she felt ready to take this step. But guilt rose up in her faster than she could calm it down. In the middle of Remy's quiet seduction, she slapped her hand across his.

"I can't do this, Remy." Persenia sat up. She shook her head from side to side and sighed. "I'm sorry, but in good conscience I can't make a mockery of my marriage."

"Listen to yourself, Persenia. Earlier you told me that your husband has had numerous affairs and could very well be with someone else even as we speak."

"That doesn't give me the okay to be like him. I'd only be contradicting myself for how I feel about what he's doing. In fact, I've been my own super sleuth, collecting evidence to make my case and have that bastard pay when I've had enough. If I do the same thing, what does that make me?"

"Someone who needs to be shown some compassion...someone who needs to know that they're loved."

"That's sweet, Remy, but I made a vow to be with Reggie until the end...come hell or high water. With all of the evidence that I've collected on him, I'm not sure that I'll do anything with it."

"So, what are you doing here? If your beliefs are so strong about your marriage to your husband, why did you tell me you were ready? In fact, you're talking out of both sides of your mouth; I'm not sure I understand. I see that you're emotionally torn, especially having not been in this situation before...I'm guessing."

Persenia looked at Remy. He was getting the best of her. Why couldn't Reggie be more like him? Persenia hit the side of her head with her hands. "Don't make me feel any guiltier than I already do. I'm confused; I'm sorry."

"It's okay. As I said, I'm not here to take advantage of you. I have another room that you can sleep in and I'll take you back to Seattle in the morning. If you'd like to take a shower, the linen is in a closet in the bathroom." Remy got up from the bed and walked toward the door.

"Wait!"

Remy turned around slowly. He had a sour look on his face, one that seemed to say, I'm through; what is it now. "Yes?"

"I don't want to be alone."

"You don't know what you want, Persenia. I'm not up to playing table tennis with you, although, I will say that the ball is in your court." Remy turned the way he started. "Goodnight."

"Please don't be mad at me. Part of my hesitation also has been wondering how Carlitta would feel knowing that her cousin is screwing her husband."

"I'm not mad, although we can't equate what's going on across the Puget Sound with what's going on here. That's a horse of a different color, but I don't want to talk about them."

"I'm ready."

"No, you're not. I'm going to my room."

"I'm ready."

Remy took a long look at Persenia. "I'm at the point of no return. I respect your feelings..." Remy stopped in the middle of his sentence. Persenia unhooked her bra and set herself free. Remy went to her and put his hands on hers. "Don't do this to prove something to me; I understand. I may be crazy because I do want you, but not like this. Goodnight." And Remy was out of the door.

Persenia stared after him, not quite understanding what went wrong. She was going to give him what he wanted. But was this what she truly wanted?

Getting up from the bed, she pulled the covers back and got in between the sheets. She lay down without putting her bra back on... her bikini panties the only adornment. The darkness swallowed her, and she lay by herself in the still of the night.

Persenia listened for any sound coming from other parts of the house, but she heard none. Positioning her head on the pillow, she found her spot. Silent tears streamed from her eyes. She continued listening, heard nothing, and fell asleep.

❧ 13 ❧

RAINY DAYS AND SUNDAYS

It was raining cats and dogs. Out of nowhere, the sky seemed to open up and drench the Puget Sound. Thank God, they'd crossed the Sound in the ferry before God let the city have it.

There was no sign of life when Remy's car pulled up to Kimiko's house. Persenia was happy that her practically brand-new BMW wasn't picked apart nor hijacked for that matter. Not waiting for Remy to come to a complete stop, she opened the door and got out—hell with the rain. Remy sat in the car, and after a few moments drove off.

The atmosphere from Vashon Island back to Seattle was numb. Barely a word was spoken, and Remy remained a complete gentleman, although it was quite obvious he wasn't as charitable and not in a good mood, Persenia thought. He'd turned on the radio and let it keep him company. Even on the ferry ride back to Seattle, he was mute, not offering much more than an *are you all right* or *would you like something to eat?*

Rushing to her car, Persenia didn't look back as Remy took off. Off and on during the night, she wished she hadn't let him leave...wished she had had the opportunity to find out what it was like being sexual with another man. She sighed, hindsight being twenty, twenty, that she hadn't been a fool and let a man she'd only met hours earlier touch and taste her prized possession that had been awarded only to her husband.

Husband! She'd turned her cell phone off and hadn't given any thought to the possibility that Reggie might call. She turned on her cell and waited for it to boot up. While she waited, she knocked on Kimiko's door.

The rain was relentless. Persenia started to shiver as the water began to soak her clothing. After a few minutes passed, she turned to go back toward her car when the door creaked. Kimiko blocked the doorway.

"Well, heifer, are you going to let me in. It's pouring down outside, if you hadn't noticed."

Kimiko stood her ground and then put her hands up. "Look, Persenia, I'm sure you have negative thoughts about what you witnessed this weekend. I don't want to be a finger pointer, but the truth is the light; you're no better than Jacoby and me. Yes, it's wrong what we've done to Carlitta, but I have no explanation for you except that Jacoby and I love each other.

Persenia looked at Kimiko with disdain. "Can I come in so we can talk about it without me shivering?"

"Oh, yeah; come in." Kimiko relaxed her arm and moved out of the way so Persenia could pass by.

They went into the living room. "If you're worried about me saying something to Carlitta, you don't need to. I feel some kind of way about it, especially with Carlitta being my best friend, but I don't have a lot of room to talk after staying out all night with Remy. But for your information, nothing happened between us. We talked and lost track of time."

"Whatever."

"Is Jacoby still here?"

"No, he's on his way back to Oakland." Kimiko put her head down. "I love my cousin. I know that what I've done is wrong. But what can I say? I'm in love with the man."

"How about come clean? At least that's a first step. I'm not sure what that will do as far as your relationship with your cousin, but confession will be good for your soul."

"Easier said than done. You know good and darn well that I'm not going to break that kind of news to Carlitta. That would put her over the edge. The truth is, Carlitta and Jacoby's marriage has been over for a long time."

"So, you were going to conveniently step in and pick up the pieces."

"Not quite the way it happened."

"Well, I don't want to know. In fact, I'm severing my ties with you. It will be impossible for me to live around a lie."

"What in the hell are you talking about, Persenia? I hear Reggie isn't the saint he's all hyped up to be. Yeah, he runs in all those big Washington circles, hob-knobbing with the congressional types and big brass. But his lure is what the female types like between their legs."

"Shut the hell up, Kimiko. You haven't a clue about Reggie or his career. My husband is off limits to you. I didn't bring up the dirty deed you're doing with Jacoby; you did. I've wasted enough time here." Persenia pulled her purse strap across her shoulder, huffed and turned around and began to walk down the hallway.

"You may drive a fancy vehicle and have more money than me, but when you cut away the surface, you're just like me. Later; I'll tell Carlitta you asked about her."

Persenia didn't dignify the dig with a response. She opened the front door and ran through the rain to the safety of her car. She was nothing like Kimiko and she hoped that when Carlitta got wind of what went on in Seattle that she'd have a front row seat to the beat down both Kimiko and Jacoby were going to get.

❧ 14 ❧

SUDDEN DEATH?

There was a hushed quiet in the nation's capital. Soon Sunday morning church goers would be springing from everywhere to make it to the house of the Lord, synagogue, temple, or whatever their place of worship happened to be. Reggie had one more short morning meeting before he'd be hopping on a plane bound for Seattle, Washington.

His uniform packed away, he sported a pair of denim jeans, a long-sleeved white shirt, and a black gabardine jacket. A black pair of Giorgio Armani shoes adorned his feet.

Anxious to get back home to announce to Persenia that they would soon be moving to D.C., he still had a personal matter that would keep him in Washington a little longer after his morning meeting concluded. Lunch with Kaleah was on the menu, and then on to catch his flight back to the Pacific Northwest.

He arrived at the Pentagon without any fanfare and rushed to the conference room for the closing meeting. Just as he was about to enter the room, he heard a voice call out. He turned, and there was Rebecca Dickerson, the red-head secretary, leaving her post from sucking up to another high-ranking officer, no doubt looking for a meal ticket before they left the city to go back to their families and life beyond Washington.

"Colonel Charleston," Rebecca said, slurring her words for effect, "do you have everything you need for the meeting?"

Reggie looked at this woman for the first time. She was young, slightly attractive, but her eyes were piercing and menacing. The color of her skin was so white that it looked like the sun had never touched it. It was what made her hair look so red. However, her fake smile was bright along with her large porcelain implants. "I'm fine; thank you for asking."

"Well, if you have some free time after the meeting and would like to get something to eat, I'm here for you. As well, I can give you a ride to the airport."

Confused, Reggie's immediate impulse was to distance himself as far away from this woman as possible. Who was she really? Why was she all in his business? For all she knew, he was staying on in Washington to attend to other affairs. But curiosity got the best of him. "Why would you do that for me when I have a service that will take me to the airport, something you've already known about in advance, I'm sure?"

"There's no motive behind me asking you, if that's what you mean."

"That's what I mean."

"It was nothing. I heard you speak yesterday, and I was quite impressed with your intelligence."

Reggie wasn't amused. "Is that due to the fact that I'm black? If so, there are many intelligent people, especially black people who are in power, own big business..."

"Like President Obama?"

"Sure, President Obama is an example, but he's the obvious example. I can give you names but what would you care?"

"I care about you."

"Ms. Dickerson, I don't mean to be rude, but I've got to get into my meeting. And, I already have a lunch date."

"With Major General Neal?"

"That's none of your business. Have a nice day." Reggie walked away, his temperature rising. Thank God, he didn't have high-blood pressure; he was steaming mad.

Before he sat down, he felt a hand on his back. He turned around and there was Kaleah.

"What was that all about?" Kaleah asked.

"I'll tell you later."

"Major General Neal," one of the officials called out, "we need to get started.

Kaleah rushed to her seat and pretended to listen, although her mind was on what was bothering Reggie. She kept glancing in his direction, but he seemed to be glued into the matter at hand.

⚜

Meeting over, Reggie grabbed up his stuff and headed toward the back of the room. He saw Kaleah approach, and he wished that there was another way out.

"Hey, Colonel Charleston, what's up with you?" Kaleah asked. "You act like you're in a hurry to get somewhere. We are still having lunch together."

Reggie looked around to see if others were listening. Kaleah's voice was raised, and the last thing he needed was someone to bring attention to him. "Actually, I was thinking about leaving for the airport and wait until my flight was ready to take off."

"What happened during the time I briefly spoke with you this morning and when I arrived this morning?"

"Let's leave it alone."

"Let's go to lunch."

Reggie sighed. "All right, if it'll make you happy."

"It's about more than making me happy, Reggie," Kaleah whispered. "I don't want you to go."

"But I have to; let's go."

Reggie shook a few hands and proceeded out of the conference room with Kaleah close by. Ready to get as far away from the Pentagon, Reggie looked up and saw Ms. Dickerson staring at him. Now his insides churned. He understood that the woman might be enamored by his good looks. But there was something more going on with her and he couldn't put his finger on it.

Surrounded by a few others, Reggie rushed from the building, forcing himself to not look back. Look back he did, and the red-head woman in question was staring at him. She pretended to pick up the contents on her registration table, but those piercing eyes didn't miss its target.

❧ 15 ❧

SETTING A TIME BOMB

G lad to be home, Persenia jumped into the shower, changed clothes and prepared for Reggie's return. She was glad that he wasn't coming home until late that evening; he'd be too tired to talk and she wouldn't be in the mood to talk either, considering everything she'd been through on yesterday.

Persenia went to the kitchen and put on the tea kettle for a cup of tea. She glanced around the house, taking snapshots of her life, only to realize that she was empty as the house seemed to be. There weren't any children's laughter or someone calling her mama every two seconds. She'd welcome it into her reality. Even the television that was presently off offered only a temporary fix.

The whistle on the tea kettle blew and she fixed herself a cup of tea. Persenia loved barbeque potato chips and went to the pantry and pulled out a bag that was yet to be opened. She took it to the table, opened it, and sat it next to her cup of tea. Sitting down, she looked out of the kitchen window into her backyard.

The rain was still falling and put her in a trance. Remy was standing before her with his arms outstretched, beckoning her to come to him.

What would it have been like to have this man touch her body and take liberties she'd only given to her husband? Certainly, love wouldn't have been attached to it...only a strong desire to satisfy the empty temple of her soul. She sighed, ate a few chips, drank her tea, and fell asleep where she sat.

Persenia's head flew up at the sound of an intruder. She sat straight up in her seat paralyzed, watching and waiting to see if her fears were founded. And in the next instant, Reggie stood in the doorway, looking at her with eyes that seemed to pity.

"Hey," Reggie said, giving Persenia a half-smile, while moving toward the kitchen table. "Are you all right?"

"Yeah, I'm fine. How was your trip?"

"The usual, but I do have some news for you."

"News?" Persenia searched her husband's face, skeptical of the news he was about to lay on her."

Reggie sat down. "I'd like a cup of tea."

"Sure." Persenia got up to put more water on the stove. As she passed the oven, she noticed that the clock said ten. It was almost midnight. Where had the time gone? She placed the kettle with fresh water on the stove and sat back down at the table.

"Do you want to hear my news?"

"Yes, I can't wait."

"We're moving to Washington, D. C."

Persenia felt as if she'd been struck by an oncoming train. "D. C.?"

"Yes, I'll be a new resident at the Pentagon. My promotion is to take place on Thursday, and I want you there in all of your fabulousness."

"When will the move take place?"

"How about next week?"

"But Reggie, that doesn't give us any time to plan...get our things in order."

"We have people who'll take care of that. You're not working and there's nothing to keep you here. I'll be glad to get out of Tacoma and away from all of this dreadful rain."

Persenia sat there dumbfounded. Blindsided wasn't even the appropriate word for how she felt. It was more like someone had dropped a bomb on her and she'd barely made it out alive to tell about it. "Well, I guess I'll have to start packing."

"That's my girl. You'll like it there."

"Will I? Doesn't the Major General live there?"

"Are you talking about Kaleah again?"

"This is the first time I've mentioned her since you've been home, but yes, I'm talking about her."

"She's not your worry. I have another surprise for you. After we've settled in, I'm taking you to Dubai and you can shop until you've done all the damage you want to do at Burj Khalifa, Burj Al Arabs, and wherever else. You'll have plenty Dirhams to spend. And if you want, will do some dune bashing and camel riding; they have those desert safaris with lots of options."

The cat had tied Persenia's tongue. She stared at Reggie, as if he'd fallen off the moon and landed in a strange place. All of a sudden, Persenia's face lit up and all of Reggie's transgressions temporarily forgiven. "Really, Reggie? No lie?"

"No lie, baby. I'm taking my wife on a much-needed vacation."

"Wow, I'm not sure of what to say no more than I'm thrilled and appreciate you for this. Thank you. I'll start packing."

⚜

REGGIE DRANK HIS TEA AND WATCHED THE EXCITEMENT ON HIS wife's face. He was glad that his news had pleased her, especially since he was about to drop a major bomb on her in the near future. It was all about timing, though, and the moment wasn't yet ripe. But when the time was right, it was going to be an explosion heard throughout the Army's military community.

❧ 16 ❧

WEST COAST/EAST COAST

The days rolled by fast. Persenia took care of all the logistics that pertained to their move. The movers were coming on Friday, and they'd be in a hotel for five days before flying out to Washington, D. C.

Persenia placed the suit that she'd prepared to wear to Reggie's promotion ceremony off to one side of the closet. She decided on a navy blue and white Chanel suit with a Chanel purse and bag to complement it. It never occurred to her that the man she met in college would one day become a General in the Army.

Moving full steam ahead with her task at hand, Persenia felt new life. All the awkwardness of the past weekend was now a blur—a fog that had dissipated into thin area. Even the secret she'd hold tight to her chest for forever about her best friend's cheating husband and her best friend's cousin the seducer, took a back seat to her pending move.

Her cell phone began to ring. This wasn't the time for interruptions, especially when she was on a roll. The phone stopped and started again and she moved over to the nightstand and retrieved it.

Thinking it was Reggie, she went in full blast. "Hey, baby, I'm making headway with this move."

"Move?" the voice asked.

Persenia pulled the phone away from her ear and looked at the caller-ID for the first time. The number wasn't familiar, but there was something very familiar about the voice.

"Persenia?" the voice said.

"R-e-m-y, is this you?"

"Yeah, I got your number from Kimiko. I had to call and say how much I enjoyed your company. While I was a tad bit disappointed that...that we didn't get to experience...or should I say get to know more about each other, I understood where you were coming from. I appreciate you being upfront with me and sharing how you felt about honoring the institution of marriage."

"While I appreciate your call, Remy, I've put our weekend in the past."

There was a moment of silence before Remy spoke again. "Listen, I understand, but I can't get you out of my mind. Persenia, I saw first-hand how unhappy you are and I want to be the one to replace that frown with a smile."

"Look, you just met me and now it's not possible for us to see each other again. I will be moving to Washington, D. C. next week."

"Next week?"

"Yes, next week. Reggie is being transferred to the Pentagon. He's being promoted and with his promotion he's been given a quick transfer. Forget about me, Remy."

"I can't. It's not that easy for me."

"Try harder. It's not as if we had an emotional connection or hot, lurid sex."

"Okay, that hit below the belt; I'm not that shallow person. You haven't any idea what you did to me...did to me inside. I met a woman who I could possibly love and spend the rest of my life with."

"I'm a fraud, Remy. I'm in love with my husband and have no intentions of ever leaving him. I'll admit that a moment of temptation almost caused me to stumble and regret that I'd even allowed myself to ever be with you...although I was very close to it. Forget what I said about all of Reggie's infidelities; in some way, I believe it's part of the territory."

"In what life? Persenia, that's crazy talk. You're saying all of this stuff to put a shield between us. You let down your guard and shared a bit of yourself...how you feel about what your husband has done and how he's made you feel. No one has taken care of you in a long time, and for once you need to think about yourself. I needed you and you need me."

"I'm married, Remy, and that's the end of it. I'm leaving this part of the world and moving forward with my life. I won't forget you."

"Don't count me out that easy. I'll be watching and waiting."

"There's nothing to wait for. I appreciate your concern and under-standing. I've got to go and finish packing. I hope all will be well with you."

"Don't count me out."

"Bye, Remy." And Persenia disconnected the line.

❧

TEN DAYS LATER, PERSENIA AND REGGIE WERE ON A PLANE HEADED to Washington, D. C. She wasn't sure why she boarded the plane. In her heart, she felt her marriage was doomed. Even before and certainly after Reggie was promoted to brigadier general, his attitude was stank. He was gone most of the time on the pretense he had highly classified meetings to attend, at least that's what he made her to believe, leaving her to do the majority of the work in getting things ready for the movers. She didn't mind, but she hated Reggie's dismissive attitude. He always seemed happy to be going to work but agitated as hell when he was at home. She wasn't sure that he was still taking her to Dubai as he promised, although come hell or high water, she was going, even if it meant traveling alone.

Their housing quarters was much older than their previous accom-modations at Joint Base Lewis-McChord. The interior looked much more promising than the exterior, which was brick, but it fit in with the aura of living life in the nation's capital. Their place was together in no time, and now, a month later, it felt like home.

Regardless of Reggie's aloofness and standoffishness, Persenia was ready to explore Washington, D. C., Alexandria, and all that Maryland had to offer, especially the crab cakes that Baltimore was known for. At this moment, she wished there was a close friend to share her excitement with. And for the first time in months, she picked up the phone and dialed Carlitta.

Persenia couldn't wait to hear Carlitta's voice. She wished her friend could pick up from where she was and come and visit, although the answer would probably be an obvious no with young kids to look after.

She heard her voice and was overcome with excitement. "Carlitta, it's me, Persenia."

"Fool, your name is flashing like a neon sign on my iPhone. It's about damn time you called me, Mrs. Kept Woman. How you be?"

Carlitta and Persenia both broke into laughter. "Carlitta, you are so crazy, but it's good to hear your voice."

"Yours too, chick-a-dee. I miss you so much; wish you were still in the Bay Area. When are you coming home?"

"I'm not sure, but if I do, it'll be sometime near the end of the year —Thanksgiving or Christmastime."

"I need to see my best friend and spend some adult time with her. How's Reggie?"

"Reggie is Reggie the big-time brigadier general. I see less of him now than I did in the other Washington. It's no big deal; I've accepted my fate as a military wife."

"That means Reggie is still being an asshole." There was quiet on the line. "You don't have to tell me. Jacoby told me that Reggie has a reputation of bedding his subordinates."

Persenia was pissed. She had never spoken out right to Carlitta about all of Reggie's misdemeanors—some should be considered federal offenses depending on where they took place. Jacoby must have talked with Reggie. How else would he have known? Sure, she'd dropped hints from time to time that all was not well on the home front, but she'd never given Carlitta any details, as she knew them, of Reggie's trysts. And Jacoby had some freaking nerve talking about anybody.

"Are you still there, friend?"

"Yeah, I'm still here, Carlitta. I don't know what you've heard..."

"Girl, Jacoby and Reggie still talk from time to time. I happened to overhear them talking one day, although it was only Jacoby's side of the conversation, but I made him spill some of the beans. But that man-thing... I mean man-code wouldn't allow Jacoby to completely diss on Reggie."

"Hmm," Persenia said. Only if she was a dog, she'd break her chain and run Jacoby's ass up a chain-link fence with barb wire at the end. He and Kimiko weren't getting away with what they'd done. This wasn't the moment to pull a cloud over Carlitta's good mood, though. She needed her friend, but she'd have to cut the conversation about Reggie short. "Why don't you come out and visit me?" Persenia asked, changing the subject.

"Girl, I've got these babies, and I'm working on my Masters. What am I going to do with them?"

"Do I really have to answer that question for you? They are not in diapers and I'm sure their grandmother would love to have three loving grandchildren for a week or two. If not, you have enough sisters who could give you a break."

"I never thought about stepping out on my babies, but momma does need a break."

"Think about it and make that plane reservation. I heard through the grapevine that you're living large down there in Silicon Valley."

Carlitta laughed. "We're close enough to it. Your idea is wonderful, but I can't come until I've completed this semester. I've invested too much money in my Master's program to put it on hold for even a week. I'm going to call Mommy tonight, though. I'll give you a call tomorrow and let you know when and if I can come. I feel it in my spirit that I'm on my way to the Chocolate City. They still call it that, don't they?"

"I'm sure they do; if not, who cares. Now get off the line and call your momma."

"I'm on it, friend. Call you tomorrow."

"Okay." And the line was dead. It wasn't quite the response Persenia was hoping to get but she could wait a few weeks. Maybe Carlitta could stay more than a week.

She was going to paint the town. If Reggie thought she was going to sit home and do nothing, he had it twisted. In fact, she decided to become fully involved in the officer wives' military circle. She would host party after party and keep Reggie on his toes. They would see her face all the time and recognize her for who she was. Brigadier General Reggie Charleston, get ready. This general's wife is getting ready to make her presence known.

❦ 17 ❦

PENTAGON CITY – THE FIVE-SIDED PUZZLE PALACE

Reggie brushed the front of his Class-A uniform as he headed into the large conference room. The second in command to Al Qaeda was killed in a Yemen strike by the United States. An impromptu meeting with the Joint Chiefs (JC) had been called to discuss present Homeland Security issues in preparation for a meeting with the Secretary of Defense who'd later advise the President. The Chairman of the JC, Vice Chairman, and the Military Service Chiefs from the Army, Navy, Air Force, the Marine Corps, and the Chief of the National Guard Bureau were all there. Reggie's job was to assist the JC of the Army.

Sitting off to the side, Reggie took a seat next to one of the assistants to the JC of the Navy. He balanced a leather portfolio on his knee that contained intelligence reports on the most recent Al Qaeda defenses. It appeared that ground troops might be needed for an upcoming offensive, and the JC's responsibility was to ensure personnel readiness, policy, planning and training of their respective military branches for combat commanders to utilize.

Reggie sighed as he listened to each respective JC impart their ideas for going forth. One of the major concerns was that Al Qaeda was operating on U. S. soil and that the Islamic Group ISIS was operating as an arm. There had been a rash of ISIS wannabes who were either heading to the Middle East as recruits or acting out on their behalf on American soil, and Homeland Security was operating in long hours to stay on top of the fray.

The babble around the table became a faint rumble in Reggie's head. Major General Kaleah Neal had been weighing on his mind. Being in close proximity—Washington, D. C.—was too close for comfort. Seeing Kaleah almost every day made Reggie's desire to be with her near top priority, next to fighting Al Qaeda. He shook his head and refocused on the issue at hand.

"Brigadier General Charleston," his boss called out.

Reggie immediately rose to his feet with portfolio in hand and rushed to his boss' side. The Military Service Chief for the Army whispered something in Reggie's ear. Reggie removed a document from the portfolio and handed it to his boss. The boss studied it carefully and held up his hand.

"We must move as soon as possible! Our attempt to get the Iraqi ground forces trained as expeditiously as possible is on a slow roll. Al Qaeda is our enemy, and we've got to make sure we are in ready mode. There's no way we can defeat the devil if boots aren't on the ground." And then he gave Reggie some instructions and an envelope, and Reggie was out of the room.

Major General Kaleah Neal would have to take a back seat for a while. Reggie was on a mission for the United States that involved the country's security. Classified information was stamped on the outer part of the tan-colored envelope he carried. He'd have his assistant, Captain Hummerbacher, get it to where he needed it to be. This was the stuff...the world Reggie loved—weeding out the enemy and being part of a task force that oversaw the operations, even if the joint chiefs operated only in an advisory capacity.

Moving fast, he almost missed her if she hadn't thumped him on the shoulder.

"Hey, where are you going? You look like the front end of a locomotive train, barreling down the tracks, destroying everything in its path."

Reggie stopped long enough to pass a smile. "Major General Neal, it's good to see you. I'm...sort of in a hurry."

"Hold up. You can't be in that big of a hurry that you'd ignore this pretty face."

Reggie leaned in and whispered. "It is indeed pretty, but you'll have to put it on ice, as I have more important things to think about at the moment."

Kaleah stepped back a couple of paces and cocked her head. "Did you really mean that?"

"Not in the way you think. The JCs are meeting, and I've got to move on something right away. I'll call you later."

"All right. I'll let you off the hook if you promise to call me."

"I promise; got to go."

꧁꧂

Kaleah watched as Reggie moved passed her and out of sight. She was overcome with joy when she learned that he would be transferred to the Pentagon. The thought of seeing him practically every day with the added opportunity of being able to share more of her—her body—with him was what she called a blessing.

Since he arrived in D. C. almost a month ago, they'd share several nights of sexual bliss. The desire to be between the sheets with him night and day was driving her into a sexual frenzy. Reggie fed her sexual prowess and fantasies, and it heated up her loins whenever she thought about him. She wanted him more than she ever thought she would. But the Reggie she'd just witnessed needed to be put in check.

She wouldn't be a woman scorned, even if she was what today's society called a side piece. To hell that he had a wife. Reggie had a list of recipients—longer than Bill Cosby's—of women he had penetrated, that included commissioned and non-commissioned officers, enlisted female soldiers under the rank of E-5, and the honorably and not-so honorably discharged. And it wasn't that she had settled for leftovers; she got the man who'd been cultivated, seasoned, and well-groomed to be in command. But she'd take him down in a New York heartbeat, if he even thought of kicking her to the curb.

❧ 18 ❧

WELCOME TO THE NEIGHBORHOOD

Persenia was thrilled to death when Carlitta called to say that she was cleared to visit the last week in May. Carlitta's mother was ecstatic about taking care of her grandbabies for a week, and Carlitta was overjoyed that she'd be able to spend some time with her home girl.

Needing to get some air, Persenia grabbed her purse and headed for the door. As she was about to step outside, a blond-haired woman appeared on the walkway. Her hair was shoulder length, parted on one side. The woman wore a pair of pink, pastel-colored slacks and a long-sleeved, cotton, white button-downed blouse. A pair of beige flats adorned her feet.

"Hello, I'm your neighbor, Julia Forbes. My husband, Major General Michael Forbes, works at the Pentagon."

"Hi, I'm Persenia Charleston. My husband, Brigadier General Reginald Charleston, also works at the Pentagon. We recently moved here."

"Welcome to the neighborhood. I'm sorry for waiting until now to come over and introduce myself, but I've been going through a lot," she sighed, "and for the first time in a long time I'm feeling more like my old self."

"Thank you for stopping by. I haven't met anyone yet, but I plan to get involved in the wives club and other volunteer activities real soon. Thank you again."

"If there's anything you need, please let me know."

"Look, Julia, I was on my way out to nowhere in particular. Would you like to come in for a cup of coffee or tea? I was probably going to get in trouble, spending money on a new purse I didn't need."

"I don't want to impose..."

"You're not imposing; I could use a friend."

"Well, I could come in for a little while and I could use a cup of coffee. My husband stays late most times, so there's no need to rush home."

Persenia swiped her hand and Julia followed it into the Charleston's home.

"Wow, you've got it decorated so nice in here. My house is plain, but it works."

"It's all in what you feel. I like vibrancy, so I'm all about colors, especially fall colors."

"I wish I had your knack for decorating."

"Maybe I can give you some pointers."

"That sounds great."

Persenia led Julia through the house to the kitchen. Julia sat at the table next to the window that looked out into the back yard. Before sitting down, Persenia put water in her Keurig coffee maker and waited for it to heat up.

"How long have you been here?" Persenia asked once she sat down.

Julia sighed. "Long enough for my husband to have screwed everyone in town."

Persenia wasn't expecting to hear that. Damn, she'd just met the woman. The last thing she needed was to hear about someone else's issues with their husband when she was having troubles of her own. But Julia looked as if she needed a friend.

"The late nights will get to you. Reggie is always going to meetings all times of days and nights."

"We've just met, but I must be candid with you. This is not the place for families. These bitches, military and otherwise, are always after our men. Yeah, they are generals and may have some great perks, but they aren't damn Donald Trump. I'm not sure if any of them own as much real estate as the Donald and for sure not the money that goes with it."

There was no way Persenia was going to share any information about her dysfunctional marriage with a woman she met only a few minutes ago. "Thank you for the warning; let me get your coffee."

Persenia crossed the room to the counter where her Keurig sat and made both of them a cup of coffee and brought it back to the table. "I have French Vanilla creamer if you like."

"Thank you. Forgive me for spewing my garbage out on you. I needed someone to talk to, but sharing my shambles of a marriage was totally unplanned." She sighed again. "Let's talk about something more pleasant."

"I agree that we should change the subject but know that if you need someone to talk to, I'm here. Who knows? I may need someone to talk to, if things are as bad as you say they are in this town."

"They are; however, I pray that you don't have to endure what I've been through. Now let's talk about shopping and the casinos. I spend a lot of my time doing both."

"I'm not much of a gambler, but I can shop until I'm down to my last quarter." The ladies laughed.

❄ 19 ❄

BUMPING HEADS

Reggie relished the life he now led. While his status as an officer always had its merits, being within the General ranks placed him in the top echelon of the military elite. The privileges were monumental, and the respect and admiration he received from others with the addition of his one star, topped everything he received when he was in the Major ranks. He was only feeling his way when he was a Lieutenant and a Captain in the Army.

Command readiness was his top priority. He made a note to have his secretary schedule a meeting with key military personnel at Fort Bragg, Fort Hood, and Fort Riley Army Bases to discuss impending deployments to the Middle East.

Setting his pen down, his mind took a break but immediately came back to his encounter with Kaleah that morning. While he was feeling this woman with an intensity that he'd not felt with any other woman in a long time, he had to remind her that all extracurricular activities had to be after hours and far away from the prying eyes of Pentagon personnel. Without a doubt, cameras were mounted in crevices on every floor and building, and the last thing he needed was for someone to view a piece of footage and make an assumption that they were an item. He was still married, at least for the time being, and had a career yet to be extended ahead of him.

Reggie reached for his cell phone that lay on his desk. He didn't want to make it a practice to call Kaleah on a non-secure line, neither did he want Kaleah to call his office and bring attention to them. She answered on the first ring.

"So glad you called me," Kaleah said. "I was a little worried that you were tiring of me already."

"What gave you that idea?" Reggie asked, somewhat agitated.

"You seemed far away...like you didn't want to be bothered."

"Kaleah, I want to be with you. I've told you that time and time again. However, when I'm at my place of employment, handling the Army's business, I'm 'Army All You Can Be.' If you feel I slighted you this morning, I apologize. I did have a lot on my mind and some serious stuff to contend with. So, are we okay?"

"Yeah, we're okay and I apologize. As an Army officer, I know better...I know how crucial it is to respect our respective offices and roles, which only makes me respect you even more for putting me in my place, in your own ratchet way."

Reggie relaxed and laughed softly. "I said I was sorry, and I'll make it up to you."

"That's better. Can you come out and play tonight?"

"It shouldn't be a problem. I'll run home, change my clothes, and come your way."

"What if wifey wants your attention tonight?"

"I'll have to give her a raincheck. I've got to go; see you tonight. I'll call when I'm on the way."

"Smooches."

An hour later, Reggie looked at his watch. Where had the time gone? It was five-thirty and he hadn't accomplished all the tasks on his agenda. He'd give it another hour before he went home. He was glad that Persenia was adjusting to their new city environment and hopefully she'd be out when he arrived home.

At six-thirty, Reggie packed his briefcase and headed out. It was a decent day in late May. The sun was on its way down with about another hour before it disappeared over the horizon. Reggie saluted several enlisted soldiers as he trotted to his car, and was happy when he reached it—so ready to get home, get out, and get it on with his love interest, Kaleah.

Traffic was extremely heavy, as it always was in D. C., but patience was a new virtue that Reggie was embracing. He wasn't going to let anyone intimidate him or have him participate in any road-rage shenanigans, even if he did conceal it behind a tight face and clenched teeth. He hated for drivers to cut him off or get too close to his vehicle. He'd used his horn one too many times on one given day and a driver in an adjacent car almost rammed the side of his vintage 1969 Mustang. Today, guns were the weapons for retaliation.

He turned off the Beltway and headed for the quaint row of houses that were set aside for generals of his rank. A brigadier general was on the low end of the general's salary totem pole and banked a modest low, six-figure salary, while four-star generals lived large, boasting chefs, gardeners, drivers, and you name it. Some of the other compensations Reggie received made him grateful of his status, though.

Pulling the car into the driveway, he noticed Persenia's car occupying the other space. The last thing Reggie wanted was an argument about where he was going and why he had to always have late meetings. Reggie sighed, picked up his briefcase from the passenger side seat, and got out of the car.

The door to the house was unlocked. He'd have to remind Persenia to keep the door locked at all times. Security precautions were first and foremost—a number one concern for upper-level officers who lived in D.C. Terrorists were looking for ways to penetrate the Washington military/political system, especially those who were directly connected to Homeland Security. Although the likelihood that someone was lurking around his house, watching and waiting for an opportunity to get in and seize what secrets they thought he possessed was probably nil; however, Reggie wasn't taking any chances.

Moving forward in the house, he stopped abruptly when he heard laughter coming from the kitchen. He turned his head in such a way to hear what was being said and perhaps recognize the other voice in the room. Persenia's laughter was distinctive, but Reggie didn't recognize the other voice.

He moved from where he was standing and walked into the kitchen, surprised to see the stranger sitting at the kitchen table laughing it up with his wife as if they were best friends. "Reggie, you're home early," Persenia said.

"Yeah, and I see you have company."

"Yes, this is my new friend, Julia. Julia this is my husband, Reggie Charleston."

Reggie extended his hand. Julia offered hers.

"It's nice to meet you, sir. My husband also works at the Pentagon."

Reggie gave Persenia a sideways glance.

"And your husband is?"

"Major General Michael Forbes," Julia said, as if she was proud of the association.

Persenia noticed Reggie's irritation.

"Yes, I know him. Do you live in the neighborhood?"

"Right next door," Persenia rushed to say, watching Reggie like a hawk.

"It's a small world. I'm going to leave you ladies to your conversation; I'm going to meet some of the Joint Chiefs before they head out tomorrow."

"Well, it was nice meeting you, General Charleston. It's time for me to go home. I've spent enough of Persenia's time this afternoon."

"Whenever you feel like stopping by, please do so," Persenia said with a smile. "We'll have to organize a shopping trip."

"I'm game."

"I'll walk you to the door." Persenia patted Julia on the back and whispered in her ear. "Your secret is safe with me. I don't discuss everything with Reggie and you have nothing to fear from me."

"Thanks, Persenia." Julia hugged Persenia and went home.

Persenia walked back to the kitchen where Reggie still stood. It was obvious he had something on his mind.

"What was that woman doing over here?" he asked, making Persenia jump.

"She came over, introduced herself, and welcomed us to the neighborhood."

"How long have we've been here?"

"What's the big deal? She seemed nice enough. Reggie, I'm here day in and day out and haven't made any acquaintances. You've barely taken me out to a nice restaurant. Maybe I was starving for someone to talk to."

"Well, she's not the one you should be spending time with."

"Give me one good reason I shouldn't. We don't know anything about her."

"That's reason enough. I don't want strangers all in our business... let alone in my house."

"This is my house, too, Reggie. Give me a damn break. She was friendly and I offered coffee."

"That was her last cup."

"So, I guess I won't be hosting any wives club meetings or any of the other hosting events that a general's wife is supposed to do."

"They will be supervised by me."

"The hell with you, Reggie. Don't try to control me. I have a degree and I'm not anybody's trophy wife for you to display when it's convenient and appropriate for you to do so." Persenia waved her finger in Reggie's face. "Oh no, don't play me like that. I'm not your fool."

"Say what you want. I'm going to change and get out of here before I say something I may regret."

"Well, get the hell on out; you're not here when you do find the time to stick around for a moment. I'm sick of this bull. I didn't sign up for this. No siree buddy. You're going to wish you'd treated me better."

Reggie threw his hands up in the air. "What are you going to do, Persenia? All that talk about hosting and running a foundation. Why don't you get up off of your sorry ass and do something instead of blowing smoke?"

Persenia's face became contorted. Reggie Charleston wasn't going to talk to her any kind of way. She went to the table and picked up the remains of her cold cup of coffee and threw it in Reggie's face. "Is that action enough for you?"

Reggie raised his hand, thought better of it, and left the room instead. "Bitch."

❧ 20 ❧

THE FOUR-ONE-ONE

Reggie couldn't wait to get away from home. The scene with Persenia had left him exhausted and frustrated. He wasn't even sure why he went off on her when there was no immediate reason to his madness. The last thing he needed was for the two wives to get together and this Julia end up telling Persenia something about him that her husband spouted off during a moment in a heated argument. Major General Michael Forbes wasn't a saint and was probably leading a second life that he concealed from his wife, but Forbes was well aware that he had secrets—secrets he could possibly use against him.

He was wrong, and he was sure Persenia's interest in his negative attitude was piqued. This wasn't the way he wanted Persenia to find out about his indiscretions and the strong possibility that their marriage was soon to be over.

Pulling up to what had become his favorite watering hole, Reggie exited his car and entered the bar. The light was dim, but he found a stool and sat. "A bourbon," he said, and nursed it like he was holding hands with the last friend he had on earth.

He decided he needed to talk to a familiar friend. As he was about to place the call to Jacoby, a call came in. Reggie let out a sigh and let the call go to voice mail. He was too agitated to have to deal with Kaleah and all of her idiosyncrasies—not tonight. And then, without notice, a woman sauntered in and took the empty seat next to his.

"General Charleston, you're here by yourself. Where is your girl toy?"

Reggie's head swung to the right. There sat the redhead, Rebecca Dickerson, who worked at the Pentagon.

"Are you following me?"

"No, I'm not that good. This place happens to be one of my favorite spots for after hours. I'm supposed to meet a few friends here. I was as much surprised to see you here as you were to see me. I didn't take you for one who'd hang out in a seedy place like this."

"I wouldn't say it was seedy, only a hole in the wall that makes a good hideaway when you want to be alone."

"So," Rebecca turned her head to the left and right as if she was looking for someone, "where is the Major General? You don't have me fooled."

"No one is trying to fool anyone. First, you need to mind your business. Second, I haven't the foggiest idea as to where Major General Neal is at this time. You need to be careful how you speak to and of a General. It might affect your job stability."

"Hmm, you might try and have me fired, but you won't be successful."

"Another bourbon?" the bartender asked.

"No, I'm on my way home." Reggie reached in his pocket and pulled out a ten, and then he looked up at Rebecca. He put the ten back and pulled out a twenty. "This is to cover mine and whatever she wants to drink. And keep the change."

"Thanks," the bartender said, retrieving the money.

Reggie turned toward Rebecca. "Remember what I said; see you around."

"Oh, you will."

Reggie moved as swiftly as he could from the place. Rebecca gave him bad vibes every time she was in his presence. There was no rhyme or reason to it, only a feeling. Getting into his SUV, Reggie navigated through the D. C. traffic and headed for home. While he needed a drink, it wasn't what he wanted at that time.

The encounter with Ms. Dickerson unnerved him. He was stumped about what seemed to be an unsolicited intrusion in his life. Intel on Ms. Dickerson would be the first order of business when he got home. He had to find out what this red-head, skinny woman wanted from him. Reggie retrieved his cell phone from his pocket. Quickly, he pressed the quick-dial number for Jacoby. On the third ring, Jacoby answered.

"What's up dog?"

"A little frustrated is all."

"What are you frustrated about? You're a General now working at the Pentagon…"

"Don't get me wrong, I'm feeling my oats being here, although my job is pretty stressful."

"Yeah, but you're in the Chocolate City. I heard D. C. is full of pretty sisters with a ratio of ten to one for each man. That's what I call stress relief and I like those odds. I forgot that you're still messing with the lady general."

"I'm still seeing her, in fact on a serious note, I want to be with her. I've decided to leave Persenia. But it's not up for discussion, as I'm not sure when."

"Man, you can't be for real. Persenia's been your wife for forever. She's been there for you, sacrificed for you…"

"And listen to the dog that's messing around with his wife's cousin."

"Yeah, but I don't want to marry her. I've got a woman who takes care of my home, kids who adore me, and a place to rest my feet when I'm not smashing the cousin."

"You're sick, Jacoby. A lightning bolt is going to fall from the sky and fry your fornicating ass to ashes…that is if Carlitta doesn't beat your ass first and throw you out into the street as an example."

"Damn, homey, you don't have to stomp on a brother's self-confidence, although if my memory serves me correct, it was you that called me. True, my wife can get as evil as hell when pushed to the brink. I wouldn't put it past her dog, but I don't plan for her to find out about me and Kimiko."

"Well, I don't have room to talk. Anyway, I'm almost home."

"I thought you had something on your mind when you called."

"I did, but it doesn't matter now. I'm in the driveway. I'll call you sometime next week."

"Okay, dog. My line is always open if you need a sounding board."

"Appreciate it, bruh." Reggie clicked the OFF button.

IT WAS THEN THAT REGGIE REMEMBERED THAT HE WAS TO MEET UP with Kaleah. "Damn," he said out loud. Persenia's badgering and running into the red-head Dickerson woman made him have a complete mental melt down. He'd deal with Kaleah tomorrow; he wasn't in the mood to fondle anyone's breasts or have sheer lustful sex just for the sake of it. Tomorrow; there's always tomorrow.

❧ 21 ❧

REALLY REGGIE?

Morning shadows pushed light through the blinds. Reggie willed his eyes to open, as he closed the lid on the remnants of the dream he had about his encounter with Rebecca Dickerson. Browsing the internet when he returned home didn't turn up anything on Ms. Dickerson, but she had a skeleton or skeletons that Reggie was going to unearth, if he had to go to the end of the earth to uncover them. At the moment, he had a more important matter to attend to.

Reggie sat up and removed the covers from his body. He looked to his left and watched a sleeping Persenia, who was sprawled on her side of the bed in a deep sleep. While he had every intention of being with Kaleah in the future, he needed to do something now for his wife, who he'd treated miserably the past several years. He wasn't sure why he was having these thoughts. Maybe it was something Jacoby said about having the concubine and keeping home separate, although he didn't consider Kaleah a concubine.

He got up and started to head into the bathroom in order to prepare for work. His movement caused Persenia to shift her position.

Reggie watched her—she seemed so innocent, almost angelic like. He moved into the bathroom, showered, shaved, before going into his walk-in closet to retrieve his uniform for the day. He returned to the room and found Persenia lying on her back fully awake.

"Good morning," she said in a voice that was hardly audible.

"Good morning. Sorry to have disturbed you."

"You didn't."

"Look, I'm sorry that I went off about Julia being at the house. I'm under a lot of stress at work, in fact, I believe I'll be going to the Middle East in the very near future."

"Don't worry about it, Reggie. I probably should've checked her out first before inviting her in."

"Maybe I'm paranoid, but we've got to be careful who we entertain, especially with me working for Homeland Security. I could be a target."

"Was it a good idea for me to move here? I feel trapped—no friends or a life of my own." Persenia sat up in the bed and brushed her hair back with her hand. The neckline of her lacy gown was pulled down, exposing her perky breasts, although Reggie seemed to not notice. "I can't do this anymore." She sighed.

Reggie continued putting on his uniform but didn't look at his wife. His thoughts were of Kaleah, but he felt sad for Persenia. He had loved her. He sat on the edge of the bed and laced his boots. In the quiet, he turned to his wife.

"I promised you a trip to Dubai."

Persenia's eyes got wide and she watched Reggie without moving.

"We could go over for a few days...over the Memorial Day Weekend. I need a change of venue, even if for only a few days." Reggie looked at Persenia. "What do you think?"

Persenia placed a hand over her chest. "I'm surprised that you're asking but I'd like that. I'll have to get my passport updated."

"I can handle that. Why don't you plan on us going? I'll call you from work to let you know if all systems are go. It shouldn't be a problem." Reggie managed a smile.

"Okay. I'll get a few things together. Thanks, Reggie. I appreciate you doing this for me...for us."

At first Reggie didn't say anything, and then he thought better of not commenting. "I owe you." Reggie collected his wallet off the nightstand and grabbed his hat. "I'll call you later." He walked around the bed to where Persenia sat, kissed her on the forehead, and was gone.

Persenia was shocked that Reggie had even given a thought to them going to Dubai. The only problem with the time period was it was the week that Carlitta said she could come. Persenia would call her later in the day, since California was three hours behind, and ask her to come the early part of June.

❧ 2 2 ❧

LET IT GO

Excitement had consumed her. This called for a shopping spree. For a brief moment, Persenia thought of inviting Julia to join her, but after going over in her mind the conversation she had with Reggie, she thought better of it. She was in a good mood, and she wasn't going to do anything stupid and spoil the opportunity to do some serious shopping in Dubai. Smiling, she got up and prepared to start her day.

Moving toward the bathroom, Persenia stopped abruptly when her cell phone began to ring. Reggie must've been serious about checking whether he'd be available to make the trip. He hadn't even waited until he arrived at the office.

Persenia picked up the phone but sighed heavily when she saw Remy's number in her caller-ID. She wanted to ignore it, but if she did, he would more than likely call again. Squeezing her eyes shut and opening them again, she sighed again and answered on the next ring.

"Hi, Remy," she said without emotion.

"I've caught you at a bad time."

"Yeah, you did."

"Well, I can call back later."

"No, we can talk now; I assure you it will be a short conversation."

"I sense that you don't want to talk to me."

"Something like that. As I told you, Remy, I'm trying to make a life with my husband. In fact, we're getting ready to go to Dubai. He's been making a great effort toward improving our marriage."

"Is that so?"

"Damn, why did you say it like that?"

"Funny thing, only five minutes ago I received a call from Jacoby."

"What time is it there? It has to be early. It's a little after eight here."

"It's after five. I'm usually up at this time, although Jacoby woke me up today."

"So, what has your call to me have to do with him?"

"He shared an interesting conversation he had last night with your husband."

"Oh really. Well, I'm not interested in anything Jacoby Morgan has to say, and you should be ashamed to co-sign on his behalf."

Remy ignored Persenia and pressed on. "You might want to hear what Jacoby shared with me. You may thank me later."

"I doubt it," Persenia said under her breath.

"So, you say Reggie is taking you to Dubai?"

"That's what I said, Remy. Now I've got to go, so if you're only taking up my time on a pretense to talk to me, I'm cutting it short."

"Please...please, don't hang up. We've met only once, but you had a profound effect on me." Remy sighed. "I'm really feeling some kind of way about you. Usually, I'm not a petty or pushy person, but by any means necessary, I'm going to try and win you over."

"For the last time, Remy, I'm a married woman, who's working on her marriage. I shared some private thoughts and events in my life with you, but as I said earlier, they are tabled for further discussion. Mine and Reggie's business is just that—our business."

Remy sighed again. "You're making me go there."

"You don't need to. Anyway, it won't cause anything to be in your favor."

"Your husband is leaving you. That's what he told Jacoby. His heart is with some high-up officer who lives there."

Persenia politely hit the OFF button on her cell phone and proceeded into the bathroom. She ignored the phone when it rang again. She entered the shower and turned the water on high until the steam oozed from the bathroom to the bedroom. The water cascaded over her body, while she stood there without any expression. She didn't even enjoy the shower, although the water massaged her tense muscles. When she reappeared from the steamy tomb, she went about her day as if she'd never been interrupted.

She wore a pair of slim-fit Levi jeans that supported her rounded hips. On top, she wore a cotton candy, pink-colored cashmere sweater and on top of it a lightweight jacket. Setting the alarm, she stepped outside and instead of getting in her car, she walked briskly to the house next door. She rang the doorbell, waited, and after a minute or two, Julia came to the door.

"This is a pleasant surprise," Julia said all smiles.

"Hi, Julia. This is last minute, but I was wondering if you'd like to go shopping with me? I could use some company."

"Girl, let me get my purse, and I'll be ready to go. I was watching *Good Morning America*, but I can catch it any day; it was about to go off anyway. Come in."

Persenia followed Julia into her house and scanned her surroundings. They stopped in the family room, and Persenia waited while Julia went to get her purse. Her house was plain and dull, nothing that spoke to the feisty, colorful, spontaneous woman Julia seemed to be. There were lots of plants in the house, but lacked any type of art or pictures on the walls. For a General's house, the furniture was old and country. It looked as if Julia and her husband had purchased it at the beginning of his military career some thirty years prior. But the room was warm. Julia's children were in college out-of-state, which made it somewhat lonely for Julia. She didn't mingle well with the other smug, stuck-up wives that felt they were a class above her.

"Okay, I've got everything. Let me set the alarm and we can go."

"All right, I'm going to get in my car, I'll be waiting for you outside."

"I'll be right there, Persenia."

𝕏 23 𝕏

WHAT'S THE URGENCY?

He saluted several enlisted men as he headed into the Pentagon. The day was dreary, but he was going to make the most of it and begin with a positive attitude. His mind moved to his proposal to Persenia. Not sure why he pushed himself to offer her a trip to Dubai, but at that moment, it made Persenia happy, and he needed peace after the strange night he had.

Damn, they have some pretty women in here, Reggie thought, as he moved toward his office without allowing his head to twist, turn and look back on some curvaceous backsides. Weak for the opposite sex was his downfall, but today he was going to turn over a new leaf...well, all except for Kaleah, who was his joy and pain. He wanted to be with her; the urge was strong. She was like hot fudge pouring over his body. Undeniably, she was that intellectual partner he didn't have with Persenia—their two heads together could conquer the world and everything in between. Reggie had to make up for not meeting with her last night.

As Reggie neared his office, he suddenly stopped. Why was the red-headed secretary standing outside of his door?

Reggie approached the door to his office and prepared to move past Ms. Dickerson.

"Brigadier General Charleston, may I speak with you a moment?"

Reggie stared at her. "What is it, Ms. Dickerson? Say what you have to say right now. My schedule is busy today."

Rebecca Dickerson scanned her surroundings and noticed that Reggie's secretary, Sandra was now staring at her. "It's best if I spoke to you privately. Major General Forbes asked that I share something with you."

"Ask him to call me if it's that important."

Rebecca stood there a moment, but Reggie had already walked away. Sandra Whitaker, Reggie's secretary, stared back and gave Rebecca a look that seemed almost lethal. Hands up in surrender, Rebecca backed up and started to say something and thought better of it.

Sandra Whitaker rolled her eyes and turned back to her computer screen and continued to read whatever she was reading before being distracted.

"Ahhh…" Rebecca began.

"You heard the General," Sandra said without turning around, seeming to enjoy Rebecca's discomfort.

"Yes, I did, but…never mind." Rebecca turned around and exited the office.

Sandra watched as Rebecca retreated, her gears seeming to go into motion.

෩

It was nine-thirty in the morning, and already, Sandra had given him ten messages. The message he thought he'd see wasn't there, although it was his and Kaleah's unwritten rule to never call on military phones to discuss personal business.

He pushed back and relaxed and went over some of the messages, but the one from his boss, the Army Military Service Chief, made him sit up straight.

Urgent! Meeting at ten to discuss major offensive—War Room. Gen. Compton.

Sandra should've mentioned this message to him right away. Twenty minutes was all he had to pull notes together from their last defense meeting. He'd call Major General Forbes when he returned to his office. Strange as the encounter was with Rebecca, it would have to wait.

Reggie hit the intercom. "Sandra, pull my files with the information on my previous meeting with the Joint Chiefs. I need them pronto. If General Compton's office should call, tell them I'm on my way."

"Yes, sir."

Within seconds, Sandra had the file in hand and knocked on Reggie's door. Reggie took the folder, glanced in it, and looked up at her. "As soon as you saw me enter the office, I should've been handed the message about the meeting that's about to happen. Do not let this happen again."

"Yes, sir."

And then Reggie headed out of the office, leaving Sandra to stew in her mistake.

He hadn't gotten far down the corridor when Major General Forbes suddenly materialized from around the corner.

"You heard?"

"Heard what?" Reggie asked puzzled.

"ISIS hit three major targets about an hour ago."

"What?"

"Yeah...four of our own were killed at a hotel in Kuwait. And they've hit the London Tube system again. It's a mess. And there was a report that they may have killed another British soldier they'd captured some time ago, but it isn't confirmed."

"Damn. Look, I've got to run. I'm on my way to the War Room now to probably discuss this very thing." Reggie looked at his watch. "I've got five minutes, but while you're here, what was so important that you had to send Rebecca Dickerson to my office to give me a message?"

"Huh? I didn't send that girl anywhere. In fact, I was wondering where in the hell she was. My phone has rung off the hook all morning and I was a little pissed off about having to answer it myself several times. I've been thinking about firing her."

"She's a strange one. My vibe tells me that something is up with this girl. Every time I turn around, she's staring me in the face. I went to this bar for a drink last night, and five minutes after I arrived, there she was. And this morning was all too strange. If you had something important to tell me, you'd pick up the phone instead of sending someone around to give me a message."

"You're right about that, Reggie. We'll talk later; I know you have to go. Rebecca's behavior is cause for concern. By the way, we have something else to discuss. Our wives. How's Major General Neal doing?" Michael winked at Reggie.

"I've got to run."

"Okay, we'll talk later."

❧ 24 ❧

HOMELAND SECURITY

Reggie listened attentively to the Joint Chiefs as they strategized about what needed to be done immediately in the Middle East. With the attack on three major interests in the wee hours of the morning to include U. S. casualties in London, ISIS had to be dealt with as soon as possible. ISIS had become a stronghold in the Middle East and the surrounding European nations, strangling the European and United States' defenses at every hand. There weren't enough Syrian or Iraqi troops being trained to defend against this new enemy who'd swooped in like a thief in the night, taking up the slack from Al Qaeda. It was almost a given that Reggie would be going to the Middle East shortly to assess the immediate situation with his naked eyes and meet with some of the commanders with instructions from the Joint Chiefs.

Fifty minutes into the mandatory meeting, there was a knock on the door. This was a closed meeting, and no other personnel were allowed to come into the room. Annoyed, the head of the Joint Chiefs nodded at his Navy counterpart, who rose from his seat to assess the urgency.

A note was passed through the door and then closed. Reggie's counterpart took the note to his boss who handed it to the head of the Joint Chiefs.

"Oh my goodness," uttered the head of the JC's.

General Compton, who sat next to the head, took the note that fell on the table and read it. Immediately, he turned in Reggie's direction, his eyes bucked and seeming to glaze over.

"What is it?" someone asked.

General Compton composed himself. "Major General Kaleah Neal was found murdered at her home this morning."

Reggie sat up straight as General Compton's words sank in. His body began to shake. He didn't remember the time, but Kaleah had called him last evening and he didn't answer. Maybe she was in trouble and he could've saved her. But it was too late now to ever know the truth of his statement. It could've been the other way around. They could've been together when the horrific event took place. Why had God spared him?

Reggie willed his body to stop shaking. He, along with the others, was visibly upset at the news. However, he didn't want to make a spectacle of himself, let alone have people speculate about his relationship with Kaleah. And then he remembered the strange conversation he had with Rebecca Dickerson this morning. Was she trying to tell him something? He had to speak with her right away...as soon as they were released from the dungeon.

General Compton wiped his face on the sleeve of his fatigues. "General Charleston, your TDY papers will be prepared right away for travel to Kuwait and Syria. You'll be leaving in twenty-four hours. General Wallace Elston will accompany you."

"Yes, sir," Reggie heard himself say.

🎋 25 🎋

PRIORITIES

As soon as Reggie left the War Room, he headed for his office. His secretary, Sandra, had already been advised to push his temporary duty, otherwise known as TDY paperwork through pronto. Learning of Kaleah's death had left him numb and without a sanctuary to express his immediate thoughts.

Agitated, he approached Sandra's desk and barked an order. "Get Major General Forbes on the horn right away."

"Yes, sir," Sandra said flatly, as she stared at Reggie out of the corners of her eyes. "I'm sorry about what happened to Major General Neal."

"Does the whole world know?"

Sandra was somewhat taken aback. She took her time, composed herself and responded. "Everybody is talking about how she was murdered execution style in her home."

"Execution style? Jesus. I only heard that she was murdered but damn...this is terrible."

"That's what the newscasters reported. The FBI has been brought in to..."

Reggie interrupted Sandra's thought. "Call Major General Forbes now. Tell him it's important that I see him right away. Do not give that message to anyone but him."

"O...Okay."

Reggie went into his office and dropped down into his seat. He picked up a little gold metallic what-not object on his desk and twirled it between his fingers. First things first. He had to find out as much as he could about Kaleah's death before he got on the plane and flew away to the Middle East. And somehow, he felt that the red-head secretary held a key to the mystery.

Blowing air from his mouth, Reggie opened the drawer to his desk and pulled out a picture of Kaleah and himself he'd hidden amongst some of his papers. Tears began to flow as he reminisced about the last time she was in his arms and how they'd made sweet love to each other. She made his body tingle; no, that wasn't an accurate account. Kaleah made his body a human land mine that could explode at the touch of her fingers. And those velvety lips and fine, fierce hips of hers changed the meaning of pleasure in his book. But Kaleah was more than what she could do for him between the sheets. She was an officer and a woman that was well respected by her peers. She could've run Homeland Security by herself, if she were ever given an ounce of a chance.

What was taking Sandra so long putting the call through? He got up from his desk and started to go to hers when the intercom buzzed.

"Major General Forbes has left the building, sir."

"What about his secretary...Ms. Dickerson?"

"She wasn't available either. Another secretary answered the line and informed me of Major General Forbes' absence."

"On second thought, call again and leave a message. Thank you." Reggie clicked off the intercom and slammed his desk with his fist. "My mind is telling me that that red-head bitch may be involved." But he had no way of knowing that to be true.

Reggie got up from his desk, retrieved all of his valuables and prepared to leave. He stopped by Sandra's desk and waited until she was off the phone.

"I'm on my way home. Have a driver bring my orders to my home.

If Major General Forbes should call, give him my cell number and tell him to call me right away."

"Alright, sir."

※

THE LAST THING REGGIE WANTED TO DO WAS GO OVERSEAS. WHILE driving blindly through the streets of D. C., anger had consumed him. He felt obligated to remain in town for Kaleah's sake. What about her family? Who was going to take care of her arrangements? Who'd be standing over her casket boohooing for a love lost?

Selfish as it was, that's how he felt. There was a hole in his soul that hurt like brand new shoes. Tears dripped onto his fatigues like a storm that was brewing and was getting ready to let loose. Who in the world wanted Kaleah dead?

He wanted to see her...view her body before he left. He wanted to look upon her one last time. "Oh God, why Kaleah?" Reggie wailed.

✿ 26 ✿

MAKING A NEW FRIEND

Barely out of the driveway, Persenia's cell phone began to chirp. Remy's name appeared in the caller-ID, and she quickly declined the call and turned her focus back to the road. Not even a minute passed before Remy called again. And again, Persenia declined the call.

"Your phone rings a lot," Julia said with a smile. "I seldom receive phone calls, not even from my kids. It's almost as if they couldn't wait to leave home."

"Thank your lucky stars that you don't have someone bugging you all the time, although it would be nice to hear from your children every now and then. You need to take a trip and go visit them one weekend."

"My children think I'm old fashioned."

After looking at the inside of her house, Persenia understood that statement. "Well, you'll have to make them understand that you miss and love them, and care about how they're fairing."

"Yeah. I'm so lonely. Michael is so involved in his work. To be honest, I'm in a loveless marriage."

"So why are you still with him?"

"I grew up in a strong, religious household and divorce is taboo. My parents were together for fifty-two years. My mother passed away one year and my father the next. There was always love in the house, and I vowed that when I married, I was going to have the same kind of home."

"Do you have any siblings?"

"One brother who's married with six children. They live in the Ozarks and are happy as a lark."

"Does your husband take you out? Does he give you the latitude to make a lot of decisions about your household?"

"Persenia, I can count on one hand how many times my husband has taken me to dinner in the last year. He's a tightwad and holds on to our money as if he's not going to get another paycheck."

"So how do you go about getting groceries and personal things?"

"I get any allowance that I use for personal things, but he goes to the commissary and buys the groceries himself, or he has someone else to do it, and he takes care of the other major household bills."

"Today, I was going to go out and purchase some new outfits for my trip to Dubai."

Julia's eyes lit up. "You're going to Dubai? I'd love to go to a place like that and enjoy myself."

"Well, we'll have to plan a trip. But back to today. I'm going to take you to a furniture store and you're going to pick out some new furniture for your living room. It really needs to be updated."

"I can't do that, Persenia. Michael would kill me. Anyway, I don't have any credit cards in my name, let alone the money to pay them off."

"You've got to have some money saved up somewhere. A girl always must have a rainy day fund."

"Well, I do have about five-thousand dollars saved. It's in an envelope in the back of my lingerie drawer."

"Julia, please. You need your own bank account and you can elect to not have statements sent to your home. Better yet, get a post office box and that way you can have private mail go there."

"I've never had anyone to advise me about these kinds of things, but I'm excited about the possibility of doing it. Let's go."

Persenia's phone rang again. This time, she shut it off without looking at the caller-ID. Since she had yet to hear from Reggie, she would wait until she returned home to get his verdict. She had a few weeks to plan for Dubai. "My phone is off and we're off to shop for furniture."

On Maryland's 295, Persenia drove toward Arundel Mills Mall. The ladies laughed, talked, and seemed to enjoy each other's company.

"Have you ever spied on your husband?" Julia asked out of the clear blue sky.

Persenia clutched the steering wheel tight, trying to regain her composure. "No," she lied. There was no way she was going to part with her secrets with a woman she barely knew. "Why are you asking? I hope I'm not being a bad influence by enticing you to go behind your husband's back to buy furniture. Your husband is a General and you shouldn't live the way you do."

"I spy on Michael. I have spyware hooked into our computer and I've even put a tracker on his car. I've followed the son-of-a-gun to restaurants where he's met young women and I have a folder full of emails that he's sent to a slew of women. He thinks I'm dumb and stupid, but I'm not that backwards. And today, I'm taking it to a new level."

"Girl, you have completely fooled me. Here I am thinking that I'm giving you pointers about how to navigate your life with your husband, when you're already a step ahead of me."

"Don't get me wrong; I love my husband, but I'm tired of the abuse. Regardless of how I've been brought up, I've been thinking seriously about turning him in to his superiors."

"Why don't you divorce him instead of messing with his career? That way, you'll get all that you deserve in alimony. If they kick him out of the military, they may downgrade his rank, which means his money will be funny. Better yet, they may not give him an honorable discharge. By divorcing him for irreconcilable differences, he'll have to pay you what a wife deserves, who's been with him his whole career as a housewife, taking care of him and the children. And he'll still have to take care of the children until they've graduated."

"Wow, Persenia. You have all the answers. It's almost as if you've been counseling others."

"Yes and no. Many women go through this as a military spouse, and in the units, I've been a part of, there have been a couple or two women that came to me with their drama. I tried to help as much as I could, considering I've never been in that predicament."

"Well, I'm going to forget about it for now and get some new furniture. I'm glad you're next door and I have someone to talk to."

Persenia reached over and squeezed Julia's arm. Even though she was country as hell, Persenia saw a different person emerge from her shell. It was in a good way. She smiled at the thought of Julia spying on her husband and following him to different places. Reggie better straighten up and fly right, if he didn't want one of those devices tailing his ass. Later for doing it the hard way.

❧ 27 ❧

HEAD OVER HILLS IN GRIEF

R eaching home, Reggie quickly moved from his car to the house. He looked around for Persenia's car, but it wasn't there. Maybe she had run to the grocery store, but if he knew his wife like he thought he did, she'd probably was participating in some retail therapy so she could look good in Dubai. He hated to break the news to her, although he had tried to call her several times.

He thought about dialing Kaleah's number just to hear her voice, but it was probably being monitored for any incoming calls as part of the police's investigation. He sat down on the couch in the family room and cried until there were no more tears. Unable to keep still, he went to the bar and poured himself a stiff drink.

Thirty minutes after he arrived home, there was a knock at the door. He looked through the peephole and realized it was the courier with his TDY orders. He opened the door and signed for the package that was in a large envelope. Without wasting any time, he opened it up and saw a white, business-size envelope resting on top of his orders.

He slid his finger through a small opening where the envelope wasn't sealed and ripped it open like a caveman. There was a one page piece of paper inside that was folded in threes, and he rushed to view the contents.

"It was from General Compton, postponing his trip to the Middle East by three days in order for him to attend Kaleah's funeral. It appeared that her family had already obtained the body and set a date for the services.

Reggie crushed the paper in his hand and found some tears from somewhere. He was grateful for the reprieve, although as soon as the service was over he'd been on his way to the Middle East. There was no way he could live his life without this woman. He wasn't sure what he was going to do.

An hour passed when he heard the front door open. He wiped his face, gathered up his package, and placed it in his desk drawer in his office. All that he'd lost today, the last thing he wanted to hear was Persenia's cheerful voice, but he was rather surprised when she went straight to their bedroom without calling out to him.

Reggie waited and when she didn't come looking for him, he got up from his desk and went into his bedroom. Instead of the happy woman he left this morning who was excited about going to Dubai, another woman who seemed to be in an ill mood met him. She turned around and stared at him.

"I called several times and all of the calls went straight to voicemail."

The countenance on Persenia's face changed slightly. "Oh, I forgot to charge the phone last night, and I was already out and about when I discovered it." Persenia put her hands on her hips and produced a faint smile. "So, what was the verdict?"

"They're sending me to the Middle East. I already have my TDY orders. We'll have to postpone the Dubai trip."

"Figured you'd come up with some sorry ass excuse." Persenia dropped her arms to her side and started for the bathroom. She shook her head and rolled her eyes. "Should've known."

"I'm sorry, P. ISIS hit three strongholds today. We've had some casualties. This is what met me first thing when I arrived at the office this morning. Also, I've got some more bad news."

Persenia's back was to Reggie. She huffed and continued to stroll toward the bathroom. "There couldn't be any worse news than we're not going to Dubai, something I had looked forward to."

"Persenia, please turn around."

She turned around and folded her arms across her waist.

"Kaleah was found murdered today."

Persenia gasped and dropped her arms to her sides. "Oh my God, Reggie. Oh my God. Who'd do a thing like that? Do you have any idea who did it?"

"Not a clue. We were in our meeting when we received the message. I was supposed to leave for the Middle East tomorrow, but my leave has been deferred until after the service, which will be in three days."

"Arrangements have already been made? And so soon after finding her?"

"Apparently. The information was in the letter General Compton sent to the house by courier along with my TDY orders."

Reggie wasn't sure why he did it, but he reached out to Persenia and held her. Reluctantly, she held him back. "Kaleah was a dear friend, a highly intelligent leader in Homeland Security, and she'll be sorely missed."

Persenia said nothing.

Reggie felt Persenia withdraw, but he held her tight. He needed Persenia to get him through the week.

❦ 28 ❧

A FOOL IN LOVE

Three days flew by, as if time was pushed forward by some centrifugal force. Persenia was surprised at how clingy Reggie seemed to be, as if they had become true best friends. She knew the truth; he was mourning a woman that Persenia believed Reggie was in love with. Although Persenia was saddened at the death of Kaleah and the brutal way in which she met her death, she was happy that she was no longer an equation in her marital triangle.

Haunting her spirit was Remy's phone call to her in which he said Reggie told Jacoby that he was leaving her. As much as she wanted to address this issue with Reggie, she thought better of it. Bringing it up now might hinder any chance of repairing their marriage.

Grabbing the black jacket that went with her black knit dress, she meandered to the family room where Reggie sat nursing a drink. He was handsome, she thought, dressed in his Class-A uniform. His eyes were somewhat swollen, like he'd been crying for some time and his mind somewhere far away.

"A penny for your thoughts."

Startling him, Reggie jumped and almost spilled his drink. "Oh, I was thinking about the trip I have to make tonight."

"How long will you be gone?"

"Approximately two weeks. It depends on what all we get accomplished." Reggie put down his drink and looked up at Persenia, who stood in front of him. "Come here a moment."

Persenia moved forward and rounded the couch and sat next to Reggie. He took her hand.

"Thank you for understanding and being my rock this week. It's been a trying time for me. Kaleah was a special person in our group and it's hard to fathom that she's gone. The police and FBI have said they're doing everything they can to apprehend the culprit or culprits involved in this horrific crime." Reggie paused for a moment and swiped at a tear. Then he looked Persenia straight in the eyes. "I loved her."

Persenia froze in her seat. She wasn't sure this was Reggie expressing his grief for a dear friend or a lover. In any event, it left her feeling empty and then unsure of how Reggie really felt about her. And then she remembered Remy's telephone conversation, in which he said that Reggie told Jacoby that he was leaving her. Right now, she was going to get through Kaleah's service and deal with the other later, especially since Reggie would soon be boarding a plane to the Middle East.

🕸 29 🕸

FAREWELL

It was a media circus. News reporters from all television affiliates were on hand to get the reactions of the military brass who'd come to bid farewell to one of their fallen comrades. The FBI and local police force were also on hand, surveying the crowd that might possibly drop clues of Major General Kaleah's assassin. There was some reason to believe that this was a terrorist action, although there were no true leads and no one had come forth to claim victory.

Kaleah's family were all in attendance—a mother mourning under large sunglasses that covered her eyes but dressed in an elegant black and a silver buntal hat with a bursting flower applique on it that dipped to the side and complimented her simple but classic two-piece St. John knit dress and jacket, surrounded by her spouse, remaining children, and a host of other relatives. For sure they would take up many of the seats in the African Methodist Church that Kaleah attended.

Dignitaries from all branches of the military tied to Homeland Security were in attendance. Besides the obvious saturation of the local police force, the President's Secret Service was also in full effect. The

Presidential motorcade arrived moments later and President Barack Obama stepped out and lent a hand to First Lady Michelle Obama, who gracefully emerged from the car into the sunshine sporting a gorgeous lightweight, pale-blue sheath and coat by one of her favorite designers, Jason Wu. The media ate it up.

Hidden behind dark glasses, Persenia stood next to Reggie as they moved through the crowd not wanting to be observed. And then she heard Reggie's name called out, and as a creature of habit, he turned his head in the direction of the caller.

"Brigadier General Charleston," the reporter called again. Reggie said nothing. "The tragic loss of Major General Neal must be a tough one for the agency."

Smoldering with anger, Reggie tried to keep it in check. Get the story...sell some papers were all that these hungry puppets of media society were interested in. He hated them with a passion, but he wouldn't act out his feelings—at least not right now.

"The loss of human life is tragic no matter whom it is, and Major General Neal's loss will be felt for a long time."

"I understand that you and General Neal were very close, closer than most."

Reggie stared at the reporter with disdain. "You need to recheck your source. We at Homeland Security are a closely-knit group."

"You're missing the point."

"One of my colleagues is lying in a casket due to an irresponsible, no-account maniac who decided to take her life—a life that had so much more to give to this country. Now get that damn mike from in front of my face." Reggie pushed the microphone aside. He took Persenia's hand, moved around the reporter, and walked into the church.

THE CHURCH WAS OVER ONE-HUNDRED YEARS OLD. ITS FADED, GRAY brick structure, stained-glass windows and old, exposed wooden beams gave it an old-world feeling. An aisle went down the center of the church and long wooden benches, covered in a purple velvet fabric, sat on either side of the aisle. A modest pulpit sat up behind the casket, and a choir comprised of elderly men and women, who were dressed in black and white, stood up and rendered several musical selections.

In the pulpit sat a number of dignitaries to include the President of the United States, the Vice President, and the Joint Chiefs. The family took up at least four rows of seats. On the opposite side sat Mrs. Obama along with a slew of high-ranking military personnel. Other military personnel and staff were also in attendance.

Persenia sat through the service, oblivious of all that was going on around her. The reporter's comment to Reggie about his closeness to Kaleah was still stuck in her head. She'd watched the commotion under the shelter of her large, black shades, taking mental notes of Reggie's obvious irritation. While she wasn't a cold person by nature, Persenia didn't feel anything, although the numerous expressions from different ones about how the life of Kaleah had affected them, how she was a pillar of the community, how she was a well-respected military officer, how she was the consummate friend and would be sorely missed clearly painted Kaleah as a woman of honor. But Persenia knew better. Kaleah was Reggie's whore no matter what the rest of the world thought about her.

Her attention was diverted when Reggie suddenly stood up, moved from beside her, and headed for the front. She watched him walk briskly, almost as if he was in a hurry and didn't want to be late. He stopped at the head of the closed casket, ran his hand across it momentarily, took a deep breath and moved to the podium that stood off to the side. But Persenia wasn't prepared for the long soliloquy about the woman whom Reggie found to be more than a friend, confidant, and an admirable soldier.

Uncomfortable wasn't the word; she was seething. If it wouldn't have made a scene, she would've gotten up in the middle of Reggie's recitation and walked out. Persenia wondered when he took the time to write something down, but when she looked back up at the podium, there was no paper. Reggie was coming straight from the heart. And then he broke down—alligator tears and all.

Persenia sat still, her eyes transfixed on the scene in front of her.

When Reggie returned to his seat, she ignored him and moved her hand when he attempted to touch hers.

President Obama gave the eulogy and brought everyone to tears. It was befitting the fallen angel of democracy, although in Persenia's mind, her wings were singed with black soot; no, covered in black soot. And then it was time to say a final goodbye, at least for the Charleston's, since Reggie had to scurry off to meet up with General Elston for a briefing before they flew to the Middle East later that evening.

Outside again, Persenia was ready to get as far away as possible. Reggie milled about, talking to this one and that one, until the hearse, followed by the limousines filled with family members, filed off of the church grounds headed for Reagan National to ship Kaleah's body to Hampton, Virginia for another family farewell and burial. And for a brief moment, she saw his body stiffen when he appeared to be looking in the direction of where a white, red-headed woman stood, dressed in a trench coat and who seemed to be staring at Reggie.

Immediately, Reggie made an about face and told Persenia he was ready to leave. Lips shut tight, Persenia followed Reggie to the car. Her temperature was boiling over as Reggie's mood that moments earlier seemed to be one of amusement and content had suddenly turned cold. Unable to assess it totally, she stopped before they arrived at the car, turned to her husband, and asked the question she'd been dying to ask.

"Were you going to divorce me if she hadn't been killed?"

The look on Reggie's face was worth at least a thousand words. For sure, he was taken aback at the question. "Where in the hell did that come from?"

"Don't play me for a fool, Reggie. I listened to you talk about that woman today, as if she was the love of your life. Anybody listening to you today would've surmised that your relationship with Kaleah went deeper than a working one. You spoke about her as if you'd been together for years and enjoyed a lifetime of memories. If I felt it after listening to you, I'm sure others did."

"You're exaggerating."

"Am I?"

"Let's go, Persenia. I've got to drop you home before I meet Elston.

I'll get all my stuff so I won't have any need to come home before shipping out."

"You didn't answer the question but maybe you did."

"Don't try to rile me up. It's been a trying day."

Persenia walked briskly, moving ahead of Reggie. She remained quiet once they got in the car and rode home.

Reggie was first in the house when they returned home. They both went to their bedroom—Persenia to take off her clothes and get into something more comfortable, while Reggie gathered his bags for his trip.

She sat and watched, as he moved about the house effortlessly and in silence, gathering up any additional things he needed. He left the room and returned with his briefcase and orders in hand. He sat the briefcase on the bed and opened it, shoving things around to make sure he had all he needed. Then he quickly changed into his uniform that he'd hung in the closet.

Finally, he placed his orders in a side pocket of his briefcase, and before he closed it, he picked up Kaleah's obituary from the dresser where he had laid it and tossed it in. Reggie closed it and then looked over at Persenia without saying a word.

Reggie gathered up what he could and took it to the car. He returned and picked up the rest.

Persenia was still in the same sitting position he left her in. She felt Reggie's gaze and looked up at him.

He stared, as if he felt sorry for her. "I'm gone. I'll call when I can." And he was gone.

๑๛๑

THREE HOURS HAD PASSED SINCE REGGIE LEFT THE HOUSE. Wallowing in self-pity, Persenia rose from the couch she'd been sitting on since Reggie made his exit. Her head ached from trying to rationalize why her husband hated her so, even in the wake of Kaleah's death. Drained and dejected, she went to her bedroom, picked up her purse from a chair where she'd thrown it, and pulled out her cell phone.

Deep in thought, she sat on the edge of her bed and looked at her phone. No longer contemplating her next move, she scrolled down her call log and found the number she was looking for. She touched the keypad with her finger and pressed it. Putting the phone to her ear, she waited.

"Hello, Remy."

❧ 30 ❧

RECONNECTING

"I was expecting your call."

"Don't flatter yourself, Remy."

"I didn't mean it in a disrespectful way, Persenia. All I meant was that I was hopeful you'd be calling soon."

"If you say so."

"So, what prompted you to have a change of heart?"

"Circumstances have changed. There's been a disruption in my household."

"How so?" Remy asked in a concerned tone of voice.

"For starters, my husband's concubine was murdered last week. Her funeral service was today."

Remy gasped and then was quiet for a moment. "I'm sorry to hear it."

"While I don't wish anyone ill will, I was hopeful for my marriage once she was out of the picture."

"Let me guess. He's mourning her loss more than expected."

Ignoring Remy's remark, Persenia steered the conversation slightly.

"You were right, Remy. He was making plans to divorce me. It's apparent he's unhappy with me, and Kaleah's death hasn't changed how he feels."

"Something is wrong with a brother that can't appreciate a woman who is dedicated to her marriage on top of being as fine as hell."

"Don't be sorry. I'm ready to move on with my life."

"What are you suggesting?"

"When the time is right, I'm going to walk away from my loveless marriage. I'm tired of the mental abuse; I deserve better. Honestly, I thought there was a smidgen of a chance for us after Reggie found out that Kaleah was murdered. He hung on to me for dear life like he needed me in the worse way, but he only used me to assuage the hurt he felt in his lousy heart for his lover."

"Where is he now?"

"He's on his way to the Middle East...no goodbyes or any concern for how I was feeling."

"So, you decided to call me."

"Yeah, that's what I did. My decision to call you wasn't only due to the stressful situation I'm in. I've had a lot of time to think, Remy, and I want to find out what a real relationship could be like. I'm not getting any younger, and my life will be over waiting on Reggie to realize that I'm the best thing he's ever had."

Persenia could feel Remy's smile through the phone. "I like what I hear, but I'm not a toy you can take out of a box, play with any time you get ready, and when you're done, toss it in a corner until the next time you feel like playing with it."

"You're right and I understand perfectly well where you're coming from." There was a long pause. "Look, why don't you get on a plane and fly to Washington? I need to talk to a friend—someone who has my best interest at heart."

"Do you mean that and is it a smart thing to do?"

"Maybe not, but who cares? I'm sick and tired of being the butt of Reggie's thoughts and dreams. I no longer exist in his world, and for the first time in a long time, I'm going to follow my heart and do me. I don't give a damn what anyone has to say. Will you come?"

"I'll be on the first thing smoking."

"Thanks, Remy. You have no idea how much this means to me."

"I believe I do. I'll see you tomorrow. I'll call you later with the details."

"That will be fine. Hurry." And the line was dead.

NO PEACE IN THE MIDDLE EAST

Reggie and General Wallace Elston were airborne on a C-130 headed toward the Persian Gulf. There was plenty of time for Reggie to reflect on all that happened that week...from Kaleah's untimely death to the reality of what was left of his marriage to Persenia. Then a visual of the red head, Rebecca Dickerson, clouded his thinking. She was the last person he wanted to think about, but somewhere in the back of his brain, that woman fit into the equation of all that had been happening to him.

It was too quiet in the plane. Reggie watched as General Elston combed the contents of a military transcript he was given at the last minute that contained details of the carnage of a few days prior with strategies he and Reggie planned to share with the commanding general over the U. S. forces in the region.

"What's on your mind, Reg?" General Elston asked, temporarily taking his eyes away from what he was reading.

"Still thinking about Major General Neal's death and who'd want her dead. It's driving me crazy to think she had to endure such a horrible end."

"Yeah, that was tragic, but the FBI and CIA, I hear, are on top of it and hopefully will have the culprit in custody by the time we return back to CONUS."

"I hope so."

"You need to read this intel before we land in Iraq. ISIS is a beast, and it's going to take more than air strikes to rip the core out of this enemy."

"With them recruiting heavily in our own backyard certainly hasn't made life easy for Homeland Security. But I'm up to the challenge."

Elston ran his hand through his completely silver mane. "Let me ask you something, Reggie. It might sound kind of strange coming from me, but it's something I've thought a lot about lately."

"What is it?"

"Fear. Do you have any reservations about constantly going into enemy territory so close to retirement?"

Reggie looked at Elston and then turned away, staring out of the plane's window. "I'm surprised that the word "fear" came out of your mouth."

"I'm sure you've given it some thought."

"So, you're going to answer for me?"

Elston laughed. "You're right; I did ask you the question. So, what's your answer?"

"Everyone has a fear of dying, whether it's on our own city streets or on foreign soil fighting the enemy. But I try not to think about it. We're leaders and must keep our fear in check, otherwise our troops will lose trust in our ability to lead as they fight and defeat the enemy. Why, other than the explanation you gave, are you giving into fear?"

"My family...my wife, especially. She's so afraid that I'm going to leave her a widow and she'd be left alone in the world. The kids are grown and gone with lives of their own. Although the military has been my life for the past thirty-nine years, I love my wife dearly. I've been thinking about retiring soon so I can give her one-hundred percent of my time—traveling to places we want to go. I even thought about purchasing a villa on some remote island. I don't want to have to forfeit the life I've planned after the military, playing cops and robbers for a war I'm not sure I believe in. What about you and your wife?"

Reggie wished he could switch the conversation to something else. The woman he wanted to spend the rest of his life with was gone. He wasn't sure how he was going to answer the question, but Elston was waiting on one.

"Persenia and I haven't had that conversation. Maybe I've taken for granted that I'll always return from a war zone unscathed. Yeah, it's presumptuous of me to think that getting killed in combat at this time in my life couldn't happen to me, especially since our travels to the war zones have been only in an advisory capacity. But we can't take anything for granted."

"No, we can't, Reggie. There's never going to be any peace in the Middle East."

Reggie turned his head toward the window. His life with his wife had been the farthest thing from his mind. He wasn't sure what he was going to do when he returned home, as his desire to get a divorce hadn't changed because Kaleah was no longer in the picture.

32

SMOOTH LANDING

A brisk wind stirred up the atmosphere. There was a hint of sunshine, as the sun's rays pushed against the heavy accumulation of clouds that covered the sky. Persenia waved to Julia as she backed her car out of the driveway. For the first time in a long while, there was a good feeling in her soul. Persenia had fixed her mind on moving forward with her life and establishing a brand-new chapter. She felt free to love.

She headed for baggage claim at Ronald Reagan Washington National Airport. Persenia was ecstatic that Remy was able to catch a Red Eye so quickly. Money could do that, and from Persenia's limited view of Remy's station in life, he wasn't short on cash.

Pulling up in front of the airline terminal, Persenia's heart skipped a beat when she saw Remy standing at the edge of the sidewalk, fine as new money, with a medium-size metal suitcase. Sunglasses covered a large portion of his face, but the muscular, tall, cocoa-brown brother she remembered from her last visit to Seattle, was one in the same.

She let out a huge sigh, not exactly sure how she was to act. A large smile broke out across her face. It was apparent that Remy was excited about being there, as a smile covered his face as well.

Remy stuck his head in the window of Persenia's BMW. "Hey, beautiful." He couldn't take his eyes off of her.

"Get in. We'll have plenty of time to talk."

Opening the back door of Persenia's car, Remy lifted his suitcase off the sidewalk and placed it in the car. Wasting no more time, he quickly opened the passenger door and jumped in. "I'm glad you called." Then he reached over and kissed her on the lips.

"So am I," Persenia agreed, recovering from Remy's sweet taste. They held each other's hand, and minutes later, Persenia drove away.

They talked non-stop, as if they'd known each other their whole lives. Not realizing that they were doing so, they completed each other's sentences and laughed for most of the trip about trivial things. Their conversation was easy and effortless and Persenia couldn't deny Remy's effect on her.

"I've got to give you fair warning. I have a nosey neighbor named Julia, but in reality, she's a good person. She's the victim of a loveless marriage, too, and I've become the friend she needed."

"So, does this mean that we will be going somewhere other than your home?"

"Yes, although I'll need to stop by my house and pick up a couple of items that I forgot to pack in my suitcase. I've made reservations at a hotel at the Washington Harbor. It would be suicide for us to stay at my house, since all the Generals who work at the Pentagon are our neighbors. Although Reggie is like gum on the bottom of my shoe, I'm not the kind of woman who'd have another man sleep in the bed I share with my husband. My stop will only take five minutes."

"I agree; I wouldn't in all good conscience want to be shacking up in a house where you and your husband call home. Although we're taking a risk by seeing each other, it doesn't seem like a total violation of our liaison by going to a hotel."

Persenia was enthralled with Remy's way of thinking, although she wondered if he was only pacifying her for what he expected to get out of their being together, even for a short period of time. She wasn't used to an athlete talking halfway proper, although Reggie knew how to turn it on and off when needed. She smiled.

"I'm glad you agree. Well, we're here. This is the Gaylord at the National Harbor. It's a nice hotel. I'll go to the house later."

"Let me take care of the expenses while we're here. I want our time together to be the perfect few days that you've experienced in a long time."

"I'm long overdue."

✢ 33 ✢

REUNITED

The valet got into Persenia's car and drove away. Remy gave her a puzzled look as the car disappeared from sight.

"Aren't you staying here tonight?"

"Why are you asking?" Persenia said with a smirk on her face.

"The obvious. I don't see a suitcase or an overnight bag."

Persenia hooked her arm in Remy's free one. She smiled as she led him to the elevator.

Remy stopped in his tracks. "Okay, fess up before we go any further. I need some kind of explanation. Don't think I didn't notice that we didn't stop at the Reservation Desk."

Laughing out loud, Persenia reached in her coat pocket and produced what looked like a credit card. "I'm a twenty-first century thinking woman. Since I don't need everyone in my business, I took the liberty to register in advance of your arrival. You can still pay the final bill." Remy laughed; Persenia stuck her hand out. "Therefore, I'm in possession of the key. Walla walla."

Eyebrows arched, Remy's smile was spread the length of his face. "I like how you think. Show me the way, twenty-first century woman."

The duo headed for the elevator, laughing as if they didn't have a care in the world. Remy wrapped his free arm around her waist and she snuggled up under his arm. When the elevator arrived, they rode it to the fifth floor.

Stepping out of the elevator, Persenia looked both ways, still cautious about what she was doing. This was no time to get careless, although Reggie probably wouldn't give a damn what she did. They moved quietly toward the door marked with the room number that matched the key she was holding, and when they arrived at their destination, Remy took the pleasure of opening the door and ushering them into the room.

As soon as the door closed, Remy let go of his suitcase he'd been clutching by the handle and grabbed Persenia into a strong embrace. Gently, he pushed her up against the wall and kissed her passionately, not giving either one of them an opportunity to come up for air or a chance for Persenia to object.

To Persenia, it seemed that hours passed before Remy let up. The only reason she hadn't pushed away earlier was that she was enjoying it too much. Remy's lips were soft and pliable, like Charmin toilet tissue was to a baby's behind. Whatever the analogy, she hated it when they finally pulled apart.

Remy sighed. "Wow, you taste so good."

"So do you," Persenia whispered in his ear. "Why don't we get comfortable? Are you hungry?"

"Hungry? Don't make me answer that question."

Persenia went to the window and closed the curtains. Remy placed his suitcase out of the way and went to the bathroom. Hearing water fall in the tub, Persenia smiled to herself. Not once had she thought of Reggie, and he not of her since she hadn't received a single telephone call from him yet. She didn't care. It was a moot point.

Anticipating what was to come, she pulled back the plush, down comforter and then stripped down to her lacy lingerie. And then she sat and waited for what she'd been craving.

When Remy appeared out of the bathroom, a white bath towel was wrapped around the lower half of his body. His brown skin glistened in the darkness of the room. As he came close, Persenia could smell the musk oil he'd rubbed over his body.

Dressed in a black-lace teddy, Persenia held her arms out for Remy. She was the seductress, seducing the gorgeous black stallion that stood before her. With the grace of a king, Remy walked to Persenia and embraced her in his muscle-bound arms, stopping momentarily to strip the bath towel from around his body.

Eyes fluttering like butterfly wings, Persenia accepted him without reservations. She felt the hardness of his erotic member pushing up against the moist passion between her thighs that itched, no begged to answer his call to claim her precious jewels.

Slowly and seductively, Remy slid the straps of Persenia's teddy down her arm, while his penis throbbed at the bit, encouraging him to get a move on. It was almost effortless in the way he removed the lacy covering, as if he was an expert in the field of disrobing women in another life—in Persenia's eyes he was the *xpert*. And when the lingerie was completely absent from her body, Remy cupped his hands around her smooth buttocks and squeezed and rubbed them like a ripe piece of fruit.

In one quick move, he swept Persenia's body up from the floor and laid her on the bed. On all fours, he hung over her, examining her body, as if for flaws, but instead admiring every inch of her sensuous specimen. His eyes remained fixed on her supple breasts with its dark, ripe areolas. Suddenly his eyes shifted toward her patch of hair that hid her prized possession and finally he smiled.

"Girl, you're so damn beautiful."

Persenia smiled back. "Thanks. You aren't so bad yourself."

Remy lowered his body, careful not to crush hers with his. First, he gingerly kissed her lips before letting go and planting kisses here and there as his mouth slid down to her breasts. He took each breast in either hand and interchangeably went from one to the other, sucking and squeezing until Persenia's panting could be heard in the next room. He continued exploring—tasting, moving south in anticipation of what Persenia was about to surrender.

And all of a sudden, Persenia's knees rose in the air and knocked

Remy in the face, blocking his view and before being able to taste and seize her sweet fruit.

Remy sat up. "I thought you were ready."

"I am. I got tired of you taking so long to make love to me...to let me feel you inside of me."

"Well, I thought you would love a little foreplay before getting to the meat and heart of what we came here for."

Persenia looked in Remy's eyes. "I'm all for foreplay, but right now the throbbing between my legs, like the throbbing between your legs is begging for us to cut to the chase and make passionate love to each other. My body is hot and about to burst, and I can't wait for you to make me brand new."

Remy laughed. "Say no more. Open your legs for me. I've been more than ready."

"Me too. But I must say this, I do want more, Remy. I want more. I'm ready for a fresh start at life and for some odd reason, I feel free to love. Now, make love to me and we'll talk about the rest later."

Persenia was in heaven—under his spell. Her body hadn't felt the heat of passion in years. Remy moved with such precision that Persenia felt like a limp rag underneath him. Her nails dug into his body as he thrust himself further into her. Before long, Persenia felt a rumbling in her gut, an intensity that felt like a fatal explosion. And then she screamed Remy's name...Remy screamed hers, the sound piercing the quiet of the afternoon. And Persenia prayed that no one would come to their rescue."

❦ 34 ❦

THE PRICE OF PASSION

Persenia was in seventh heaven. The afternoon was spent well and she fantasized what it would be like being with Remy forever.

He was more than she'd bargained for. He was a smooth lover and he made her insides tingle like no one had before, and that included Reggie. He aroused her in the worst kind of way, and while her sudden thirst for him was lust initially, she could see their relationship becoming something much more. But, of course, it was too soon for her to give it a lot of thought. It was only one afternoon.

Showered and feeling great, Remy stepped out of the bathroom in his birthday suit, confident and fulfilled. Seeing his clean, buffed body with its bulging muscles and the scent of his cologne permeating her nostrils caused Persenia to collapse on the bed. The heat between her thighs betrayed her eagerness to make love to him right then and now, although she was almost dressed, since she'd jumped into the shower first. Willing her body temperature to drop, she was happy when Remy finally put a towel around his waist.

"Let's go to the bar and get something to drink and then we'll go out to dinner."

"Okay. Hurry up and put some clothes on before I jump your bones."

"We can cancel going down to the bar and hibernate in here the rest of the night."

"We'll have the rest of the evening to love on each other. Now get ready. I'm also hungry."

Remy laughed. Without saying another word, he put on a pair of creased jeans, a long-sleeved blue shirt, and a black linen blazer.

⚜

REMY AND PERSENIA WERE IN A PLAYFUL MOOD AS THEY SAUNTERED down the hallway toward the bank of elevators. Several other couples stood watch, engaged in colorful conversation, as they approached.

Ding. The elevator arrived and they prepared to get on. Persenia froze as she gazed into the eyes of her next-door-neighbor, Julia, who was all dressed up—hair twisted and pinned on top of her head; professionally made up, to include eyeshadow in hues of black and gray, and long, black glue-on eyelashes; and a short, clingy dress that left nothing to the imagination. Standing next to her, almost breathing in her ear, was a middle-aged man who was a mixture of Middle-Eastern and European decent. Julia's face turned red as a beet and she seemed petrified upon seeing Persenia, although Persenia was as petrified, not wanting to be exposed. Although Persenia had never met Julia's husband, it was a sure bet that her companion wasn't her husband. Julia flashed her eyelashes as some kind of signal, and Persenia ignored her. Julia slipped out of the elevator without exchanging a word.

Puzzled, Remy tried to snuggle next to Persenia as they stood at the back of the elevator. "What was that all about?"

"You won't believe my luck. That woman is my next door neighbor and I believe she wasn't with her husband."

"Oh, hell, what are we going to do?"

"I'm going to give you the key. I need you to go back to the room and get my purse, so we can run to my house and pick up my stuff and then go out to dinner. I can't hang around in this hotel."

"I guess this means we'll have to be locked up in the room for the next few days." Remy smiled.

"No. I'm sure Julia won't be here the whole weekend, although I have no way of knowing that unless I ask her. I'm going to take you sightseeing and we're going to have a good time while you're here."

"When is your husband returning?"

"Hell, I don't know, Remy. He barely said goodbye, let alone told me how long he'll be gone." Persenia paused. "Please don't think terrible of me, but a couple of times I actually prayed that...that he'd get killed over there."

"That wasn't a good thought, especially not said out loud."

Ding. The elevator stopped on the lobby floor. "I'll wait for you in the lobby." Persenia got out while Remy made a return trip to their room.

Nerves were getting the best of her, as she waited for Remy to return. She strolled to a group of plush chairs and sat in one, looking all around. Two minutes passed when she felt a hand tap on her shoulder.

Persenia jumped and looked over her shoulder as Julia came around and sat next to her.

"Persenia, let me explain." Julia sounded exasperated and her face was beet red.

"Really, Julia, you don't have to. My mouth is sealed. I won't say a word to anyone. Whatever you're doing here is your business."

"I don't want you to think that I'm some kind of floozy, who says one thing but actually cheats on her husband. If you knew..."

"Julia, you have your reasons. I'm not one to pass judgment on another. Honey, you do what you've got to do. I will admit, you've got taste."

For the first time Julia smiled. "Armand makes me come alive. Look, I've got to go. He's in town only tonight and I'm taking an opportunity to have some fun, since Michael went TDY for a week. So, what are you doing here?"

As Persenia prepared to give Julia a loose answer, she saw Remy in her peripheral vision. She gave him a look and he walked in the direction of the bar. That was a close call.

"A good friend of mine flew in today, and I'm meeting her for a few drinks. I was coming from her room when you saw me. I came down to the lobby to make a personal phone call and check my messages. I'm waiting for Reggie to call me. I haven't heard whether he arrived in Iraq. Hopefully, he'll call in a few minutes. As soon as my girlfriend comes down, we're going to go to the bar and get a drink and then to dinner." It wasn't the total truth, but sounded plausible as an answer.

"I hope your husband calls you. Can you imagine both of us ending up at the same place on the same day?"

Persenia smiled and shook her head. "Girl, no." She saw a man staring at them. "I think your gentleman friend is coming this way."

Julia jumped. "Ah...ah, let me go. I'll talk to you at home."

"So, was it an afternoon delight?"

Julia bit her lip and then smiled. "A girl never tells. Bye." Julia got up from her seat and Persenia watched as she and the gentleman strolled out of the hotel.

She breathed a sigh of relief. That was a close call.

ॐ 35 ॐ

WHERE DID THE TIME GO?

The next five days were a blur. Persenia and Remy enjoyed each other's company, so much so, they seemed as if they were one. Without any real concern of being discovered, save Julia, the couple explored the wonders of Washington, D. C.

They strolled down the Washington Mall, making stops at the African-American Museum, the Museum of Natural History, the Aeronautics Space Museum, and several others. They took pictures in front of the White House and swore out they caught a glimpse of President Obama and Michelle. Hand in hand, they admired the statues of prominent Americans that were littered throughout the busy thoroughfares, ending up on the steps of the Lincoln Memorial, as the statue of Lincoln, sitting on his presidential laurels, stared down at them.

"Of all the monuments that dot the city, I like this one the most," Remy said. "It's so imposing and has history written all over it."

"I would agree, however, we have yet to see the statue of Dr. Martin Luther King, Jr., and sight unseen and in my heart, I believe that statue will mean the most to me."

Remy smiled at Persenia and kissed her in front of all the other tourists who marched up and down the Lincoln Memorial steps. They pulled apart quickly when they heard the click of a camera nearby. A thin woman with red hair, dressed in black leggings, a long-sleeved white blouse, and a short denim vest smiled at them. "I couldn't help myself," she said. "There's nothing like beautiful love."

Persenia managed a smile and looked from the redhead to Remy. She put her arm in his and held on tight. She whispered in his ear. "It's time to go."

Without going to the top of the stairs to view the monument up close, the couple turned around and jumped on one of the sightseeing buses. They didn't speak and kept quiet for more than fifteen minutes, until Remy spoke.

"I'm not sure what's bothering you, Persenia, but I'm hungry. Why don't we go to the Capitol Grille and get something to eat? We'll take a taxi. Martin Luther King will be here tomorrow, that's if you want to still see it. I forgot that quick; today is my last day."

Persenia sat in total contemplation. She wasn't mad at Remy. The day was fantastic. In fact, she wondered where the week went. She turned and looked at Remy whose face looked confused, as he waited for her to respond to his request.

"I'm hungry too. Sorry for the change in my mood. That girl taking our picture bothered me."

"She was probably a tourist from Iowa who's never seen a black person before and can't wait to get back to her Midwest white friends to show our happy black asses to them."

Persenia laughed out loud. "Only you would come up with that scenario. My thought was that Reggie might have someone spying on me. Am I being paranoid?"

"Yes, ma'am, that redhead is a perfectly harmless human being. She and her friends will look at our pictures, laugh, and reflect on what the lens captured. Besides, Reggie hasn't called you once since I've arrived. I seriously doubt that he's even stopped to think about your feelings, let alone wonder what you're doing."

A dull ache surfaced in Persenia's head. She hated that Remy was probably right, although she hated even more that she heard it out loud.

"Look, I didn't mean to come off as being harsh, bashing that sorry ass husband of yours. It was only a statement of fact. Let's get back to the redhead. She couldn't help that we were two good-looking chocolate people, who have more going on for them than her cows-in-a-pasture friends."

Persenia laughed again. "Okay, Remy, I made more of the situation than it deserved. I don't even know anyone in D.C. except for my next-door neighbor, who almost busted me. Maybe I was a little paranoid. Now let's go eat. I can't take any more. You're too funny."

"Are you having a good time?"

"This has been a fantastic day and I don't want it to end."

"I've got to leave tomorrow." Remy waved his hand. "Here's a cab; talk about luck."

The cab pulled to the curb. Remy opened the door and they got in. Persenia was quiet until they were buckled into their seats. Remy told the cab driver where to go and they were off. Instead of talking, they turned toward each other and kissed, smacking so loud that the driver snapped his finger for them to bring the noise down a decibel. They laughed.

Lunch at the Capitol Grille was romantic, even amidst all of the chatter from high-profile clientele that sat talking politics, world issues or scheduling some kind of rendezvous with a mistress or male side piece. Persenia had soup and half of a club sandwich, while Remy munched on a nice cut of steak. They both ordered a glass of Chardonnay. Persenia didn't want time to race by; she prayed the day would last forever. Time spent with Remy was not only a valuable commodity, it was the best she felt in years.

Remy leaned over and whispered. "I want to suck on those plump, juicy breasts of yours."

Persenia smiled, then giggled as Remy made crazy faces at her. She caught a small piece of her sandwich that was dangling in her hand before it landed in her soup. "I want you, too," she said, looking around to see if anyone was listening. "I want to electrify your soul so that you won't want to leave. I'm hooked into you, man, and I'm not certain what I'm going to do about it."

"You can leave him."

"It's not that easy, Remy."

"What are you afraid of?"

"I'm not sure. Well, the truth is, I've been a kept woman most of my marriage to Reggie. I've done a lot of volunteer work but have barely spent a year on any paying job. I wouldn't put it past Reggie to cut me off completely, although I have rights since I've spent almost twenty years as his wife."

"You don't need him. I can provide you with anything you may need."

"Again, it's not that simple."

"So, what is it? Do you still love him and have no plans to ever leave him?"

Persenia sighed. "No, Remy, it's not like that. Reggie doesn't know how to love. Well, let me take that back. He didn't love me. The one person I believe he truly loved was recently killed. I was even foolish enough to think that with Kaleah gone...out of the picture, Reggie would redirect his attention toward me."

"So, you do have hopes that your marriage can be saved."

"I'm sure this must look strange to you, Remy, but I'll be the first to say that my marriage can't be salvaged, and truthfully, I don't want it to be. I'm not even sure about our future, but I will say that I feel some kind of way about you. You've got my heart fluttering...got me stuttering all over myself."

"I feel some kind of way about you too, Persenia...in fact I'm pretty sure it's love. My heart is beating for you. All you have to do is claim it. I honestly hope that my coming out here wasn't a total waste. I'm all up for a booty call, but this was more than that."

"I'm married."

"Not for long."

Persenia smiled and took a sip of her wine. "I'm feeling you, too."

"I'll wait."

✠ 36 ✠

TOO CLOSE FOR COMFORT

Reluctant to see her love interest go and unable to detach herself from him, almost as if he was her child going off to college for the first time, Persenia hugged and kissed Remy. She watched as he disappeared in the long line at the air terminal, her arm extended in a long goodbye. Face long, Persenia reflected on her week with Remy and how much she'd come to love this man, although she refrained from admitting it out loud.

Just as she turned to head out of the airport, her cell phone rang. She reached in her pocket, pulled out her phone. Sitting in the window of her caller ID was Reggie's face...a face that she despised. Nearly a week had gone by without a word from her husband, and at the moment she was feeling mellow and on a high from her time with Remy, Reggie decided to call.

Her first impulse was to let the phone ring, but on second thought, Persenia decided to take the call and listen to Reggie's lies.

She moved outside and opened the line. "Hello," she said without any feeling.

"Persenia, this is Reggie."

"Yeah. So, are you just now getting to Iraq?"

There was a long pause before Reggie finally answered. "No, but it's been go, go, go since we touched the ground. I'll be here for approximately another two weeks."

"Okay."

"Look, I'm not sure if you heard...if it was in the newspapers, but we've had intelligence that alludes to the conclusion that Kaleah's murder might be connected to ISIS."

Persenia couldn't believe her ears. His one phone call, late as it was, came without even an "*I'm sorry that it took so long to call*" but rather a disrespectful update on his dearly, departed girlfriend. Really?

"I've waited a week to hear if you made it to your destination and that you're sorry for taking so long to call. Instead, I've got to hear you talk about what may have happened to Kaleah. While I'm sorry that she was brutally murdered, she's not on my first list of concerns."

"I don't even know why I called you. Should've known you wouldn't have an understanding ear. Talk to you later." And the line was dead.

Persenia ears were still ringing, long after the line was dead. The nerve of that trifling man, Persenia thought. Why had Reggie bothered to call her in the first place?

Racing to her car, Persenia nearly fell as she neared her car. After clutching the side of the car, she steadied herself, and then, out of the corner of her eye, she noticed a woman looking at her...a woman with red hair. She couldn't be sure that it was the same person she saw yesterday at the Lincoln Memorial, but for sure she had red hair and had been staring at her. She turned away, but when she looked back, the woman was gone—vanished into thin air. Now a chill came over Persenia, and she hopped in her car and drove home as fast as she could.

Finally arriving home, Persenia pulled into the driveway and waited for the garage door to open. Before she was able to pull into the garage, Julia was running to her side of the car. It was as if Julia had been sitting by her window waiting for Persenia to come home and share some secret she couldn't wait another minute to tell.

Aggravated, Persenia let her window down, all the while only wanting to be alone inside the comfort and warmth of her home.

"What's up, Julia?"

"I was worried since I hadn't seen you in a few days. I rang your bell several times, and when you didn't surface I became concerned."

"There was no need to be concerned. My girlfriend and I decided to go to the Baltimore Harbor and spend a few days."

Julia seemed offended. "Well, I'm glad you're alright."

"I am. Now, I'm going inside and put my heels up—maybe take a nap since I've had so much fun these past few days. Is everything okay on your home front?"

Julia looked around as if to make sure no one was listening. "Yeah," she whispered. "My friend was here that one night. Michael came home a few days ago. He's been in a miserable funk. It has something to do with that General that was killed a couple of weeks ago."

Persenia was now interested in what Julia had to say. "Let me pull my car in the garage and get out." Persenia pulled the car inside, turned off the ignition, and got out. She'd wait to get her suitcase after Julia was gone since she had a ton of packages in the trunk. She wasn't up to Julia's interrogation.

"So, what did you hear about General Neal's death?" Reggie had been anxious to share some news with her earlier, but her heart wasn't into listening to her husband lament over his dead girlfriend.

"My husband, Michael, said that her death may be ISIS related and that the connection may have been compromised through Homeland Security."

"Your husband and Reggie must work in the same area. Reggie doesn't share anything with me."

"Yes, he works closely with your husband. Michael doesn't share hardly anything that goes on with me either when it comes to his work, but he seemed really disturbed by this bit of news. He says your husband is in Iraq because of an incident that occurred on the day they found the General's body."

"It's true that Reggie is in Iraq. For Michael, not to share a lot with you, you seem to know more than I do about what's going on at the Pentagon."

"Not really, and I wouldn't have known that much if Michael hadn't come home shaking in his boots. That's why I was worried about you."

Persenia sighed. "Thank you for sharing that with me. I'll make sure to check in with you next time."

Julia's neck jerked at Persenia's last remark. "I wasn't trying to check up on you."

Persenia patted Julia on the shoulder. "That remark wasn't meant to say that you were. Excuse my attitude; I'm tired. However, I'm glad you thought about me, and I think we need to check on each other often."

"Okay," Julia said quietly. "I've got to get Michael some lunch. I'll talk to you later."

Persenia's mind raced as she watched Julia exit her garage. As soon as Julia was out of sight, she let down the garage door, entered the house and turned off the alarm. She was happy to be home, but Julia's conversation was still fresh on her mind. And then she remembered the redheaded woman, who'd been lurking near her car when she was leaving the airport. And was yesterday a coincidence?

Before she was able to catch a breath, Persenia's cell phone rang. She reached inside her purse and pulled it out and saw Carlitta's picture on her caller ID.

"Hey, girl, have you decided to come visit me?"

"P, how about in two weeks? My mother says she can watch the kids for as long as I need."

"That's wonderful."

"Everything alright? You seem out of sorts."

"Everything is cool. Why wouldn't it be?"

"I hear things."

"Things like what?"

"Things like that General that was killed a few weeks ago in D. C. was Reggie's woman."

"I don't know what you're talking about, Carlitta. Reggie is in Iraq. I'm here trying to keep busy. My life has been a little dull and it would be nice to have my best friend here to keep me company."

"Do I need to come earlier?"

"That's up to you. Let me know when you've made your plans so that I can have everything ready."

"Okay, that'll work."

"How's Jacoby and the kids?"

"Good...the same. Busy making that money." Carlitta laughed.

"Alright, I'll see you in a couple of weeks."

"I'll send you my itinerary when I book my flight. Love you, P."

"Love you too."

Persenia looked at the phone and then dropped it on the bed. So, what had Carlitta heard and who was the carrier pigeon? Had Reggie called Jacoby after he'd hung up on her? Surely, Jacoby wasn't running his mouth to Carlitta when he had committed the world's worst deception right under her nose. Persenia was sick of all of them.

37

WHEN IN IRAQ

Reggie stared at the phone after disconnecting the call to his wife. His mind was already battling the news that Kaleah's death might be directly related to ISIS, and the one time he'd reached out to Persenia for support, she was non-existent. Persenia was dead to him, and as soon as he returned home, he would put her out to pasture—give Persenia her final walking papers. He didn't give a damn what his superiors thought or anyone else for that matter. To him, his marriage was a fraud, and with Kaleah gone, it wasn't going to change how he felt about Persenia.

Meetings had gone well with the ground commanders. Next, Reggie and General Elston were shuffling off to Syria in the next hour or two for a short briefing with a few key people about special ops and air offensives. President Obama had now given orders to deploy Special Ops to Syria to intensify the U.S. strategy to help local forces defeat the enemy.

In the distance, Reggie saw General Elston moving in his direction. As hard as he tried, he couldn't put thoughts of what had happened to

Kaleah out of his mind. Why was she targeted? Maybe it wasn't ISIS as everyone was so eager to believe.

His demeanor changed as Elston approached. He put on his tough outer shell to mask his feelings.

"Ready to head to Syria? These guys are good here."

"Yeah," Reggie said solemnly.

"Thinking about your friend, the Major General..." General Elston said as a matter of statement.

"Yeah, no, yes. It's so unreal that she would be a target. Why not you? Why not me?"

"Who's to say that we aren't, Reggie? The CIA and Homeland Security are working hard to get to the core of Kaleah's murder." Elston tapped Reggie on the shoulder. "Right now, we have a mission to complete. Remember, we're deep in enemy territory. Any one of us could be next."

Reggie looked at his comrade. In his heart, he knew that every word of what Wallace Elston said was true. He was a general and he needed to think like one. Man up and do what Uncle Sam had hired him to do.

"You're right," Reggie finally said. "Now let's get some chow. I hope CWO McClain has his crew fixing us a good meal."

"Yeah, that chow was good for being in the desert. McClain ought to open up a chain of restaurants whenever he gives up his boots for civilian service."

"Right about that, partner. Let's go eat so we can fly in and fly out."

"You're the man, Reggie. I wouldn't want to be on this mission with no one else but you."

The two shook hands and headed off to the mess hall.

✿ 38 ✿

HOMEGIRLS

Before Persenia had time to put her time with Remy into perspective, two weeks had passed and her home girl, Carlitta's flight had arrived. Reggie hadn't made it home from the Middle East, but word was that he was due soon.

As Persenia drove up to the American terminal at Dulles Airport, she saw Carlitta with her hands on her hips, engaged in conversation with someone she'd probably met on the plane. That's how Carlitta was; she didn't know a stranger. Two Samsonite luggage pieces sat next to her and when Persenia blew her horn, Carlitta nearly tripped over them to get a good look at the person who'd interrupted her conversation.

Persenia parked, jumped out of her BMW, and rushed toward Carlitta. They embraced like two long-lost sisters. They hugged and kissed each other's cheeks, until a traffic officer reminded Persenia that her car was running and she needed to get in it and move.

After placing the luggage in the back, the two best friends got in the car and drove away.

"Girl, look at you," Carlitta said, eying Persenia and slapping her on the shoulder. "You still look like the girl you were in high school. I'm all fat and pudgy from having all those kids…"

"All of what kids?" Persenia countered. "You only have three." Persenia laughed.

"Girl, they're a lot of work. I wish Jacoby would take more time with them."

"So, how is Jacoby?"

"He's fine. He works too damn much if you ask me, although I do like…no…love the money. He's gone a lot…flying to this place and that, setting up software systems for all of these growing companies, so he tells me. Seattle must be booming; he's up there all of the time. I've asked Kimiko if Jacoby ever stops by and say hello."

Persenia didn't say anything right away. Listening was one of her great attributes. She learned so much by doing so. As she was about to speak, Carlitta started again.

"The funny thing about coming to see you was that Jacoby was against it."

"Why?" Persenia asked, curiosity getting the best of her.

"I haven't the faintest idea. When I told him I needed this vacation, he suggested that I go somewhere else. I even asked if he was afraid that Reggie was going to "f" me behind your back."

Persenia's face became expressionless. She didn't want to read Carlitta right after she'd just landed, although Carlitta had already overstepped her boundary. Reggie's philandering wasn't a secret, and if there was to be a discussion about it, she'd be the one to lead it. "No you didn't, girl," Persenia finally said.

"I did, P. He was acting so stank about it. How long has it been since we've seen each other?"

"Ahhh…"

"See, that was my point to him. It's been ages. You and Jacoby have always liked each other, and I didn't understand what the fuss was all about. Hell, it didn't matter; I was going to see my bestie, regardless of what Jacoby said. I mean, he offered no explanation, and I told him to move his ass out of the way; I was getting on that plane. Shoot, I'd already paid for the ticket; I wish he would have tried to stop me." The ladies both laughed.

"So, are you guys all right? Marriage still good...still hot?" Persenia laughed in spite of herself.

"Yeah, we're doing okay. The sex is getting less and less. I've been using these sex toys that I purchased at these parties a couple of my girlfriends have given. I haven't even told Jacoby about them. It keeps me happy, and I give him what he wants when he wants it."

"Sounds like trouble in paradise to me."

"Why would you say that, P? Because we don't do it every day doesn't mean our marriage is crumbling. Jacoby takes good care of the kids and me. I don't have to want for anything. He's a good father, when he's home. My basic complaint is that he's spending too much time on the road instead of at this nice house we have."

"Maybe when he makes that million, he'll settle down some."

"Girl, if he makes that million, he'll want another million and so on and so on.

"You're right. Let's talk about something else. I can't wait to take you shopping, hit the casinos, and enjoy life in the DMV."

"The DMV? Doesn't DMV stand for Department of Motor Vehicles?"

Persenia started laughing and couldn't stop. When she did, she let out a sigh. "It does, but in this neck of the woods, it also means Washington, D.C., Maryland, and Virginia."

"Oh, that's clever. I got it."

The ladies were quiet for a minute. Carlitta was enjoying the drive until she nodded off and her head dropped to her chest.

"We can't have any of this."

"What...what...what?" Carlitta asked in staccato, opening her eyes and looking around. "What did I miss?"

"Girlfriend, you're too funny. No sleeping on our sightseeing tour."

"We're going to have to sightsee tomorrow. I was up early with little sleep, trying to get my babies situated before catching my flight. I feel like half the day has already passed me by, plus the fact that I lost three hours going east."

"At least the sun is out longer and anything beats those dreary Washington days I had to endure, no matter what month it was. I hate

I missed the Cherry Blossom Festival this year. But I'm liking this May weather."

"Who sang that song "Rainy Days and Mondays" always get you down?"

"The Carpenters."

"Yeah, yeah, I remember now. That's how Jacoby described Seattle —always raining."

Persenia didn't respond. The conversation always seemed to come back to Jacoby. If only Carlitta knew what a sorry, good-for-nothing dog he was. She'd let her get away with assassinating Reggie's character for now, although it was the truth, but before long, Carlitta was going to be exposed to the truth of her own husband. Reggie might "f" Carlitta behind her back, but Persenia truly doubted it, but for sure, Reggie's good friend, Jacoby was doing the same thing.

✦ 39 ✦

WELCOME HOME

The cool wind whipped about his face and gave Reggie and eerie feeling. Coming home wouldn't be easy; it meant that he'd never see Kaleah again, and her spirit haunted him.

Reggie and General Elston moved from the tarmac on the airfield to the waiting cars that had been dispatched to pick them up. Night time soothed his thoughts somewhat, but now that he was home, he wasn't looking forward to a confrontation with Persenia, since she'd been in a foul mood the last time he spoke with her. Hopefully, she'd be in the family room reading a book, and he could go about his business and be left alone.

All the lights were on in the house when the driver let him out in front of his residence. Reggie's first thought was to pull his car out of the garage and go somewhere for a drink. The last thing he wanted was to engage in conversation. Blowing air from his mouth, he proceeded into the house.

Seeing no one when he entered, he walked stealthily into the house, not wanting to attract attention. For a second, he thought about calling out to Persenia but refrained when he heard voices and then laughter. He moved slowly and found the source of all the chatter.

He frowned as he came upon Persenia and his best friend's wife, Carlitta, sitting at the kitchen table. Carlitta had gained a lot of weight, and the cheerleader body that used to wow the guys on U.C. Berkeley's football field was completely gone.

Sensing a presence, the ladies looked up abruptly as Reggie moved further into the kitchen.

"You're home," a not so surprised Persenia said, giving Carlitta a backhanded look.

"Yes, I am," Reggie replied, and then turned to Carlitta. "And when did you arrive? Persenia said nothing to me about you coming to Washington."

"Kind of hard to do, Reggie, since I've only had one phone call from you since you left here three weeks ago." Persenia rolled her eyes and turned away.

Reggie ignored Persenia's nasty remark and turned again to Carlitta.

"I arrived in town a few hours ago," Carlitta said. "I told Jacoby I needed a break and wanted to visit my best friend." Carlitta and Persenia smiled at each other.

"So, how long are you staying?"

"A week."

"A week?" Reggie looked at Persenia. "I guess you plan to show her the town."

"Yes, I'm going to show Carlitta a good time while she's here; I've missed her."

"So, what is Jacoby up to?" Reggie asked finally sitting down in a chair that sat between the two ladies.

"You should know; I'm aware that he talks to you all of the time."

Both Persenia and Reggie sat silent, waiting for Carlitta to continue.

"I really haven't the faintest idea what Jacoby is doing," Reggie finally said. "We pick up the phone to say hi every now and then, but that's about it."

"Reggie, look at me," Carlitta said. "Tell me to my face that you didn't know that my husband was cheating on me."

Persenia's eyes grew wide and she looked at Carlitta as if she was in shock. The few hours they'd been together, Carlitta hadn't once mentioned anything to her about Jacoby having an affair. Having the knowledge firsthand as a witness to Jacoby's triflingness wasn't the same as being told by his wife that she was aware of what he'd been up to. What else did Carlitta know?"

"I'm sorry to hear that," Reggie offered. "My boy hasn't once mentioned to me about any extracurricular activities he's involved in."

"My situation isn't to be taken lightly, Reggie. You see, I overheard Jacoby talking to you on the phone one night, and told him..."

"Hold up, Carlitta. You're in my home and I trust you're going to be careful about the selection of words you're getting ready to use."

Persenia stood up and looked between Carlitta and Reggie. "What's going on?"

"Nothing, babe. Your best friend is going through some anxiety about her husband's affair and she thinks I know something."

"What about you, Reggie? That one star on your shoulder don't scare me. You and Jacoby have swapped stories about being with other women. I heard you on the phone."

Persenia surprised everyone. "Carlitta, you are in my home, talking about my husband. I won't have it."

"P, that's what' wrong with you. Reggie has been..."

"I'm not putting up with this shit," Reggie blurted out. "She's out or I'm out."

Persenia held up her hand. "Hold on, Reggie. I'm not going to tolerate this either." Persenia looked at Carlitta. "Maybe this visit wasn't such a good idea."

"So, who are you trying to protect?" Carlitta asked Persenia, as she stood up and pushed her chair back from the table. "You've known for years that Reggie has been cheating on you, and yet you let him get away with all kinds of hell."

"And what's Jacoby doing?" Persenia asked, as she put her hands on her hips, ready for battle. "Jacoby is no saint. In fact..."

"In fact...what? What were you going to say, P?"

"I wasn't going to say anything. I want you to quit your ranting against my husband. Whatever Reggie and me have going on, it's our damn business not yours. Now, I've had it up to here." Persenia took her hand and swiped it across her chest and the tears began to flow. "This visit was supposed to be about two friends having a good time and enjoying each other's company. If that's not the case, we'll have to terminate this visit."

Carlitta looked shamed. She huffed and then held her head down. "Persenia, Reggie...I'm sorry. I've been holding my emotions inside for so long and the dam broke. Forgive me; I don't know who that person was you saw a minute ago. I promise it won't happen again."

Persenia rubbed the back of her head with her hand and sat down. Reggie glared at Carlitta and then looked at Persenia.

"I need to get out of here and get a drink before I do or say something I might regret."

※

REGGIE GOT IN HIS CAR AND DROVE OUT OF HIS DRIVEWAY LIKE HE was heading to a two-alarm fire. Steam rolled from his nostrils and the desire to hurt someone wasn't far from his mind. How could Jacoby have been so careless, although it was probably true that Persenia had long since known that he'd been with other women and chose not to say anything.

❦ 40 ❧

HAVEN'T I GOT NEWS FOR YOU?

Needing to get off the road, Reggie stopped at a local restaurant that had a bar and entered. Even for a Thursday night, the crowd was slim to none. Thankful there wasn't anyone he knew, Reggie scooted on top a stool and ordered a beer.

An attractive African-American woman, who appeared to be in her mid-to-late thirties slid on the seat next to him. Her long, weaved mane wrapped around her face just so; in fact, she reminded Reggie of the former pageant queen who was on the Real Housewives of Atlanta. Reggie tried to ignore her, as his mind went elsewhere. She played footsies with him until Reggie had enough and offered to buy her a Martini—her choice. The woman smiled, but Reggie didn't offer any conversation in return.

His first order of business was to call Jacoby and put him in check about running his mouth around his wife. He didn't appreciate Carlitta coming into his home as a guest, hurling accusations that she couldn't substantiate. There wouldn't be any way to prove it, but it seemed to him that a seed was planted, and he didn't want to give Persenia any ammunition to paralyze or destroy his career.

He finished his first beer and then drank another, finally getting up from his seat. Sensing the woman wanted more, he told her he was married and offered to buy her another drink. Before he could move from the bar, she placed something in the pocket of his jacket.

Conscious of others around him who might have a listening ear, Reggie left the restaurant and got in his car. Fishing for his cell phone from the holder on his belt, he dialed Jacoby's number and waited.

"Has my wife gotten on your nerves already?" Jacoby said, with laughter in his voice.

"That's not even the half, brother. The woman had a mental breakdown in my kitchen. Thing is, I didn't even know she was coming."

"What do you mean Carlitta had a breakdown? She is the only sane person I know."

"Well, your sane wife was ranting and raving about how you were having an affair and she tried to put me in the same category with you. She was getting ready to give the four-one-one to Persenia behind some stuff she heard us talking about on the phone."

"What do you mean she overheard me talking about having an affair...? Oh crap, I remember the night when she may have overheard."

"Well she said without any filter that she was eavesdropping on one of your conversations with me. If she heard anything, it could've only been what she heard you say out loud."

"Did she say who I was supposed to be having this affair with?"

"Obviously she doesn't know that you're getting it on with Kimiko."

"Damn."

"I had to get out of the house fast. Persenia was shook up and I didn't want her to start asking me any questions."

"So, Persenia didn't say anything?"

"That's the surprising part. She defended my ass. Told Carlitta if she didn't stop bashing me, her visit was about to end."

"Whoa! That was serious talk."

"It didn't sound like best friends to me."

"Well, dog, I hear you. I'll be sure and not to have a conversation about our misdeeds under the nose of my prying wife again."

"Likewise. I still have some climbing up the general ranks to do. I'm not ready to get busted on a humbug. But in due season, I'm going to ask Persenia for a divorce."

"That'll devastate her."

"It will, but I believe she already has an idea that our marriage is over. Hell, it's been over for years."

"Well, I don't plan to divorce Carlitta, not now or in the near future—three kids too many to be paying child support. Like Johnny Taylor used to sing, *it's cheaper to keep her*. Both men laughed. "But I'll be careful. I've been thinking about letting go of Kimiko anyway."

"You can have your cake and eat it too, as long as you're careful."

"Yeah, that's true, however, since Persenia is aware of our affair..."

"What does Persenia know, and how in the hell does she know?"

"She saw us together when she stopped by Kimiko's one weekend while you were in D. C. I did my best to keep Carlitta from making this trip. I was afraid that Persenia would spill the beans."

"Hmmm, Persenia never once mentioned anything to me about having seen the two of you together. Maybe she figured you were there to visit Carlitta's cousin...nothing more. Surely that wouldn't be cause to have a conversation about it, although I would've thought she would have said something. She was aware that you were in Seattle on business, right?"

"Why would she say anything to you? While your dog ass was playing these women like they're some kind of new discovery, Persenia met someone that weekend...a friend of mine. And I do believe she spent the night with him. But I will say this dog, as an Army officer, I don't understand how you've been able to get away with the underhanded bull crap you've been doing."

Reggie held the cell phone to his ear and let Jacoby's words penetrate his brain. For sure he didn't say that Persenia had been with someone other than himself. "Look, brother, I appreciate the four-one-one, and I suggest you keep a lid on your wife's mouth. To answer your question, though, I have a talent that most of these women love."

"That's a for sure dog barking. You can't be that good."

"These women love it, but as you were aware, I was doing one woman exclusively and now she's gone. Kaleah was the only one who knew how to break a brother down."

"Sorry about your loss. It's probably for the best."

"That was a distasteful thing to say, but I'm going to let you slide since there's no way to bust you in the face."

"Well, I better go. I picked up the kids from my mother-in-law, and they are screaming at each other. I've got to get them some Happy Meals from McDonalds or something. But don't worry about Carlitta. I've got it under control." And the line was dead.

JACOBY'S WORDS ABOUT PERSENIA BEING WITH SOMEONE DISTURBED him. He hadn't taken care of her in so long, that he hadn't noticed that Persenia might be receiving attention from somewhere else.

He had to find out if what Jacoby said was true. Persenia was part of the Washington deal that would put him on the path to four-star general. She had always been an upstanding woman, who fit the culture that was carved out for the spouse of a military officer. Persenia knew how to throw good parties, and she was the perfect hostess who other generals admired.

There was no way Reggie was going to let Persenia screw up what he was destined to do.

❧ 41 ☙

BEST FRIENDS

The house was quiet, except for the television that had been tuned to BET. *The Game* was on for its last season. Kelly Pitts and Chardonnay Pitts were consoling Tasha Mack, whose father had died while watching TV, in fact, he was still sitting on the couch waiting for the coroner's office to pick him up.

Persenia and Carlitta sat across from each other, neither one having said a word in the past twenty minutes. Persenia had no idea what Carlitta was thinking, but Persenia was breathing a sigh of relief that Carlitta didn't know that she knew that Jacoby was having an affair with Kimiko. Carlitta's quietness was probably more out of embarrassment.

First to break the silence, Persenia got up from her seat. She glanced across at Carlitta, who seemed to be feigning sleep, but opened her mouth and asked any way.

"Would you like something to drink—water, soda, wine, or something stronger?"

Carlitta batted her eyes. "P, I feel so bad. You invited me into your home and I acted a pure fool. I didn't mean to go off on Reggie. I guess seeing him sitting there, acting as if he didn't know what I was talking about, was the last straw. For me, he represented all men who cheated on their wives, who with their superior attitudes think they can do whatever they want and get away with it. I'm not saying that there aren't good men in the world; there are. Mine was a good man until...whenever."

Persenia sat back down. "So, when did you find out that Jacoby was cheating on you?"

"Girl, go and get us some wine, and then I'll tell you the whole sorted story."

"Ok." Persenia went to the bar and plucked two wine glasses from the small shelf in the bar area. She chose a bottle of Pinot Gregio that she had set in the bar to chill earlier in the evening and poured some into each of the glasses. She returned and found Carlitta wiping her face with a Kleenex.

Carlitta took the glass of wine by the stem of the glass and drew it to her lips. "May we toast to our friendship...to best friends. I certainly hope I didn't do anything to cause a rift in what has been a lifelong friendship.

Persenia smiled. "We can do that. I'm still your best friend, no matter what. Now, regardless of what Reggie is, he's still my husband. The Lord and I will deal with him. Now, let's drink up. To best friends."

"Yes to best friends," Carlitta said. "She sipped her wine and smiled at Persenia. Thank you again for inviting me."

42

I WANNA KNOW

The girls were in deep chatter when Reggie returned to the house. He took off his jacket and hung it up, and made a beeline to the family room. It appeared that Persenia and Carlitta had made up, which Reggie was somewhat grateful.

Startled, the ladies swung their heads around when he entered the room.

"I didn't expect to see you so soon," Persenia said, surprise written on her face.

"I hated how I left here," Reggie replied. "After one drink, I decided to come home and apologize." In the back of his mind, the words, Jacoby's words, kept resounding in his ear—*Persenia met someone that weekend...a friend of mine. And I do believe she spent the night with him.*

With wine glass in hand, Carlitta stood up as Reggie began to go into his planned spiel. "Reggie, it's me who owe you an apology. I'll admit I've been frustrated for some time, after realizing that my husband has been unfaithful to me, but I shouldn't have taken it out on you. And...I'm sorry if I said those things about you...things I had no business uttering, and for that I do apologize."

Reggie was overwhelmed, although he knew his ass was in a sling. Everything that Carlitta had said about him was true, although the truth was worse than anything that Carlitta divulged.

Reggie flapped his hand. "Sit down." He sat at the other end of the couch that Persenia was sitting on. "No need to apologize." Reggie looked at Persenia and then back at Carlitta. "Let me apologize for my behavior. That was unbecoming of the person I am; I got caught up in the moment.

"I'm sorry that your visit has been tainted because of your knowledge of Jacoby's affair. Yes, I was aware, but I'm not in a position to be a rat." Reggie searched for words, looking around the room at nothing in particular. "I'm not completely innocent, in that I've taken other women out—job related—who wanted more than a casual night out." Reggie looked at Persenia. "And I'd like to apologize to my wife for those indiscretions, although they were meaningless."

Persenia stared at Reggie as if he was a stranger. Her lips didn't move and her eyes stared blankly into space.

Reggie scrunched up his face and dismissed Persenia's non-reaction. "Persenia, I understand your silence, but hopefully we can talk about it later and move forward. Together, we're going to let this town know that the Charleston's have arrived.

Persenia took a sip of her wine and looked at Carlitta. She rolled her eyes and took another sip.

Quiet ensued and Reggie resorted to watching what was on the tube.

⊗

RETREATING TO THEIR BEDROOM AFTER ANOTHER HOUR OR SO OF watching television, Reggie couldn't wait to find out if Persenia had been unfaithful to him. Persenia had thrown a boomerang and he needed to know if what Jacoby told him about her being with someone else was really true. He had no room to ask anything with all of the women he'd slept with during their marriage.

Persenia rushed to the bathroom and shut the door. Reggie could hear the water running but he waited. He pulled off his clothes, hung them up, and sat on the edge of the bed. When Persenia reappeared, Reggie didn't waste any time getting to the point.

"Persenia, do you love me," he asked.

Her hair protected by a head scarf and her body wrapped in a gold terrycloth robe, Persenia turned and looked up at Reggie. A puzzled look and then a frown crossed her face, but she refused to say anything.

Reggie stood up and went to her, grabbing her hand and pulling her toward the bed. "Baby, I hate that you had to hear what I said about dining with other women, but that's all it was. True, they may have thought that something might have come of it, but never in a million years would I betray my trust to you."

Persenia pulled away from Reggie and began to wave her finger in his face. "Do I look like a fool to you? Not me...not me, Reggie. I don't know what fool you've been serving that lie to, but know this. You can hide behind that one-star pinned to your shoulder, but I know the real Reginald Charleston. Believe that. So, go and tell your lies to someone else. Dear husband, you've been cheating on me for years and taken me for granted, and yes, I've tolerated your foolishness. But take me for a fool no more; your time is ticking."

Reggie couldn't believe his ears. Persenia was bluffing, and he was ready to turn the cards on her.

"So, have you been unfaithful to me? All this pointing the finger in my face makes me believe you're trying to hide an indiscretion of your own."

Persenia tried to keep her composure at Reggie's words. "Nice try, Reggie. Don't try to hide behind your whoring-ass ways to turn the tables on me. I have nothing to hide. I'm sure that your whoring buddy, Jacoby, may have told you that I was with his friend...a friend he brought into the picture to set me up to hide his own indiscretion. But nothing happened." And she would never tell that she and Remy had recently celebrated the best time together.

"Did you spend the night with him? I wanna know...now."

"Oh, you slay me. Remy, that's his name, was a true gentleman..."

"I can't believe that you uttered another man's name in my house."

Persenia threw her hand in Reggie's face. "...and at the time, I needed someone to talk to. You don't have any idea what loneliness can do to a person. And since Remy was all ears, attentive, and considerate of my emotions, I shared my feelings about how my life has been with you—tortured, loveless, and humiliating."

"All right, I'm not going to listen to anymore..."

"Shut the hell up. You're going to listen to every word I've got to say. You started it; I'm going to finish it. For your information, I enjoyed talking to Remy. There was nothing at home for me to go back to, so I rode with him on the ferry to Vashon Island. It's beautiful, Reggie, but how would you know? Your trifling ass has never taken me anywhere."

"I've had enough."

"No, you're going to listen since you brought it up. We were unable to make a return trip back to Seattle; the last ferry had already left. I panicked but ended up staying the night...in separate rooms; and nothing happened," she lied. "The next day, I picked up my car from Kimiko's house where your boy was still playing tittiewinks with his wife's cousin. What's your story? Do you treat your women as well?" Persenia held her finger up as Reggie tried to speak. "There have been many women that you've bedded. Some have even had the nerve to call and tell me all about your prowess with them. Now, let me be clear, don't ever grab my arm again if you don't want to be reported for spousal abuse."

"I've given you all of this and so much more, Persenia, and you threaten me? We've been married for nearly twenty years, and you betray me with another man. And you're crazy if you think I believe that you were in another man's house all night and didn't do anything."

"Just because you're a whore, Reggie, doesn't mean that I'm one. Nothing happened between Remy and me. Jacoby so wanted us to get it on so that his black ass would be in the clear, but not so. Believe what you want, brother, but it's your ass you should be worried about. It would be a shame if your house of cards suddenly tumbled down at your feet. Many high-ranking officers have...oh, never mind." She waved her hand in his face.

"And what does that mean?"

"Reggie, I'm tired. Carlitta and I have a busy day tomorrow. Suck on a lemon or something. You'll figure it out. Or better yet, why not find another whore to be with now that Major General Kaleah Neal is no longer here to feed your sexual fantasies."

Reggie brought his hand up in the air and immediately put it down. "Do it, if you dare," were Persenia's last words for the night.

Venom coursed through Reggie's veins. How dare she talk to him like he was a nobody, threatening him like she held the cards? After all, he was a general in Uncle Sam's army and held a powerful position. He'd invested too much time in the military...his career for his "house of cards" to come crashing down around him. He got up, went to the bathroom, and slammed the door.

❦ 43 ❧

DO THE RIGHT THING

R eggie was gone when Persenia got up the next morning. A ray of sunshine shone in her room, and she smiled. The conversation she had with Reggie on last evening was now on the back burner; it was time to get up so she and Carlitta could get their day started.

"Carlitta, get up," Persenia shouted.

Now in all of her nakedness, she rushed to the bathroom. There was an urgency that her bladder needed to satisfy. In three short movements, her body began to glide across the bathroom tile but with good acrobatic skills, she was able to maintain her balance without falling. Something was stuck to her foot.

Huffing and puffing, Persenia lifted her foot and peeled off a piece of paper that was stuck there. Mad as hell, she looked at the torn paper that looked as if it had been ripped out of a pocket calendar. Curious, Persenia turned it over, and there in plain view was a ten-digit number, obviously a phone number, without name the first. Persenia cursed.

Hurriedly, she turned the water on in the shower. After a couple of seconds, she got in. Steam from the hot water drowned out Persenia's curses. Reggie was a rat that she was going to snare in a trap. She was tired of his foolishness and she didn't give a damn if he was a one-star general, although Persenia rather enjoyed the perks that went along with their life as it was now. But in due season, the rat was going to eat some poisonous cheese. And for a moment she thought of her week with Remy—the best week she'd had in a long time.

Turning off the water, Persenia took her time and opened the shower door, enjoying the effects that the steam from the hot shower gave her. Then she jumped as a distinct rat-a-tat on the bedroom door met her ears. She should've known it was Carlitta, her shrill, loud voice interrupting her thoughts.

"You all right in there?"

Persenia allowed herself to relax. She plucked one of her plush bath towels from the linen closet, wrapped it around her, and went to the bedroom door and opened it. Carlitta was leaning so hard against the door that she almost fell to the floor when Persenia opened it. The ladies laughed.

"I didn't know if I had to come in there and get you. It seems like I've been hollering your name for an hour with no response."

"Carlitta, you exaggerate too much. I was barely in the shower fifteen minutes. You need to sit somewhere and write a book about your life."

"That sounds like a good idea, P. I'd embellish the hell out of it, all the while getting my revenge on Jacoby. But, P, my life...my marriage has been a good one for the most part. Jacoby has taken good care of me and the kids. He's taken me on fabulous vacations and built a beautiful home for our family. He doesn't complain too much about the money I spend, and I don't want for anything."

"That's all well and good, but how does your heart feel, especially in light of all his running around with women..."

"Hold up. Jacoby has been with only one woman, even though I don't know who she is."

"How can you be certain that this affair is the only one?"

"I know."

"Carlitta, you only found out because you heard him talking to Reggie. That doesn't mean there haven't been others."

"Look, let's not fight. I love Jacoby with all of his flaws. I choose to be happy, and I'm going to forgive him this one indiscretion."

Persenia looked thoughtfully at Carlitta. *What a fool.* Carlitta could believe whatever she wanted to believe; it was on her. "I don't want to fight either. Let me put some clothes on and we'll go out for breakfast." She went to her bed and lifted up the blouse she'd placed there. "I've got this cute gold blouse with the ruffle going down the front that's going to look fabulous with these white slacks I'm going to sport today. Wear something cute so we can take a bunch of cute selfies."

"Okay. I love you, P." Carlitta hugged Persenia around the neck. "We've always been friends and we'll continue to be until the end. Thanks for always being there for a sistah. I understand you have my best interest at heart, but I've got this. Jacoby and I will weather the storms of life together. Now hurry up; I'm famished."

Persenia smiled. There was no way in hell that she was going to let Reggie off the hook. When the time was right, she'd make her move. Who knew when that would be? It could be two, maybe three years from now. She was looking at the dollars and cents and the other benefits that would keep her well beyond her marriage to Reggie. Once Reggie was a thing of the past, there wouldn't be another man she'd give her hand to in marriage...or would she?

❧ 44 ❧

SOMETHING IS AFOOT

The thought of Persenia being with someone other than him never crossed his mind. She seemed to exhibit no real interest in anything in particular, let alone another man, but his mother always said to watch out for the quiet ones. He'd been so busy doing everything a grown man could do and covering his own ass after the fact, that not once had he noticed anything peculiar in Persenia's behavior. It may have been a one-time event, but he had no way of knowing. He'd keep an eye out, but right now he had some fixing that Olivia Pope couldn't help him with.

45

MIND YOUR OWN BUSINESS

Acloudy sky couldn't put Persenia in a bad mood. Her best friend was by her side, and for now, everything was alright with the world. The hustle and bustle of Washington D. C. and Maryland life was much more accepting to her than the dreary Pacific Northwest. Tourists seemed to be everywhere, exploring the various venues that comprised the Smithsonian—the African American History and Culture Museum, African Art Museum, Air and Space Museum, American History Museum, and the Natural History Museum to name a few. It was only a few weeks ago that she shared those experiences with Remy. She missed him.

"I'm enjoying this vacation, P. The Lord knew I needed a break from the kids and my husband. I've never wanted to live in D. C., but I'm having the time of my life capturing all of these historical monuments with my camera lens. I was most impressed with the statue of Martin Luther King Jr. and the Lincoln Memorial."

Persenia smiled. "There is a culture that's all its own here. Like in the Bay Area, L.A. and New York, this place has a flavor you can't duplicate.

The tourists that come to this city are different from the ones who flock to L.A. and New York. Even if and when these tourists visit other places, they know how to become immersed in the culture they find themselves in."

"I hear you on that, P. A Coney Island dog from New York is completely different from the food trucks in L.A. with their wings 'n things, tacos, burritos..."

"Carlitta, stop. We haven't been too long finished breakfast and now I'm hungry all over again. For lunch, we're going to drive to the Baltimore Harbor for some crab cakes that are to die for. Moe's Seafood makes the best."

"Child, let's ride. You don't have to paint the picture for me; I'm licking my fingers."

"Alright, now. And when we've finished dining and doing a little shopping—they have all the big stores right at the harbor. I'm also taking you to Arundel Mills, home of one of the largest casinos in Maryland. And it's busy twenty-four seven. They even have a Cheese-cake Factory inside if you want to stop a minute and fatten up on one of their meals and sink your teeth in a luscious slice of Adam's Peanut Butter Cup Fudge Ripple Cheesecake..."

"I'm already there."

They both stopped when Persenia's cell phone began to ring. A surprise registered on Persenia's face. She took the call off of Bluetooth and answered.

"Hi, this is a surprise."

Carlitta glanced at Persenia, a glint of wanting to know who the caller was in her eyes.

"Yes." Pause.

"I'll call you back later. I'm navigating through D. C. traffic with my best friend, and I need to keep my eyes on the road." Pause.

"Okay." Call completed.

"So, who were you talking to in that sickening, sweet voice you use when someone is admiring you?"

"Girl, please. Nothing about you has changed. You're still nosey."

"So, aren't you going to tell your best friend? For sure it wasn't Reggie, especially after your conversation last night."

"You've been wrong before. Anyway, Reggie and I may have made up last night."

"Save that empty talk for someone else. You're wasting my time. Out with the goods."

"It was someone I met recently."

"Since you've been in D.C.? I can't believe you're holding out on me. Where does he live?"

"Carlitta, calm down. I met this someone while I was having lunch one day, she lied. Casual conversation was all that we had and exchanged telephone numbers. I was surprised to actually hear from him. We haven't communicated since the day I met him at the restaurant."

"Oh, okay. There's nothing wrong with having a male friend to confide in."

"Listen to you, Miss Going to Kick Jacoby's Ass. I'm not entertaining a friendship with this man. It was fun when it happened. I may or may not call him back."

"With all of Reggie's dirt..."

Persenia's hands went up and stopped Carlitta in her tracks. "My relationship with my husband is off limits. Now, if you expect me to treat you to some wonderful seafood this afternoon, you'd better sit back and behave."

Carlitta sat with her mouth closed. Persenia took her eyes off the road for a second and looked at her best friend. She didn't give a damn what Carlitta was thinking, it was her war to rage against Reggie. She needed to mind her business and get her own house in order. Besides, Remy was her secret, and if she had to lie about the caller on the other end of the line, she'd do whatever she had to in order to protect what they had together. Anyway, Carlitta could never keep anything to herself.

❧ 46 ❧

TWO DOWN

Persenia cruised down the Beltway, anxious to get to Baltimore. She hated the traffic, but it was part of the drawback of living in a city full of politicians; high ranking military brass; and what was home to the National Security Agency (NSA), the Pentagon, and the whole Washington regime to include the biggest political machine that was housed on Pennsylvania Avenue, its address known to tykes as young as five years old. Even with that knowledge, she cursed under her breath as she had to put on brakes and come to a complete stop. They were less than twenty minutes away from their destination.

"Is the traffic always this bad?" Carlitta asked.

"You live in the Bay Area and you're going to complain about traffic?' The ladies laughed.

"You have to catch it just right. It's one in the afternoon, and the lunch crowd isn't back in their offices yet. But it makes no difference to the time of day, this place is always like this."

"It looks like we're going to be sitting here for a while."

"Yeah, I see blue and red lights flashing ahead in the distance. Lord,

I hope it isn't a bad accident. In fact, it looks like the commotion is near the exit for the NSA."

"They don't need any more headline news."

"Yep. Well, we're moving a little bit. I'm going to turn on the radio to see if I can get some feed on what's going on."

"That would be great since we're getting ready to stop again. These road blocks are keeping me from sinking my teeth into some good Maryland crabmeat."

"You're funny, Carlitta. Hush, here's a news flash."

The car was silent as the announcer droned on about stepping up security due to the Memorial Day weekend and the precautions each person should take in making sure their holiday was safe. But it was the last statement the announcer made that made Persenia stop talking and listen attentively to what was being said.

"At the top of the hour, we will bring you up-to-date information on the execution-style slaying of Major General Michael Forbes, who worked for Homeland Security. This is the second such execution-type slaying in a month. Major General Kaleah Neal was killed in a similar fashion—the common denominator being that they both worked for the same agency with the U.S. Army."

"What?" Persenia shouted loud enough that the car seemed to shake.

"What is it, P?"

"Oh my God; oh my God, Major General Forbes is my neighbor." Persenia began to hyperventilate.

"Julia's husband?"

Foot still on the gas, Persenia jerked her head in Carlitta's direction. "Yes. Both he and Kaleah Neal worked with Reggie. I wonder what's going on ahead?"

Persenia's first thought was to call Reggie to see what information he had or if he was even aware that Michael had been killed. She sighed. Of course he was aware. Reggie was probably on pins and needles.

"Ahh, Carlitta, I think we should postpone our trip to Baltimore."

"Really, I was looking so forward to going, but if..."

"Nevermind; let's go and get some crab cakes. It'll take my mind off of this bit of news." But Persenia knew it wouldn't.

"We're moving again. Let's go and eat some crab legs and whatever else," Carlitta sang.

Persenia was quiet. When they approached the place where the police cars were flashing their blue and red lights, two tow trucks were uploading cars on their carriages, while another was pulling away. Passing the remnants of the wreckage, Persenia drove on, although her mind was on Michael and Kaleah and who might have had them executed. She cringed. Would Reggie be next?

❦ 47 ❦

WHAT'S THE POINT?

Before leaving Moe's, Persenia excused herself from the table. While Carlitta was having the time of her life, her stomach churned, wondering if Reggie was alright...if he was in danger. She stepped into the lobby and called him.

The second she heard Reggie's voice, she wished she hadn't called. "I guess you heard about Michael Forbes."

"Of course, I've heard. What is it you want?"

"You don't have to be rude, Reggie. I'm only concerned about your safety. With Kaleah and now Michael being murdered, it...it has hit too close to home."

"I'm sorry; yes, I'm worried too. My mind has been spinning in circles, wondering why someone would want Kaleah dead. She was a brilliant woman—a woman who could run rings around half of these higher ups. I miss her."

Persenia shook her head, as Reggie droned on and on about his beloved Kaleah. She hated the ground he walked on and for a moment wished it was him instead of Michael Forbes that had been killed. Sure, she told Carlitta that she wanted to work on her marriage, but in all truth, she despised the man and whether she was wrong or right, she honestly wanted to be with Remy.

"Persenia," Reggie shouted. "Were you listening to me?"

"What did you say?"

"Look you called me. I'm fine...I'll be fine. The CIA should be close to catching the culprit. I'll see you at home."

"Yeah." And she shut the case to her cell phone.

❧ 48 ☙

HE'S NOT WORTH THE THOT

She was sick and damn tired of Reggie's blatant disrespect. Kaleah was dead, and there was nothing he could do about it. In the back of her mind, Persenia felt that her husband and Kaleah were lovers, and now that she was dead, it only meant that Reggie would be on the hunt for another female soldier to do all the things to him that she wouldn't.

"Earth to best friend. It can't be nothing but Reggie mess. Did you talk to him?"

"Carlitta..."

"Oops, I promised not to meddle in your affairs. My stomach is full of crab cakes and I've got a new Michael Kors bag; I'd say I'm going to keep my thoughts to myself. I've got to make another trip to B-More, P; had a great time."

"You're so crazy, Carlitta. I'm glad you're here. Otherwise, I'd probably be choking the mess out of Reggie right about now. I'm sorry that Michael is dead...that Kaleah is dead, but the bitch is gone and he needs to get over it."

Carlitta remained quiet, picking at her teeth with her fingernail.

"Girlfriend, that sorry ass sucker acted like it was my fault someone took her life."

"Okay, enough. You can look at it two ways—be happy that she's dead or be sad for Reggie because his THOT will no longer be able to give him nail-biting sex."

"You aren't making it any better, Carlitta. And for God's sakes, what is a THOT?"

"Please tell me that you, the Brigadier General's wife don't know what a THOT is?"

"I said I didn't. For your information, my circle of friends…"

"That you don't have…"

"My circle-of-friends don't go around talking trashy talk."

"Who said a THOT was trashy?"

"By the mere fact that it came from your mouth made it so." The ladies laughed. "What is a THOT girlfriend? School your buddy."

"It means—that ho over there."

"Shut up, Carlitta. Lord, we've taken Ebonics to another whole level."

"Girl, the white girls are even saying it. Watch, it's going to be in Webster's Dictionary in the next few years." The ladies laughed again.

"Well, I hope you enjoyed your outing today."

"I did although your friend's death put a little crimp in our day."

"She wasn't my friend; she was Reggie's THOT. And she's been dead a month. Michael is the one they found murdered today." Quiet engulfed the car.

Persenia moved easily on the Beltway without having to put on brakes every two seconds. There were two miles to go before it was time to exit the freeway. Although she had fun entertaining Carlitta, Michael's death was in the back of her mind.

The thick rows of pine trees that lined the street signaled that the next right turn was theirs. As Persenia approached her street, a sudden chill came over her. She continued on until she was in front of the house. Reggie's car was in the driveway, and she let out a sigh.

Carlitta gave Persenia the eye. "Fifty dollars that says Reggie will be on one-hundred. I swear I can't figure out how he made it this far in the military. Anyway, he's not worth the thought."

"Ten dollars is all I'm going to give you since there's no doubt in my mind that he's out-of-control, pining for that woman. What about your boy toy?"

"I don't have a boy toy, Carlitta. Please don't go around saying that stuff out loud, especially to Jacoby."

"Just messing with you friend."

Persenia turned the motor off. "Well, since we're here let's go in."

"I'm full of crab cakes and got a Michael Kors bag hanging on my shoulder," Carlitta sang. "I'm happy."

❧ 49 ❧

JESUS KEEP ME NEAR THE CROSS

With the sun slowly dipping into the west, a medium height Japanese maple tree that stood in the front yard cast a shadow on the house. With a slight breeze moving through the leaves, the shadow looked like an animated creature—a boogey man on a silent movie screen.

The ladies laden with their packages moved toward the front of the house, still chatting about the day's events. With key in hand, Persenia reached for the door handle to unlock it.

The door moved when she touched it.

"Reggie must be in a real hurry to get out of here if he didn't shut or lock the door. I can't believe it with him all the time screaming about Homeland Security."

Carlitta giggled.

The ladies moved into the foyer. It was quiet as a mouse. Carlitta shut the door behind her while Persenia continued toward the living room.

"Reggie!" Persenia called out.

Thump.

Aeowwwwwwwwwwwwwwww," Persenia yelled as she fell to the floor, her bags flying from her hands. "No, no, no..."

Carlitta approached a screaming Persenia cautiously. Her Michael Kors bag fell to the floor and the crab cakes that she'd relished eating earlier that afternoon heaved up from her mouth like a tormented volcano. "Oh my...oh my God. P, is that..."

"Call nine-one-one now."

Persenia breathed heavily as she tried to pull her body up from Reggie's fallen one. Blood oozed from his mouth and head. It rushed from his body like a tributary forcing its way upstream. She willed herself to touch his neck with her finger for any signs of life. There was a pulse, although faint, as he lay lifeless, even under her weight. And then she saw what appeared to be a hole in his neck where a bullet was possibly lodged.

Hyperventilating, Persenia tried to catch her breath. "Not Reggie too, Carlitta. Not my Reggie. Lord, please don't let it be his jugular vein. Jesus keep me near the cross. Why? Why, would someone want to hurt Reggie?"

Carlitta stood trembling although her hand gripped her cell phone as she spoke with the nine-one-one operator. "Yes, there's a pulse. The address is..." Carlitta pulled the phone away from her ear and looked down at Persenia. "Sweetie what's your address?"

Persenia called it back to her while begging Reggie to get up.

"The EMS team is on its way."

⚜

BLOOD COVERED PERSENIA'S GOLD BLOUSE, ALONG WITH HER TEARS. "Reggie and I were going to make it as husband and wife, Carlitta," she said as if she was in a vaporless cloud. "We would've had to work hard at it, but in my heart of hearts I felt it would've only been a matter of time before it happened. We even argued about it."

Carlitta stood there and let the tears roll. There was no way Persenia could've thought that Reggie was going to stop his adulterous ways and that they were going to heal their wounds. She understood her friend was hurting. It was a sad commentary of a woman who once knew her own worth but had let a man, albeit it her husband, reduce her to a mere puppet. She had to call Jacoby and tell him the bad news.

❧ 50 ❧

NUMB

The EMS moved swiftly and whisked Reggie to the National Naval Medical Center in Bethesda, Maryland. He was still alive and the cardiac and surgical teams were doing all they could to save him. Doctors who saw him upon admittance were extremely pleased that Reggie's carotid artery was intact. He'd lost a lot of blood, but his prognosis was not yet determined.

News of Reggie's attempted assassination hit the Pentagon like a torpedo, interrupting the crisis at hand, which was the group ISIS's assault on U.S. and European strongholds around the globe. But this latest development—Reggie's near death—so soon following the deaths of Major General Neal and Major General Forbes was puzzling to everyone at Homeland Security, especially with Forbes' death having transpired that very afternoon also.

Members of the Joint Chiefs called an impromptu meeting the next morning to discuss the recent deaths, speculating that not only were there implications of a terrorist connection threading the two murders and attempted murder, but that it seemed to have the appearance of an inside job. No one could immediately grasp what had happened to the two, and terror and fear had spread rampant throughout the ranks at the gangland style way in which both Michael and Kaleah had been reported to have been killed.

Rebecca Dickerson, Major General Forbes' secretary, strolled to Reggie's office. Reggie's secretary, Sandra, sat in her seat like a granite statue, numb at the news of her boss' near demise. Her tear stained face was void of expression when Rebecca approached. She looked almost as drab as the wooden desk and metal filing cabinets that sat against a puke-green wall. Sandra looked up as Rebecca stopped in front of her desk.

"Sandra, I'm sorry about General Charleston. Have you received any updates?"

"He's holding his own. The last word I received was that he was being taken to surgery. How is General Forbes' wife doing?"

"I'm sure not well. I understand her children will be arriving soon. She's being cared for by the women in her wives' group. Have you heard anything about who might have done this?"

There was a thin glaze of water in Sandra's eyes—a look that said she was in dreamland. As if she'd finally registered what Rebecca asked, Sandra cocked her head and looked up at Rebecca. "Not a word." Sandra looked away and sighed, and then got up from her desk. "This is too much. Oh my God, I can't wrap my head around this."

"Yeah, everyone is devastated by the news."

"By the way, General Forbes and General Charleston were looking for you yesterday. I left a message for you to call."

"I had to run to a meeting. I didn't receive the message, though."

"Look, I need to step away from my desk for a moment. I've got to get some air. Would you mind answering my phone for me? I'll only be gone five minutes. Everyone is calling about General Charleston's condition."

"Sure, Sandra, I'd be more than happy to sit until you come back. Take your time. Norma is covering for me."

"Great. I promise I won't be but a few minutes."

Sandra walked out of her office. As soon as she was out of sight,

Rebecca poured through papers and files that were on Sandra's desk. Coming up empty, she got up from the chair, looked to see if anyone was watching and slipped into Reggie's office.

51

WHEN THERE ARE NO WORDS

There were no words or any amount of pampering that could console Julia. There was a hole in her soul. The man that she loved for the last twenty-something years had been taken from her—tragically. Even all of Michael's indiscretions took a back seat to the grief Julia now felt—her lover, her friend, her husband now a whisper in the community.

A knock at her open bedroom door caused Julia to raise her head up from her pillow. With downcast eyes, Persenia stood staring at her friend, no doubt wishing there was something she could do or say to make Julia feel better.

"Come sit down on the bed, Persenia." Persenia moved from the doorway and sat down on the side of the bed and gazed at Julia. "My heart is broken. Regardless of what you saw several weeks ago, Michael has been my whole life." Julia dropped her head. "I've loved him; I've hated his guts, but he was still my husband."

Persenia reached over and patted Julia's hand. "I didn't get to know Michael, but I do understand. Reggie and I have a long history together—some good, some bad, but my heart still hurts."

For a moment, Julia didn't say anything. "How is Reggie?" She was somewhat jealous that Reggie got a chance to live, while Michael had to die.

"He's hanging on by a thread. Everyone is praying."

Julia lifted her head and stared at Persenia without saying a word. She'd wondered in the back of her mind if that attempt on Reggie's life and Michael's death coincided with Kaleah's. They all worked for Homeland Security and handled strategic arrangements, as it concerned the current fight in the Middle East of which she had little knowledge of, but her heart told her there was a connection. She felt that Persenia may have had the same thoughts.

"There's a thread linking the three of them," Julia said absentmindedly. "The CIA needs to be doing their job. If I can see, I'm sure they can. The answer has to be right under their noses."

Persenia rubbed Julia's back. "I agree wholeheartedly, but we're going to have to let them do their job."

"Yeah, I guess you're right."

"Do you need any help with arrangements or other things? I've placed the food that a few ladies brought over in the fridge. You need to eat something."

"No, my children should be arriving within a few hours or tomorrow. Right now, I want to lie down and forget this even happened."

"Okay, however, I can assist. I'll be next door if you need me."

Julia lay back down on the bed and Persenia covered her up. They both turned when the doorbell rang.

"I don't want to see anyone."

"It's probably your children."

"Okay."

Persenia left Julia and went to answer the door. Without asking who it was, she opened the door and on the doorstep stood a redhead woman. This wasn't a coincidence, for that Persenia was sure. She scanned the woman's facial structure, her stature, as if this would be the grounds for admittance—her self-imposed security measure.

"What's your name?" Persenia asked.

"It's Rebecca Dickerson. I'm Major General Forbes' secretary."

Not wanting to be rude but not being able to help herself, Persenia stared at the woman. The woman's spirit had an offbeat vibe that put Persenia on alert, but she wasn't her guest. She wasn't sure that Julia should entertain her.

"I've seen you before. Don't you recognize me?"

"No," Rebecca said emphatically. "I've never met you before."

"Oh, you have," Persenia insisted. "And you know that you have. Wait here. Mrs. Forbes is resting at the moment and doesn't want to be disturbed. But I'll ask if she'd like to see you, in that you worked for her husband."

Stoic was the look on Rebecca's face. She stood still without a reply or an acknowledgement.

Persenia left Rebecca standing at the door but didn't ask her to come in. She went to Julia's room, but she was fast asleep. When Persenia returned to the door and opened it all the way, Rebecca Dickerson was no longer there. Persenia stepped outside and looked around, but there was no sign of the woman. It was déjà vu—the same scene that played out in the airport parking lot. Without a doubt, Ms. Dickerson had to be the same woman. But what was her purpose?

❧ 52 ❧

THE PIECE IN THE PUZZLE

Homeland Security and the CIA were working overtime to find the culprit or culprits who'd killed Generals Neal, Forbes, and the attempt on Charleston's life. There was a commonality between the three: they all worked for Homeland Security at the Pentagon and handled secret information.

News media from every affiliate were on hand to capture any updates as they broke, but so far there were only speculations, and ISIS was at the core. There were also rumors deep inside the Pentagon walls that there was a breach and the CIA and Homeland Security were working in tandem to find the mole, eradicate it, and get on with business.

General Compton, Reggie's boss, was confounded that he'd lost two of his major staff members in less than a month, while another was hanging on by a thread. It was consistent thinking amongst the rank and file that whoever did the ugly deed was after something—something they thought Kaleah, Michael, and Reggie had in their possession. The targets were so closely linked that it had to be someone on the inside helping someone on the outside—the mastermind—to facilitate the crime.

The intercom buzzed, and General Compton pressed the button.

"General Compton, General Wallace Elston is here."

"Thank you, Jackie. Send him in."

"General," Elston said, taking a seat in front of Compton's desk. "How can I assist?"

"Wallace, you and Reggie were together for three weeks in the Middle East. What was his temperament? Did he display any actions that might convey that he might be worried about something? You get the idea."

"Well, for the most part, Reggie was himself, although I do recall a conversation that we had about Kaleah Neal's death. He kept questioning as to why it happened, but I remember, specifically, that he asked, "why not you" speaking of me and then he said, "why not me" speaking of himself. Reggie and Kaleah were real close."

"Very close from what I understand, but I didn't bring you in here to talk about Reggie and Kaleah's relationship." General Compton took a deep breath. "And you don't recall anything else that might've been minute at the time, but with what's happened might be something more and worth investigating?"

General Elston shook his head. "No, General. Nothing that I can pinpoint." There was a momentary pause. Elston snapped his fingers. "Reggie and I had a long conversation about fear. I asked him if he feared going into enemy territory so close to retirement."

General Compton sat up in his seat and looked at Elston. "What prompted you to ask him that?"

"It was more for myself than for Reggie. I've had a lot of thoughts about dying at the hands of the enemy and I wanted to know how Reggie felt, is all. We handle a lot of sensitive stuff and I had just concluded reading the "Classified" document that briefed us on our mission."

Elston sat back in his chair, contemplating for a moment and then looked up at General Compton. "But you know, General, something just came to me. It was right before a meeting of the JC's. Reggie was trying to find Michael. It had something to do with Michael's secretary."

"The redhead girl?"

"Yes, she's the one."

"I'm not sure if you were aware, Wallace, but Michael was seeing her on the sly. I don't understand it. Can you tell me why you'd want to compromise yourself, especially when intel is a large part of your job and your career could be in jeopardy?"

"Look, I don't want to come off as being insubordinate, but I've known you a long time, General. Are you going to tell me that you've never stepped out on your wife?" General Wallace Elston had possibly pushed too far. "I mean, you asked the question."

"You are on the borderline of insubordination, Wallace. I realize it's an epidemic within the military ranks, low to high...high to low, but we're talking about Major General Michael Forbes at the moment. Let's stay on task." General Compton sighed.

General Elston raised both hands. "You're right, General. Michael Forbes was on the edge of a cliff. And somehow he fell over, which is not to say it's related to his infidelity."

"What do we know about his secretary? What's her name?"

General Elston snapped his fingers, trying in vain to remember. "Oh, oh, ah, ah, ah...Rebecca Dickerson. Yeah that's it."

"Find out all you can on Ms. Dickerson and report back to me. I want you to handle this personally. As soon as Reggie is able to communicate, the FBI will want to interview him. We're going to get whoever did this."

"Will do, General Compton."

"I'd like to have the information within the next twenty-four hours."

"Yes, sir." Elston rose from his seat and retreated from the room.

53

LAUGHTER IS THE BEST MEDICINE

Trips to the airport were becoming a regular thing for Persenia. Jacoby was flying in to lend support to her and be a big brother to his ace, his best friend, Reggie. All of the rhetoric about getting a divorce was something now out of a fairy tale. It was funny how life played tricks on you, right when you decide what your destiny should be.

In the wee hours of the morning, Persenia talked with Remy. She ran down all that had transpired up to Reggie's brush with death. Her heart ached because she longed to be with Remy, although her obligation at the moment was to be with Reggie. She sensed Remy's emotions as he tried to keep in check what this all meant—being with Persenia might not happen. They hadn't etched anything in stone—no timetable as to when they'd be together, if that indeed was the case. But she did love him; she'd at least admitted it to herself. But she was still in love with Reggie no matter how good the time with Remy had been.

"How do you feel about seeing your husband after all that's transpired, especially after our conversation about his indiscretions?" Persenia asked Carlitta.

Carlitta stared out of the window, ignoring Persenia until the question was asked again.

"P, Jacoby is my husband. Sure, I've been harboring some feelings, in fact, I'm torn up inside. But I owe it to my babies to keep the family intact and forgive their father for his small indiscretion."

Persenia stayed on course but refused to say any more on the subject. She knew her best friend, and if she was a psychiatrist, she'd say that Carlitta wasn't happy about Jacoby's mess and she wanted answers. The unfortunate thing about Jacoby's mistress—the one she was aware of—was that it was Carlitta's favorite cousin. And when and if she found out, it would tear her to pieces.

"Well, we're almost there. If anybody can bring Reggie back from the dead, it will be Jacoby."

Carlitta laughed. "You're right about that, P. Those guys were like Abbott and Costello in college."

"Girl, they were more like Alfalfa and Spanky of *The Little Rascals*." The girls broke out in laughter.

"You're wrong for that, P, but you hit the nail on the head." Carlitta put her hands over her mouth, as she tried to keep from choking and coughing. "Yeah, honey, that's who those fools remind me of; they were a hot mess."

"Those were good memories, Carlitta. Good memories."

"Yeah."

"We're here." Persenia followed the signs to the Baggage Claim area. As soon as they pulled up to the terminal, Carlitta spotted him, holding up a directional sign. She pulled to the curb.

Jacoby knocked on the window and Carlitta rolled it down. Persenia hit the lever for the trunk. In all of thirty seconds, Jacoby deposited his suitcase and was sitting comfortably in the backseat of Persenia's car.

"Hey, babe," he said to Carlitta, who responded with a weak hi and kept her body face forward.

"This is a nice ride, Persenia. My boy spared no expense in loading up this bad boy for you."

Persenia tried to ignore Jacoby. He'd seen her car before—in Seattle. But he hadn't been inside, so she thought better of not responding. "I like it."

"So, how's my boy doing? Reggie has nine lives, you know. That dude always comes out smelling like a rose, regardless of what befalls him."

"Well, he's not smelling like a rose," Persenia interjected. "I'll say he's a trooper or more like a survivor; that I'll agree. But he's hanging on by a thread. I hope your face will bring him back to life."

"Well, I aim to be the rope that's going to pull him through. What's up with you guys...Carlitta? It feels like we're in a vacuum with no air."

"Maybe we are," Carlitta said, matter-of-fact.

"Okay. I guess I'll be quiet for now."

No one said anything for the next fifteen or twenty minutes. And then Persenia spoke up, not enjoying the "vacuum" they were in. "Jacoby, practice some of your good jokes. We've got to do all we can to make Reggie laugh, although I'd settle for a smile."

"I'll pretend like we're Abbott and Costello."

The girls started laughing and couldn't stop. Jacoby sat back and digested it all.

❧ 54 ❧

THE WOMAN WITH THE RED HAIR

General Elston returned to his office, sat down, and examined in his head the meeting he had with General Compton. He kept turning their conversation over in his mind—the desperation in Compton's voice to get to the bottom of the turmoil that had erupted on their immediate turf. Certainly, he wanted to know who killed his friends, Kaleah and Michael, and who attempted to kill Reggie, but it was Compton's orders to get information pronto that had Elston stumped, especially since Homeland Security had a special team that was handling this matter, along with the CIA and the FBI. Maybe the CIA and FBI were riding Compton's back.

Wallace Elston's first thought was to interview Rebecca Dickerson, but he didn't want to give her any reason to think she was being investigated. But on the other hand, he did want information about Michael's demeanor prior to his death. He'd ask Reggie's secretary as well.

He pushed through some papers on his desk and came across a manila envelope that was marked "Confidential – For Your Eyes Only." What was it doing in the middle of his desk?

Not wasting another moment, Elston picked up a silver letter opener that stood in a beautiful sterling silver holder his wife had given him for some occasion or another. He sliced the envelope open with one flick of his wrist and pulled out the contents.

Inside the manila envelope was a white business envelope and Elston was taken aback at the return address. Taking out the contents, Elston poured over the document—a letter from a former service buddy, Four-Star General Richard Dickerson. There was that name again—Dickerson. *Damn, what a coincidence,* Elston thought, as he began to read the letter. He hadn't seen or heard from his friend in years. Dickerson was a highly decorated officer in the U.S. Army, having served in the early stages of Desert Shield after the invasion of Kuwait. Elston read on.

> *Wallace, it distresses me to write this letter to you. I have reason to believe that my daughter, Rebecca, who also works at the Pentagon, may be engaged in some kind of criminal act against the country. I got wind of it when I accidently intercepted some text messages from her phone onto my computer when she came home recently. She has a cousin named Jarod Biscolli, my wife's brother's child, who I've determined from the texts may have been recruited by ISIS.*

That last sentence made Elston sit up straight and then look back down at the paper again. Could this be for real...right under their noses? Without wasting any more time, Elston continued to read.

> *I believe Jarod is using another name, but I'm not privy to it. I tried to talk with Rebecca about it without letting her know that I had acquired the information from her very own smartphone, but she became belligerent, refused to talk to me, and left the house. She must have returned to D.C.; she never even said goodbye to her mother.*
>
> *I'm afraid for her. She seems to be headed on a path of destruction. I'm asking a favor as a friend to help my daughter. She's a bright young woman and I, nor her mother, who has no knowledge of this, would not survive if Rebecca was arrested and had to go to jail should she be involved at a level that would do harm to the U.S. See what you can find out for me. When you're able, please contact me at this number 202-435-5555.*

Thanking you in advance,
Richard Dickerson

Wallace Elston couldn't believe that he'd gone from getting an order from General Compton to sitting on a land mine. Hell was getting ready to split wide open. Elston sat despondent; he was between a rock and a hard place.

"If that red-headed bitch killed my friends, I'm going to serve her up for dinner," Elston said under his breath. "I don't give a damn whose daughter she is. If she's bad enough to sit amongst us and wreak havoc on this agency, I'm going to give it back to her."

Elston turned in the direction of his computer and logged on. His top-secret clearance allowed him to access sensitive information. When he came to the page he was seeking, he dropped Jarod Biscolli's name where prompted. Less than a second passed when the name Rasheed Ali Rashamrandon came up in association with Biscolli. Homeland Security had been watching him for a while, as he'd recently returned to New York from Syria. As Jarod Biscolli, he had a police rap sheet that included being picked up for selling drugs. At the present, there was nothing in the record that tied him to the Pentagon.

Bingo, there was now a connection. Pieces to the elusive puzzle were starting to fall into place, if indeed Rebecca and Biscolli were the links to the bazaar happenings on sight. And thanks to the letter from an old friend, they were about to get some answers.

Elston hit the intercom. "Sarah, ask Rebecca Dickerson to come to my office. Tell her I need to ask her some questions about General Forbes. No, just ask her to come to my office without any explanation."

"Yes, sir."

55

OUT OF THE WOODS

A couple of days had passed since Reggie was rushed to the hospital with severe injuries to his neck and internal organs. It had to be the hands of the Lord who altered what most thought would be sure death. But Reggie struggled through, and while he still had an uphill battle, the doctors felt that bar any unforeseen events, he had a fifty/fifty chance of coming out of it whole.

All piled into Persenia's car, the trio headed for the hospital to see Reggie. Persenia looked to her left and noticed that cars lined Julia's driveway. She'd stop over tonight and see her. Michael's funeral was set for tomorrow morning and she dreaded going.

As they headed for the Beltway, Persenia surprised Jacoby. "I'm glad you're here, Jacoby." She felt Carlitta staring at her. "You're what Reggie needs right now—a good friend."

"I'm always down for my boy," Jacoby said, with a smirk on his face. "Reggie and me go way back—in fact we all do, and I've got to be there for him, like I know he'd be there for me."

"Without a doubt, he'll appreciate that you came to see about him."

"I also came to check up on my baby. Right, Carlitta?"

"If you say so, Jacoby. If you say so."

"P, what's up with your girl? My wife left home one way, and since she's been here, she's changed."

"Let me answer that for you, P," Carlitta said, jumping into the conversation. "I told Persenia about you having an affair."

Jacoby didn't say a word.

"Cat got your tongue?"

"This is not the time or the place to discuss what should stay behind our closed doors."

"You wanted to know, Jacoby, and I told you. It's one of the reasons I had to get away."

"So, what do you have to say, P, about Carlitta's announcement?"

"Jacoby, that is between you and Carlitta."

"I'm sure you had plenty to say."

"Why are you jumping on, Persenia? This is your mess."

"Girl, please," Persenia began. "I'm not paying Jacoby any mind. As I said, I have no comment on the subject."

"Umph," Jacoby said under his breath.

Quiet ensued until they arrived at the hospital. Carlitta and Jacoby followed Persenia, as she led them to Reggie's room.

Persenia turned toward her friends and held up a hand. "We aren't bringing any mess into Reggie's room. My husband needs the friends who love him to help him in his recovery." She looked between Carlitta and Jacoby. "Y'all comprehend?"

"We got it, P," Carlitta said, and squeezed Jacoby's hand.

The trio marched through the door. To their surprise, Reggie's eyes were opened, although he was looking out into space. His head turned when he saw them, and a flicker of light...a flicker of hope burned in his eyes.

"Hey," Reggie whispered. "The devil tried to kill me, but I'm still here."

"You're looking good, dawg," Jacoby said, trying not to make Reggie laugh, although it appeared that Jacoby was somewhat disturbed by what he saw. He went to Reggie and gave him a light-weight fist bump on his shoulder.

"Well, I'm not quite out of the woods, but the doctors tell me that I'm going to live."

"Glad to hear it, Reg," Carlitta said, coming to his side and placing a kiss on his cheek.

"How are you feeling, baby," Reggie asked Persenia. "Come closer."

Persenia walked over and stood next to the hospital bed that was already crowded with his closest friends. She put her hand on top of Reggie's. "Happy to see you smiling; it's going to be all right."

"When is Michael Forbes' funeral?"

"Tomorrow; I'm going to represent our family. You worry about getting well. Jacoby will keep you company."

"Let his wife know that I'm thinking of her and the family and that I'd be there if I weren't in the hospital." Reggie squeezed Persenia's hand.

"Okay."

There was light laughter as Jacoby told some off-color joke. Even Carlitta seemed to be loosening up, acting as if she and Jacoby hadn't been ill with each other earlier. Persenia smiled, happy that their being there—more so Jacoby's being there—was aiding in Reggie's healing. *Out of the woods* were the words she hung on to for the rest of the day.

✻ 56 ✻

TWENTY-ONE GUN SALUTE

"I'm glad you decided to attend General Forbes' funeral with me, Carlitta. There's been too much death and tragedy and with Reggie's near miss, I can't take much more."

Carlitta sighed. "I didn't want you to go alone, P. Besides, I'm sure Jacoby wanted some alone time with Reggie."

Persenia slid her black dress off the hanger she'd been holding and stepped into it. "Would you zip up my dress?" She pulled her hair up off her neck.

Carlitta zipped up Persenia's dress. "All done." There was a pause. "I wish my body was still in shape. You still have your college, shake-it up, body on you."

Turning around to face Carlitta, Persenia put her hand on Carlitta's shoulders. "You've got your babies; I don't have any...something I always wanted. You've enjoyed a great family life for the most part, but mine has been troublesome for the past number of years. Be careful what you ask for, Carlitta. The grass isn't always greener on the other side."

Carlitta let go of a smile. "Right you are, P. I'll remember that from now on. But I am going to a gym as soon as I return home. No longer will I take my husband for granted. Can't have his eyes wandering."

Persenia looked away. She hated keeping information from Carlitta that would certainly break her heart. But it wasn't up to her to share that her cousin, Kimiko, was her husband's side piece. It wasn't her place to do so, even though her heart had begged her to.

"Don't worry about, Jacoby. He has a good woman...wife, who loves her children and only wants the best for her family. You made the ulti-mate sacrifice by allowing your body to carry those precious pieces of cargo to full term and present them at your husband's feet. Tell him to kiss your big ass, if he doesn't like it."

Carlitta burst into laughter. "P, you are too funny. Let's get up out of here before we won't be any good for anyone."

Persenia hugged her friend and off they went.

❦

Major General Michael Forbes had a Catholic service. It was a little more solemn than Kaleah's but the military brass was well represented. President Obama was present, minus Michelle, and he gave a short recitation about Forbes' service in the military, stopping to salute and thank him for his service to the United States of America.

Persenia kept staring at the back of Julia's head, as she sat sobbing through most of the service. She was flanked by her children and other loved ones. Persenia's heart went out to her. And within forty-five minutes the service was over.

"Let's go," Persenia said, wanting to distance herself as soon as possible from all of the grief-stricken people. "This could've been my husband."

"But it wasn't. Be thankful. Looking at Reggie in the hospital bed made me remember the guy who used to play football in college. He was good-looking, kind of smart, and winked at me a couple of times. I might've married him, P, if he'd asked me." Carlitta laughed at her own choice of words.

"Well he didn't; he married me."

"Persenia, I was only joking. Lighten up. I did have a secret crush on him though...that is until Jacoby came and snatched me up. Maybe you ought to show more gratitude to Reggie. He's always loved you, P. I remember him saying he was going to give you the world."

Traffic noise was at a premium, but Carlitta stopped and took notice when Persenia called out to her.

Persenia was staring at Carlitta with hands on her hips, like she didn't have any good sense. "Uhhh, you're not getting it, are you? Don't play devil's advocate with me now, Carlitta. You've been signifying on Reggie since your ass rolled into D. C. Don't play me like you've suddenly got a soft heart for him."

"It's not that; it's what President Obama said. "He said, '*Life is too short to worry about what your neighbor is or isn't doing. The question becomes what impact have you made that could affect the world for good.*' It was that one little phrase that made an impression on me...about how I want to think and view the world in the future, P. I want to be a better person, a better mother, and a better wife. And you have to decide if you're going to be the angry black woman for the rest of your life...if you're going to continue to hate Reggie, which will keep you from moving forward. You either want or you don't. But if you're going to try and make a life with Reggie, you've got to talk to him, forgive him if it comes to that or rest with the fact that it's all over and move on."

Steam seemed to pour out of Persenia's nose. "So, is that what you're going to do for your precious Jacoby? I don't believe you, Carlitta. Don't sit in judgment of me. You have no idea what my life has been." She was about to say something else but refrained from doing so. Persenia continued to stand and stare.

"Look, P, whatever it was that Reggie was out there in the world doing, who am I to judge? Sure, I'd probably like to thump him upside his head for being such a jackass to my best friend, but what's the point? I need to mind my own affairs and get them in order. I've got to live for today like there's no tomorrow."

Persenia ingested what Carlitta said. She turned around and continued walking toward her car. "How can the doggone pot call the kettle black when her fornicating husband was doing her cousin right up under her nose," Persenia said under her breath. "What a fool."

"What did you say, P?"

Persenia threw her middle finger in the air. "I said, instead of saluting Michael Forbes, I gave a twenty-one-gun salute to Major General Kaleah Neal, an upstanding woman, citizen, and role model for all women who have a desire to be with another woman's husband because they don't have one of their own," Persenia lied, although deep down inside, that's what she felt.

Seeming not to understand where Persenia was coming from, Carlitta stared at her for a moment before rolling her eyes. Persenia sighed and pressed on without waiting for a response from Carlitta, although there was no need for one.

$$\maltese \quad 5\,7 \quad \maltese$$

DANCING WITH THE RED DEVIL

General Elston approached his office and walked inside the outer office. Before entering his office, he stopped in front of his secretary's desk.

"Jackie, ask Ms. Rebecca Dickerson to come to my office."

"She went to Major General Forbes' funeral, but I'll check to see if she's returned."

"Find her. I want to speak with her the moment she sets her feet in this place. And that's an order." Elston walked into his office and slammed the door.

A surprised look crossed Jackie's face. She sighed, picked up the phone and punched in the number for Rebecca's office. The phone rang and rang until Jackie finally hung up. She sighed once again, got up from her seat, and went to the door of Elston's office and knocked.

"What is it?" said the voice from behind the door.

"General Elston, it's Jackie."

"Come in."

Jackie slowly pushed down on the handle and walked into Elston's office. "There's no answer at her desk."

Elston looked at Jackie. "An apology is due. I'm sorry for my rude-ness. After attending first, General Neal's funeral and today, General Forbes', I'm madder than hell that someone is murdering my friends, my co-workers for in God's name I don't understand why. I'm so fed up with society...our world today. Why can't we all get along, Jackie? Why?

"Again, I'm sorry. I need for you, however, to go to Major General Forbes' office and find out when Ms. Dickerson will be returning to work. I realize they are burying her boss today, but it didn't constitute two full days off from work. She didn't respond to my call on yesterday."

Jackie managed a smile. "Yes, sir, I'll go to her office now."

"Thank you, Jackie."

⚜

JACKIE RETURNED IN LESS THAN TEN MINUTES, WITH REBECCA Dickerson following at her heels. "Just a moment," Jackie said. She hit the button on the intercom. "General Elston, Ms. Dickerson is here to see you."

"Ask her to come in."

Rebecca watched Jackie closely. She detected a vibe that didn't sit well with her. Pushing her thoughts to the back of her mind, she entered General Elston's office and stood in front of him.

"Have a seat," General Elston offered, extending his hand while pointing at the seat that sat in front of his desk.

Rebecca didn't say a word. She casually took the seat that was offered and quickly surveyed her surroundings. For sure there was a vibe in the place that she didn't like.

"I guess you're wondering why I asked you to come, Ms. Dickerson."

"I am," Rebecca said, her face void of expression.

"As you're probably aware, there is an internal/external investiga-tion being conducted of Major General Forbes and Neal's deaths."

Rebecca fidgeted in her seat.

"If you can remember, I'd like to know what General Forbes' demeanor...his attitude was like prior to his untimely death. Did he seem to be in any undue stress or did he make any remarks to you that might have caught your attention?"

Rebecca lifted her chin slightly and gave Elston a brief onceover with her eyes. She bunched up her lips and then released them. Shaking her head back and forth, she finally answered. "No, sir, I can't think of anything that would have made me think that something was going on with him. He seemed his normal self. Sure, there were the usual stresses of the job, but nothing out of the ordinary."

"Did he ever mention anything to you about an ISIS threat... perhaps on a personal level?"

Careful not to rush into an answer, Rebecca pretended to contemplate the question. She squeezed her lips together and then looked up into Elston's eyes. "No, he's never had a conversation with me regarding ISIS. I doubt seriously that he would since I'm just a secretary that carries out his orders."

Elston looked at the red-headed young woman with a thought-provoking face. Rebecca wasn't in the least bit thrilled to be where she was, in fact, she felt rather uncomfortable.

"Did you have any other questions for me, sir?"

"Yes, I do. First, how close were you and the Major General?"

"I'm not sure I know what you mean," Rebecca shot back.

"It was a simple question, Rebecca. How close were you and General Forbes? Rumors have it that the two of you were more than boss and secretary—maybe even lovers."

Rebecca stood up. "Sir, I don't mean to be disrespectful..."

"Well, sit down," Elston said, not waiting for Rebecca to complete her sentence. "I'll let you know when you're free to leave."

Rebecca sat back down, but now her nostrils were flaring. She didn't like one bit the tone of Elston's voice and the course the line of questioning was going. General Elston would soon find out that she wasn't one to be played with and that she wasn't some lost puppy off the street seeking a secretarial job that she could take or leave.

"I'd like for you to answer my question," Elston said, cutting deep into Rebecca's thoughts.

"Whatever rumors may be circulating about me and Major General

Forbes are lies. I had a good rapport with General Forbes; that's all. Nothing more than that."

"I knew your father, General Dickerson. He's an old buddy of mine —Desert Shield."

Rebecca looked away from Elston. Her hands began to perspire. She was temporarily estranged from her father, but by Elston bringing up his name meant something. Elston was fishing. He had a nibble and he was throwing bait at her to see if she'd bite. But she wasn't going to give Elston the satisfaction he was searching for. She'd answer the questions and hopefully he'd see that she couldn't help him in his investigation of Michael Forbes' death.

"Oh, it's a small world."

"A small world indeed. When was the last time you spoke with your father?"

"What does my father have to do with Major General Forbes' death?"

"Did I say it did? I merely mentioned that I know your father. You're trying to make an assumption."

"General Elston, forgive me, but I'm not sure why I'm being questioned. It's been a long day. I lost my boss a few days ago and seeing him stretched out in that church today made all the images and stories told about him on TV so real. It's been tough and I don't know what else I can tell you."

"Alright, Ms. Dickerson, you're free to go. Should you come across anything that might be useful in our investigation, please don't hesitate to contact me."

"Sure," Rebecca said, rising from her seat. Without wasting a minute more or another breath, she was out of there.

෧෫෨

GENERAL ELSTON WAITED A FEW MOMENTS AND THEN HIT THE intercom. "Jackie, dial CID for me right away."

"Yes, sir."

Only a few minutes had gone by when the intercom buzzed. "General Elston, your caller is on the line."

"Thanks, Jackie. Hey, Thurston, I want a 24-hour tail on the red-headed devil that goes by the name of Rebecca Dickerson pronto. I believe she's going to lead us right to Forbes' and Neal's killer."

"I'm on it, General."

✿ 58 ✿

ISIS IN CRISIS

Rebecca Dickerson moved swiftly from General Elston's office back to her own. She sat for a moment, wondering what angle Elston was working from. What did he know or was he only suspecting? Why in the world had her father's name come up? Was that an attempt to scare her? She was committed to her task and nothing and no one was going to stop her.

Picking up the package with the TOP SECRET documents that she'd confiscated from Reggie's and Michael's office, she headed out of the building, observing her surroundings as she proceeded to leave the Pentagon grounds. Getting the documents was a piece of cake. For one, she manned the TOP SECRET files for Forbes, and with Reggie Charleston's office feeling the brunt of his near fatal end, she was able to slip in and retrieve what she'd been looking for. Her cousin would reward her handsomely for the information she was able to extract for the enemy. Reggie Charleston got off easy, but the new enemy, General Wallace Elston, had to be dealt with now.

Rebecca hadn't detected the two officers who'd been assigned to tail her. They smiled at her at the entrance to the building upon her departure. As soon as she had gone some distance, the officers made their way to a car that was stashed near the building and was in pursuit.

A smile of contentment crossed Rebecca's face. She reached for her phone and looked up her recent phone calls and found Jarod's number. She touched it with her finger and hit the phone icon to place the call.

"Rashamrandon," Jarod said, giving his Islamic extremist name.

"It's me, Becka. I've got it. A piece of cake; Smooth as silk."

"Good, cousin. We'll meet up later...say two o'clock."

"Why not now? I'm ready to get paid."

"Patience. I'm putting something else in place. I don't want to talk about it on the phone."

"Okay, I understand. I may have another problem; I'll tell you about it when I see you."

"Okay, gotta go." And the line was dead.

Little did Rebecca know a tracking device had already been attached to her vehicle. That's how fast these operatives worked. Even if she got away from them, they'd always be able to locate her. Right now, they followed her around the city, seemingly wasting time. And then she took off on a side street in the middle of town, not too far from Howard University, a Historically Black College and University, but 1st Lieutenant Bratcher was right behind her. Suddenly, Rebecca pulled to the curb in front of one of the colorful row houses, got out with a package stuck under her arm and disappeared inside.

"I guess we'll have to wait until she reappears," 2nd Lieutenant Thurston said as he took binoculars from a side pocket and turned it toward the house Rebecca had entered. Thurston picked up a Pentax camera with a high-powered lens attached to it and began snapping pictures.

"Any signs of life?" 1st Lieutenant Cleveland Bratcher asked.

"Not yet. I wonder what's in the package. I'm going to send a text to General Elston and let him know that she carried a package out of the building to her car and into this house. Our orders were only to follow, take pictures, but not apprehend."

"If that bitch had anything to do with killing our guys, I'd like to put a bullet through her heart."

"I feel the same way, Bratcher, but we're only investigators not the MP's. What is a good-looking redhead like her doing tied up in this mess?"

"I hear that it may be ISIS related."

"Don't let me find out that it's the truth, I'll blow her brains out myself," Thurston said. "It's bad enough that we have to go over to the Middle East and fight these monsters, but to have our own people eliminate Americans for an unjust cause."

"I'm going to ram Jihad right up their butts."

Thurston sat up. "Get ready, our redhead is making a move."

"And with that package under her arms," Bratcher added.

Lieutenant Thurston snapped away. "She's talking on the phone to someone. What's the chance we take that phone from her?"

"I was a good pick-pocket back in the day, although I don't want you telling anybody," Bratcher said, putting the car in gear.

"I'd say let's do it, but our orders are only to follow and get intel. I've got the address and the coordinates of this first stop recorded and so does that box underneath her car. Let's go; she's moved out. Make sure we maintain a safe distance behind her."

❧ 59 ❧

LOVE... A LONELY COMMODITY

Reggie was smiling when the ladies entered his hospital room. Sitting on the side of Reggie's bed was Jacoby, with his back to them.

There was quiet, as Reggie looked at Persenia, waiting to hear how Michael's service went. Reggie still wasn't up to much talking.

"It was a nice service," Persenia began. "The usual was there, including the President. It was short and sweet. I felt for Julia; she cried through the whole thing."

Jacoby didn't turn around. He listened with his back to the ladies, as if he was detached from the day's events.

"So," Carlitta began, "what have you guys been talking about, although, it appears that Jacoby has been doing most of the talking."

Reggie looked at Carlitta, turned away and began to look at Jacoby.

"Nothing much," Jacoby said, keeping his tone light.

"That's not what Reggie's eyes are saying. So, Reg, did Jacoby tell you who he's been messing with?"

"Carlitta, don't do this," Persenia begged. "What about all that talk about what Obama said this afternoon? How soon we forget."

"I...I know."

Jacoby stood up and faced Carlitta. "Reggie has been through a terrible ordeal, and you're going to come in here and start some shit that you can't cash? Give me a damn break, woman. I love you, Carlitta, but I'm tired of putting up with your sarcasm...your, *I don't give a crap,* attitude. You're the kind of person that makes a man want to find peace somewhere else."

"So, is that what you did, Jacoby? Did you go find peace with someone else?"

"I didn't say I did that, I was giving you an example of what drives men wild and crazy and makes them do foolish things."

"I guess you're innocent in all of this. I guess you've never said anything to hurt my feelings or treated me in such a way that I felt this small." Carlitta pinched her fingers together for emphasis.

Jacoby sighed. "Yes, I've done something that I'm not so proud of but it doesn't mean that I've stopped loving you."

Carlitta was quiet. She went to Reggie's bedside and rubbed the blanket that covered his legs. "I hope you get well soon, my brother."

Reggie smiled and then peered in Persenia's direction. She stared back without saying a word.

"I hope they catch whoever has a bounty on our men's heads," Persenia finally said. "If you guys don't need anything else, I think I'm going to run to the house and change my clothes. Are you coming, Carlitta?"

"No, I'm going to stay with the men. You go ahead; I'll be alright. Maybe we can get something to eat later."

"Okay," Persenia said. "I won't be too long."

Before heading out of the door, Persenia stopped and turned around. She went to Reggie and placed a kiss on his forehead. He squeezed her hand. And then she left without looking back.

As soon as Persenia got in the car, she pulled out her cell phone. She chose the number she wanted and hit the CALL button. She waited and a smile crossed her face.

"Hey, baby, I've been waiting for your call."

"I miss you, Remy."

❧ 60 ❧

A VIEW TO A KILL

Lieutenants Thurston and Bratcher kept a vigilant tail on Rebecca Dickerson as she darted in and out of traffic. There didn't seem to be any rhyme or reason to the route she was taking; she seemed to be going nowhere in particular. They rode through the heart of the seat of government, along New York Avenue with its row of foreign Embassy's. They passed monument after monument, noting a homeless man dunking a tee-shirt in the dirty fountain water, with a pair of socks draped over the small concrete wall that circled the statue.

It was early June, and summer would be declared in a few weeks. The sun was still high in the sky, although it was six in the evening.

"Where in the hell is this woman going?" Bratcher asked, not expecting an answer. "We're going to run out of gas before we get anything concrete."

"We've got plenty of gas. In fact, I say let's lose her for a minute and pick up the signal in about an hour, that is unless she makes a stop."

"Okay, let's get something to eat. I'll keep driving until we get to Fourth Street and cut away for something to eat."

"That sounds good," Thurston said, taking out his binoculars for one last look. "Hold it, Bratcher. She's stopping. Keep driving past her car and circle the block. Who's she connecting with on New York Avenue?"

Bratcher drove past and had to go down two blocks. "These damn one-way streets."

"Hurry up. The last thing we want to do is lose her, especially if she doesn't get back into her car."

Bratcher had to make a series of turns because of the one-way streets in order to put them back on the portion of street they needed to be on. They drove and spotted the car sitting on the curb, however, Rebecca Dickerson was nowhere in sight. Bratcher quickly drove past and repeated what he'd just done. When they returned to New York Avenue, they were in luck and pulled into an available parking space several cars behind Dickerson's. They sat and waited.

And then they saw her retreat from a building with a young gentleman at her heels, laughing like they were familiar. Thurston's fingers clicked a dozen pictures a second.

"Bratcher, the guy has a manila envelope in his hand."

"Umm," Bratcher said. "See if you can zoom in closer."

"I got it all in my view." *Click, click, click.* "Damn, did you see that?"

"Damn, did he just shoot her, Thurston?"

Click, click, click. "Yeah, she's on the ground."

"And he's getting away in her car. Should I follow him?"

"No," Thurston said. "Call 911 and then call General Elston. I'm going to keep clicking."

"We better get away from here before the police descend upon this place. Any minute, someone is going to discover her body."

"Okay, Bratcher, make your move. I'm going to capture a few more photos."

Bratcher put the car in gear and drove slowly past the spot where Rebecca Dickerson now lay lifeless on the street.

"She's lying in a pool of blood," Thurston said. *Click, click, click.* "Let's get out of here."

ତ୍ୟୁତ

AN EMERGENCY MEETING OF THE JOINT CHIEFS WAS CALLED. Pandemonium had yet again hit the Pentagon. General Compton and General Wallace Elston sat together on one side of the conference room.

"Gentlemen," General Compton began. "We've been compromised. Ms. Rebecca Dickerson, Major General Forbes' former secretary is believed to have stolen confidential documents from Major General Forbes and Brigadier General Reggie Charleston's offices. She was seen carrying a package out of the Pentagon earlier this afternoon and was seen later with a man, who she may have given the package to. This is not confirmed. I do know, however, that Ms. Dickerson was killed at the hands of the man she was seen laughing with only moments earlier.

"A tracking device was placed underneath Ms. Dickerson's car. At present, our guys have informed the FBI and with the aid of several SWAT teams have surrounded an apartment in Bethesda, Maryland where the suspect is believed to have driven to. We are presently waiting for an update.

"I tasked General Elston with obtaining any information he could find on Ms. Dickerson. It wasn't only coincidental that he received a letter from retired General Richard Dickerson, alluding to the fact that his daughter, Rebecca Dickerson, might be tied to an extremist group. The timing was uncanny. General Elston also found out that Ms. Dickerson has a cousin, a Jarod Biscolli, with ties to ISIS, who recently returned from Syria. And now she's dead."

❧ 61 ❧

STATE OF ALERT

Persenia was happy to be by herself for a moment. She'd been on the phone for nearly two hours talking to Remy. He was a breath of fresh air, and the more she thought about her happiness, she saw Remy in her future.

Hanging up her dress, she stopped when she heard her cell phone ring. Persenia picked up her phone and saw Carlitta's face in the window. If she could be granted a wish, it was that she could let the call go to voicemail and ignore all calls other than Remy's. Carlitta was getting on her nerves with all of her wishy-washy thinking. One minute she hated Jacoby; the next minute she didn't want to live without him. That was okay with her, but Carlitta wasn't there to negotiate her life with Reggie.

She answered the phone. "Hey, are you ready to get something to eat?"

"Yes, P, Jacoby and I are tired. The doctor gave Reggie a heavy sedative and he's out cold. Both Jacoby and I are hungry. I wouldn't mind having some of those crab cakes we had the other day."

"I'm not in the mood to travel into Baltimore this time of day, but I'll take you to Carolina Kitchen. The food is pretty good."

"Sounds good. We'll be waiting on you."

"I'll be there in a few." Persenia hung up the phone.

To keep her company while she slipped into something more comfortable, Persenia flipped the television on. It was eight-thirty in the evening and the prime-time shows were on. Right in the middle of her favorite comedy, the network broke into the scheduled show and announced that they had a special report.

Persenia pulled on a pair of jeans and was about to throw on a light-weight blouse when she heard the newscaster say that a person of interest, who might be linked to the murders of Major Generals Kaleah Neal and Michael Forbes' and the attempted assassination of Brigadier General Reginald Charleston and worked at the Pentagon, was murdered this evening. She stopped what she was doing and stared at the newscaster.

"The country is in a state of high alert," the reporter said. "This evening, Ms. Rebecca Dickerson was murdered on a main street, not far from the White House and other government offices. Ms. Dickerson was being tailed by military agents and had stopped to make contact with an unknown person. The agents were eyewitnesses to Ms. Dickerson's murder."

A picture of Rebecca Dickerson appeared on the screen and Persenia grabbed her chest. "She's the redhead that kept showing up wherever I was," Persenia said aloud.

"Ms. Dickerson was said to be in possession of a package when she left the Pentagon early this afternoon. She was also in possession of this package while being tailed, however, the unknown assailant clutched a like package when Ms. Dickerson was gunned down.

"We will follow-up with this story as soon as..."

Persenia quickly shut the television off. Her nerves were on edge again, and she thought about how close she'd come to possibly being a victim. Now the woman was dead? But what did that mean? Were there others after her or was it a scare tactic to get next to Reggie?

Without letting another minute go by, Persenia dialed Remy.

"Hey, sweetheart..."

"Listen, Remy. Remember that redhead that kept snapping pictures of us at the Lincoln Memorial?"

"Yes."

"What I never told you was that I saw her again in the airport parking lot. Well, she was killed this evening, and the reporter said that she may be linked to ISIS. I believe the target was really Reggie, but now I'm scared as hell."

"Do you want me to fly back to Washington?"

"I wish that was doable. I'd feel a lot safer. Jacoby and Carlitta are here so that's out of the question. Have you said anything to Jacoby about coming out here to visit me?"

"Hell no; that's our secret. I don't want Jacoby anywhere near our business. This is between you and I."

"Great. He has such loose lips."

"I'm surprised at him. How are he and Carlitta getting along?"

"So, so. Carlitta's acting like Jacoby was due his one indiscretion, although I can see her seething under that cloak of hers. She wants to hang onto her marriage; and I applaud her for that. But if she ever finds out that Kimiko was/is her husband's lover, Jacoby will be without a penis. Better yet, Carlitta will make him commit hara-kiri. My lips are sealed."

"Baby, I wish I could be with you right now. I'd hold you in my arms and offer all the comfort you need."

"Why is it that talking to you calms me down?"

"You trust me, and I want you to always trust me. I've got you."

"Thanks, Remy. I do trust you. Now, I've got to go and pick up Carlitta and Jacoby. I'm almost afraid to leave since the newscaster said we're in a state of alert."

"The country will be until they capture whoever it was that did that woman in."

"There's a chance that this person might be the same one who gunned down Reggie, Kaleah, and Michael. The FBI and CIA haven't breathed a word about who's behind it, although the word ISIS keeps coming up. If this guy that was reported to have killed that girl is the one, I hope they catch him soon. I'm sure Reggie is still on edge."

"Unfortunately, there are others out there waiting in the cut to be brave for ISIS. It's a damn shame. Be careful, and again, you can always trust me, Persenia. I love you."

"I love you, too." And the phone was dead.

Persenia was in love with Remy; her heart and her head told her so. And when Reggie got back on his feet and this ISIS crisis was over, she was going to ask him for a divorce. There wouldn't be any more wondering and waiting for the day when their marriage would get better. And hell with the pictures she had as blackmail. She'd wasted too much time already, and she was choosing to be happy.

❦ 62 ❦

DRAGNET

A ll of Washington, D. C. was out looking for Rebecca Dickerson's killer, as well as the assassin or assassins of Major General Michael Forbes and Kaleah Neal. The city was under siege, but now there was an optimistic lead on the string of tragedies.

Dragnets weren't only set up in D. C. but all portals leading in and out of the city. If this was the work of ISIS, these homegrown terrorist cells could be operating anywhere. The FBI and CIA were working overtime to apprehend anyone related to the recent incidents.

General Elston pondered the events leading up to Rebecca's demise. He poured over his memory of their brief interview. Rebecca was cocky and arrogant. The only time she seemed to be somewhat normal was when he mentioned her father, although her arrogant attitude returned in an instant. It was apparent she was hiding something.

His thoughts were interrupted by the intercom. "Yes, Jackie?"

"General Compton is on the telephone."

"Thank you." Wallace Elston waited until the transfer was made. "General Compton?"

"Wallace, today might be a good day."

"Why do you say so?"

"The SWAT team has our target holed up in an apartment in Bethesda. He ditched the car Ms. Dickerson had been riding in with the tracking device, but the agents were on top of it when he made the switch. This guy is clever, however. He was aware that he was being followed and probably figured that there might have been a device in or on the car that pinpointed his location. Not only did he slide in and out of the car in a matter of seconds, he slid in a third car that was observed by one of the many agents we had tailing him."

"I'm happy that we're close to apprehending this lunatic."

"Me too, Wallace. Our one hope is that we can arrest him alive. We need to know if others are involved and how far this underground, salamander organization reaches. Surely, he isn't operating under his own orders."

"Yes, and there's a matter of the package that possibly contained military secrets. I'm sure that's why Forbes, Neal and Charleston were singled out. I spoke to Charleston's secretary, and she told me that Rebecca had come to the office on several occasions, trying to get an audience with Charleston, as well as making strange inquiries."

"That must be it. We've got to get the documents before they're passed off to someone else. But I'm reassured, however, that this fool will not elude our dragnet."

"I wonder if Charleston saw the face of the person who attempted to kill him."

"Good question, Wallace. Let's get someone out to the hospital pronto to see what he knows. Has anyone gone out to see him?"

"I have no idea, but I'll be happy to go out and check on Reggie. I should've been out there before now. I'll call you when I've returned."

"Alright, General Elston. "Let's kick this sucker in the ass so we can get on with other business. Give Brigadier General Charleston my regards."

"I will, General Compton." And the line was dead.

❧ 63 ❦

MOVING ON

I t was late afternoon when Persenia finally emerged from her bedroom. There was no sign of Carlitta or Jacoby, as she roamed around the house. Maybe they were making an attempt to put their marriage on auto-pilot and ride the waves of love. Persenia smiled at the thought of the two of them getting it on.

Walking outside to get the newspaper, Persenia stopped short when she saw Julia talking with her children as they loaded up their car. For a brief moment Persenia watched, and her heart went out to the family.

Not wanting to disturb their goodbyes, Persenia rushed to pick up her newspaper where the paperboy had thrown it. As she stood up, Persenia heard her name."

"Hi, Persenia," Julia said, waving her hand.

Persenia watched as Julia's daughter and family backed out of the driveway. "Hi, Julia, how are you feeling? I'm sorry for not being there for you, as I would've liked. With Reggie in the hospital, I'm spending a lot of time there."

"I understand perfectly well and it's all right." Julia sighed. "Now comes the hard part."

Persenia went over and gave Julia a hug. "It'll be all right. Michael's service was beautiful."

Tears began to trickle down Julia's face. She swiped at her tears and looked up toward heaven. "Although my husband wasn't a saint, I miss him a lot."

"You heard what happened to his secretary."

Julia pulled her thoughts from out of the clouds. "Rebecca?"

"Yes, Rebecca, the redheaded devil."

"Why do you say that, Persenia?"

"You haven't seen the news. She was killed yesterday. The news being reported is that she was possibly connected to ISIS and may have been killed to keep other identities a secret."

Julia put her hand to her mouth. Her eyes became large, round circles. "You're kidding me. But...but do you think she is somehow linked to Michael's death?"

"I don't know what to think, but the FBI is suggesting that she may be a direct link."

Julia became enraged and turned beet red. "I suspected Michael of having an affair with that bitch."

Persenia scrunched up her face. "You mean to tell me that he was seeing his secretary?"

"That's what I said and it's exactly what I mean. I never saw them together, but I saw plenty of text messages from her to him and vice versa that were spicy, lewd, and disrespectful, to include pictures of her naked tits."

"She was using him, Julia. That woman was following me. I wished I had told you this earlier, but at the time it didn't make sense. Everywhere I seemed to be, she would crop up out of nowhere. I won't rest until I find out the truth, but that bitch is at the center of Kaleah and Michael's death, and Reggie's brush with it."

Julia sighed. "I'm glad she's dead. She had no business messing with a married man. And her tits were nothing to grovel over—two teaspoons full of nothing that you could barely put in your mouth. I always thought Michael was partial to those oversized, silicone boob jobs."

Persenia started laughing and couldn't stop. "You are so funny when you get mad, Julia. Oh my goodness; my side hurts."

"But now I see what you mean. Since I've known my husband, he was always attracted to big tits. Mine were a nice size—not gross, but he enjoyed them, if you know what I mean."

Persenia bent over from laughing so hard.

"So it bears to mind that...that evil woman was using Michael."

"But it appears his taste may have changed, Julia. Michael didn't know that the girl was in cahoots with ISIS. He went for the itty, bitty, titty girl because she paid his tail some attention, not even realizing he'd fallen in her trap."

Julia sighed. "It's a damn shame. Well, I'll be leaving you shortly. The man is gone and I have to move out of military housing."

"Now, that's a shame. You served as many years for Uncle Sam as Michael did, making sure your husband maintained his sanity after fighting all of those wars and entertaining the itty, bitty, titty committee."

"You're going to hell for that, Persenia."

The ladies hugged. "I wished we got to know each other sooner," Persenia interjected. "I'm going to miss you. If you want to stay in the city a little longer, you're welcome to stay at my house."

"No, I've got to get away from here—as far away as I can. I'll be fine, though. I'm going to stay with my son awhile. After that, I'll make up my mind about what I'm going to do."

"Call me anytime; you've got my number. I'm going in and get the rest of the crew together so we can visit Reggie."

"Give him a hug for me. Whatever your husband has done, forgive him before it's too late."

"I'll keep that in mind," Persenia said feebly. "She was going to forgive Reggie, but the truth of the matter, their time had come and was now gone—no quick fix. There was no going back. Reggie had made it perfectly clear that although Kaleah was dead, his feelings for her hadn't changed. He didn't love her and what she had for him was no longer. Someone new had stolen her heart.

❧ 64 ❧

THE INCONVENIENT TRUTH

When Persenia entered her house, she was expecting to find the house as peaceful as she left it. She heard foul language and a barrage of insults coming from the guest bedroom. Not to appear to be a snooper, Persenia steadied her legs and turned her good ear toward the sound.

"You sorry-ass mother....... You've been f'ing my cousin. I hope the both of you go straight to hell."

"Carlitta, calm down."

"Don't touch me, if you value your life at this moment. In fact, don't ever touch me again."

"You're reading more into this than need be."

"I've got ears, Jacoby," Carlitta screamed from behind the closed door. "You're such an idiot. What fool would be stupid enough to have a conversation with a side piece when their wife is in the vicinity? I was in the bathroom and the shower water was going. But I heard your cell phone ring before I entered it and I stood at the door and listened to your conversation."

"Whatever you heard, you've distorted the truth."

"Oh, I know what I heard, Jacoby Morgan." Carlitta pushed her finger into Jacoby's chest. "I heard you call out Kimiko's name and tell her how much you loved her. It was all I could do to not come from behind the door and stomp your ass in the ground. Oh, yes, I listened to the whole conversation."

"And..."

There was scuffling and a thump. Persenia moved closer to the door to get a sense of what was going on. Then there was a knock against the wall and Persenia jumped. The movement beyond the door didn't sound healthy and without wasting another second, Persenia went to the door, turned the knob, and pushed her way in.

"Jacoby, what in the hell is wrong with you? I can't believe you are beating up on a woman," Persenia said.

"I was protecting myself from the jackal," Jacoby hissed. "You tell her to keep her hands off of me."

Persenia glanced at Carlitta, who was huffing and puffing.

"The sorry-ass mother..."

"Ahh, ahh," Perenia said with caution in her voice.

"Guess who that no-good-for nothing animal was having an affair with, Persenia? You wouldn't believe it in a million years."

Persenia regretted that she barged in on Carlitta and Jacoby's scuffle. Now she was in the middle of their war, and she didn't want any parts of it, although hands down, she'd take Carlitta's side.

Jacoby cocked his head toward Persenia and smirked. "Persenia is smarter than you think."

Persenia gritted her teeth and shot Jacoby a nasty look. "I hope you guys can talk it out. This is not my concern."

Carlitta's cheeks were puffed up and she placed a hand on her hip. "Please don't go," she begged. "I'm so pissed off at this moment, I could kill someone."

Persenia took in a deep breath and sighed. She put both hands up and pleaded with Carlitta. "No, I don't need to know. Why don't you kiss and make up?"

Jacoby's face was twisted in bunches. He leered at Persenia, as if to say, *you're getting ready to be thrown under the bus.* "Is that because you already know and haven't shared your knowledge with your best friend?" Jacoby offered.

"What is he talking about, P?"

Persenia glared at Jacoby.

"Tell her, Persenia. Tell your BFF that you already knew who I was having an affair with. And how does she know? She was an eyewitness to the fact."

Carlitta came and stood in front of Persenia—her face only inches away, waving her finger in her face. "What is he talking about, P? Did you know about my husband and cousin and never shared it with me?"

Persenia shrugged her shoulders. "If I had told you what I'd seen, you would've been devastated, Carlitta. I was torn. How in the world could I hurt my best friend?"

"Probably because you had something to hide as well. Carlitta, your BFF is no saint. She stepped out on Reggie during the same time she discovered I was having a rendezvous with Kimiko."

Tears began to stream down Carlitta's face. "Is it true?"

"I felt I couldn't tell you, Carlitta, although I should've told you against my better judgment. And for your information, Jacoby is a bold face liar. He called one of his friends to meet us at a restaurant so that he could cover his ass. I had gone to Seattle to visit Kimiko and never suspected that I'd find your husband all cozy up in her house.

"I was conflicted about the whole thing, but I couldn't bring myself to tell you. Two of your favorite people were involved in something that was so disrespectful and I knew it would hurt you to the bone."

"Oh, give me a break, Persenia," Jacoby said, interrupting Persenia's flow. "She spent the night with the guy, and now she wants to pretend like she's little Miss Innocent."

"I spent some time with him, but I didn't sleep with him or see him again."

Carlitta started walking in circles, trying to put her mood in check. Then she stopped in front of both Jacoby and Persenia. "You spent the night with this mystery person but you didn't sleep with him, although you were well aware that my husband was sleeping with my cousin. This is making me crazy and I want to go off on y'all. How in the world can you condemn Reggie when your crap stinks too?"

Persenia jumped in before Jacoby could get a word in. "I don't blame you if you hate me at this moment, Carlitta. There's no excuse for what I did. I went to Seattle to see a friend. I was lonesome, as Reggie and I have been distant for a long time. I had no plans to even be with Remy. He was easy to talk to and we took a ferry ride but couldn't get back to our starting point as the last ferry had left. That was the only reason why I was with this guy. But your husband is a different story, but that's his story to tell. And for your information, Reggie and I have already talked about Remy, although all the whores he's bedded over the years couldn't touch my one indiscretion, regardless of the fact that I didn't sleep with him."

"Whatever," Jacoby said.

"I'm packing my stuff and going home," Carlitta said. "This is the worst vacation I've ever had. Persenia, our friendship card is in the wastebasket. You and Jacoby can both kiss my black ass."

Carlitta turned her back on the two. She pulled her suitcase from out of the closet and began to throw things in it. Abruptly, she turned around. "Jacoby, you might as well get on a plane bound for Seattle. You're not welcome at my home anymore."

"I pay the bills."

"I don't give a damn. When I get finished with you, you'll be grateful that Kimiko can put you up."

"Let's talk about this, Carlitta. The relationship with Kimiko is over."

"When did you decide that? Two seconds ago, when you suddenly realized you'd made a mistake because your ass was busted wide open? Boy, give me a break and get out of my damn way. I hate you."

Jacoby sighed and then stormed out of the room. Persenia heard the front door open and closed and then turned to Carlitta. She folded her arms and tried to speak.

"Carlitta..."

Carlitta threw her hands up. "I don't want to hear a word you have to say. You're a fraud...you're a low-down dirty bitch, P. I've been pouring my heart out to you, but your tired ass knew all this time that Kimiko was f'ing Jacoby. You stood right in front of me, like you're doing now, while I ranted and raved about my husband's indiscretion. What kind of friend are you?"

"An inconvenient one... at the moment. Sure, I could've run and told you what I'd witnessed, but I was trying to keep you from the pain of knowing. As the saying goes, no good deed..."

Carlitta threw a hand up in Persenia's face. "Please save the rhetoric. You're dead to me. I'm going to catch the first thing flying out to California, at Jacoby's expense. Don't worry about taking me; I'll take a taxi to the airport. You ain't got to do another damn thing for me. I'd hate to inconvenience you. Now, if you'll excuse me, I've got packing to do."

Unfolding her arms, Persenia left the room, shutting the door behind her. Her world was falling apart, but she was going to put it back together again. Raising her voice so that Carlitta could hear, she belted out, "ungrateful huzzy. You've got to be careful who you ride and die for; everybody ain't worth riding and dying for."

❦ 65 ❧

GIVE HER SOME SPACE

Silence engulfed the house. You couldn't hear a peep out of either Carlitta or Jacoby. Persenia was aware that Jacoby had re-entered the house, however, all was now calm. Maybe Jacoby had persuaded Carlitta to stay, but seconds later she heard a door opening and the wheels of several suitcases being dragged across her hardwood floor.

Sitting in the kitchen with a cup of tea in her hand, Persenia looked up when Jacoby entered the room.

"Carlitta is set on leaving; she's got a four o'clock flight. The taxi should be here any minute and I'm going to ride to the airport with her."

Persenia looked at the clock on the stove. "It's only noon. She's going to leave now?"

"With possible traffic delays and still having to check-in, it'll be four o'clock before you know it."

"Is she still mad?"

"Mad isn't the word, P. Her wall of defense is taller than the Empire

State Building. I'm going to let her cool off, but I do want to make sure she arrives at the airport safely—duty calls."

Persenia looked at him thoughtfully. "You should've thought about that before...well you know."

"I don't want to get into that now. Carlitta is in the living room. It appears that she wants to speak with you. Give her some space."

"She can have all the space she needs," Persenia said sarcastically.

Both Persenia and Jacoby looked up when Carlitta peeked her head in the doorway. "You don't have to worry about me, darling. As I said, you are dead to me and you can kiss my black ass."

"So be it, Carlitta. It's been nice knowing you." Persenia turned her head and took a sip of her tea.

Carlitta stood a few seconds longer, stared at Jacoby, and headed out of the kitchen. "My taxi is here."

❧ 66 ❧

HOME GROWN TERROR

Sweating profusely, Jarod Biscolli aka Rasheed Ali Rashamrandon, sat shaking in the bedroom of one of his fellow accomplices. His jaw was tight and his face twisted in rage, as he uttered the word Jihad over and over, vowing to take out the devil, whoever in the world that happened to be. He stood up and paced back and forth, waiting for Amon Alizee to return to the room.

An arsenal of weapons to include AKA assault rifles, semi-automatic handguns, missile launchers, hand grenades and suicide vests were stockpiled in the bedroom like it was Fort Knox. A small army could annihilate a city in record time.

Irritable and frustrated, Rasheed stepped to the side of the one window in the bedroom and took a peek out of it. No one was visible, but he knew the feds were out there, waiting to mow him down with their assault rifles. But he had plans for them, especially now that that he had to quickly regroup and make new ones.

Regret ate him up inside. Having to kill Rebecca was a concession he hadn't anticipated making. She'd done a lot of the leg work, securing classified documents that would be beneficial to his leaders. And now he was without his favorite cousin, but he accepted the fact that Rebecca was a price he had to pay—a casualty in the war against the government.

Rasheed jumped when Amon's footsteps hit the landing outside of the bedroom door. He was anxious to get as far away from this place as possible, as he was determined to finish his mission.

Dressed in military style clothing, Amon rushed through the door ready to bark the next set of orders. He was slightly higher up in the organization than Rasheed, although they operated together for most of their efforts. Amon, an attractive thirty-year old although his features were somewhat rugged, was of Syrian descent, having come to America with his parents. He was well educated and had been close to completing his master's degree from Vanderbilt in Political Science when he was approached and swayed into becoming a participant in a different kind of political regime.

"We're going to the basement and escape through a trap door that connects to a neighboring house," Amon said with authority, picking up an automatic machine gun, a couple of grenades, and a vest. "We will remain there for two hours."

"Good. I wasn't aware that we had that capability."

"Yes, this was designed for a moment like this. Another contact will pick us up once we get the signal. I'm sure the feds are going to make a move, especially if we don't resurface soon. We'll have to leave the weapons behind, but there are more of those to be had. I'm not at liberty to share the location."

"When are we leaving?" Rasheed asked.

"Now," Amon said firmly. "And put the vest on."

Without any further questions, both Rasheed and Amon adorned their bodies with the booby-trapped vests and weapons of choice. Quietly they slipped out of the bedroom, down a set of stairs, and then another set of stairs that led into a dark basement.

Rasheed could hear movement outside, but he followed Amon, moving stealthily through the maze of darkness until Amon suddenly stopped. He touched Rasheed with his hand and then put it to his mouth to indicate quiet. Slowly, Amon removed a small area rug that covered a trap door. The two men entered and dropped a couple of feet to a flat surface.

There was a passage way that was dank, dark, and only large enough to crawl through. Easing their bodies through without touching the detonator on their vest, Amon and Rasheed slowly crawled through. More than fifteen minutes passed, and they were still crawling. And then Amon, who was at the lead, whispered to Rasheed.

"We're at the end. I'll need you to lift me up and I will open the door once we get to the flat surface. Hopefully, all will be well, and we'll be able to get out of here in the next few hours."

"Alright," Rasheed said. "I'm ready."

✿ 67 ✿

ATTENTION

The nurses swarmed around Reggie like bees after nectar. He heard their chatter in the room, as they checked on him while he pretended to be asleep. The black nurses were especially turned on by the brother who was on their watch, who happened to be a one-star general with his fine self. Although Reggie was still recovering from his wounds, it didn't stop him from smiling on the inside.

"Girl, I'd like to hit that once or twice."

"Watch out, Gladys, the Lord, along with your husband, is going to strike you with several bolts of lightning."

"I'm going to hit that and ask for forgiveness later, Renee. And anyway, Quintin don't care; he's too busy trying to win big money at the gambling place. He lives and breathes that place, although he only has two wooden nickels to rub together." Renee laughed. "But this brother here," Gladys began again, is too fine a specimen to be laying up in here without some good, tender loving care. I want to jump in the bed, crawl up next to him right now, and kiss those juicy lips of his. He looks like an angel."

"I'll admit he's a good-looking brother. If I wasn't saved, sanctified, and filled with the precious, Holy Ghost, ooh have mercy, I might be willing to see what he could do for me." Renee threw her hands up in the air.

Gladys laughed so hard she had to grab her sides to keep from hurting. "Yeah, girl, I'm a cougar in residence. I'll take care of this big boy and make him well. Get in line, Renee."

The ladies laughed and so did Reggie, although they couldn't hear him. He kept his eyes closed, enjoying the women's antics.

Suddenly there was quiet. Reggie squinted and then took a peek.

"General Reginald Charleston, you can't be sleeping with all of these pretty ladies standing around admiring you. Attention!"

The ladies laughed. Reggie took his time opening his eyes, as if General Elston's voice was the cause of him being awakened. He stared out and placed a smile on his lips. "General Wallace Elston, what brings you out to see me? I thought you all had abandoned the new black General."

Elston laughed. "Excuse us ladies." The nurses scurried from the room and General Elston closed the door behind them. "So, how do you feel, Reggie?"

"I'm feeling much better now. If you asked me that question a couple of days ago, I'd of told you that it felt like I had been hit with a grenade...that my number had been pulled to meet the Lord. My body felt like it was missing parts on top of being sore all over."

"Well, you don't look bad, and I'm sorry that I'm finally getting over here to see you. With having to attend Michael Forbes' funeral and the fiasco with his crazy secretary, Rebecca, it's a wonder I've had time to stop and bathe."

"I'm glad you stopped and bathed. What's up with Rebecca? That's the redhead, correct?"

"Yeah, she's the one. She's dead."

Reggie flinched. "What do you mean dead?"

"I can't say it any plainer; she's dead as a doorknob. Two of our operatives tracked her downtown to a house close to Howard University, and when she came out, this guy shot her dead on the street and then jumped into her car and fled. But he had a package in his arm, a package that looked much like the one Rebecca carried from the Pentagon, although we have no way to prove it yet."

"Damn," Reggie said, looking into space. "What caused you to go after her?"

"A number of things, Reggie, to include the way she was acting after Forbes' funeral. General Compton asked me to check her background, and things have been snowballing ever since.

"I spoke with your secretary, Sandra, today. She said that Rebecca Dickerson had come to your office on several occasions wanting to speak with you. Sandra said that she had made some weird statements. Did you by chance talk with Ms. Dickerson?"

The color seemed to drain from Reggie's face—almost chalk-white but for only a second before returning to its original color. Sitting up as straight as he could he stared General Elston down. "So, Wallace, are you trying to say that this Rebecca had something to do with Kaleah's death... Michael's death?"

"We're not positive, but all roads seem to point to her. I'm not saying she actually killed Kaleah and Michael, but her fingerprints seem to be on this one. Unfortunately, she was killed before we could get any concrete answers. The feds have her killer and possibly someone else tied to the event cornered in a house not too far from here. Also, I received a letter from her father, someone I know, that somewhat pointed us in her direction."

"Oh my goodness. My head told me there was something strange about her. I met Ms. Dickerson at a restaurant when I came a few months ago prior to my permanent assignment. She was with Forbes." Reggie thought it not important to mention that General Kaleah Neal was with him, since General Forbes, General Neal, and now Ms. Dickerson were all dead and couldn't speak on it. "And then I saw her registering people at the conference the next day. Initially, I didn't think anything of it, since I found out that she was Michael's secretary, but I got the distinct feeling that she was trying to hit on me."

"She was trying to hit on you so that she could get next to you and extract information."

Reggie arched his eyebrows and then shrugged his shoulders.

"You're probably right the more I think about it. It seemed that everywhere I turned, she was there. I remember going to a restaurant or a bar after having an argument with my wife and who should I see? None other than Ms. Dickerson, and she was flirting as usual. Normally, I would be flattered, but she'd made several advances at me by this time, and I was concerned. But the particular day that comes to mind was on the day that we had been hit overseas by ISIS. Ms. Dickerson came to my office in person to tell me that General Forbes needed to speak with me. Why didn't she use the telephone? I never did get to speak with Michael since I was on my way to attend an emergency meeting of the Joint Chiefs."

General Elston sighed. "I remember Michael saying he needed to talk to you. So, you have no idea what Forbes wanted nor did you have any meaningful conversation or conversations with Ms. Dickerson."

"No, Wallace, I didn't. My main concern was staying away from Ms. Dickerson, as I thought she was a gold digger trying to get into my pockets."

General Elston laughed. "Yeah, and probably somewhere else."

Reggie smiled and then changed his facial expression when the door to his room opened and Persenia walked through it.

General Elston moved away from Reggie's bed, met Persenia as she moved forward, and extended a hand. "Good afternoon, Mrs. Charleston."

Persenia shook General Elston's hand and slightly bowed her head. "The same to you, General Elston. How's my husband doing today?"

"I think his color is good." Both Reggie and General Elston snickered.

Persenia stared from one to the other, not getting the joke.

"That was an inside joke," Reggie said, looking up at Wallace Elston.

"I gathered that much," Persenia said unamused.

"Look, I'm out of here. I'll check on you later, Reggie. Mrs. Charleston, take care of this soldier. He's very important to us." And then General Elston was gone.

"So what did the General have to say?"

"Nothing much. He felt bad about not coming out here earlier to see me."

"Oh, I see."

"What's up with you? You seem a little stiff and...and where is your girl and Jacoby?"

"We had a little disagreement and Jacoby is on his way to the airport to see Carlitta off. She's upset at me because I withheld some information from her that as a friend she thought I should've shared with her."

"What are you talking about?"

"I'm not in the mood to talk about this now, Reggie."

"It must be about Jacoby and Kimiko."

"Even if it is, I don't want to have this discussion with you. You need to get well so you can get out of here. Oh, our next door neighbor has moved out. I feel bad for Julia."

Reggie didn't say anything for a moment. He looked away, staring out of the window, as if looking for answers.

"What's on your mind?"

"To be honest, I'm scared. General Elston thinks that ISIS might've been behind Michael's death."

"And Kaleah's also?"

"Yes, and I feel safer in this hospital room."

"You're going to have to go home sometime, Reggie."

Reggie sighed and then looked up at Persenia. He patted the bed. "Sit down."

Following Reggie's orders, Persenia sat down.

"Now that I have your attention, I need to say something to you."

Persenia sat still, holding her breath. Her eyes bored into Reggie's and she waited.

"I want a divorce. Our marriage is over."

Slowly, Persenia rose from the bed. She pouted for a minute and then gave Reggie all of her attention. "You could've saved me a trip and called on the phone to tell me this wonderful bit of news. You're right; our marriage is over and you've saved me from having to say the words myself."

Tears began to drop from Persenia's eyes. She moved toward the door and turned around. "I hope you rot in hell." And then she quietly left the room.

Reggie stared at the wall opposite of where he was laying. There was no Kaleah to fill the void, but he had nothing left to give Persenia. They merely existed in a loveless marriage, and he wanted to spend the next years of his life in peace. He looked up when the door opened.

Nurse Gladys moved toward the bed. "It's time to take your temperature and blood pressure, General Charleston."

"I'm ready."

Gladys smiled, her pearly whites on display for anyone to see. She was medium height, medium build—a tad bit chunky for his taste—but she still had a pretty face, nestled in a cappuccino complexion. She was hilariously funny. "Alright, give me your arm."

Gladys wrapped the blood pressure bag around his arm and gave it a few pumps. Then she pulled out a thermometer to stick into his mouth. At the same time, Reggie pulled the thin covers from off of his body. When Gladys turned to place the thermometer in his mouth, she looked down and almost dropped the thermometer.

Gladys blushed. "Is that for me? You're standing at attention."

Reggie smiled. "Stop being coy; I heard what you and the other nurse were saying about me."

Gladys blushed again. "If I could turn red right now I would. Let's get your temperature. And I'm going to have to take your blood pressure all over again." She placed the thermometer under his tongue and released the blood pressure bag from his arm to get it started again.

His hand now free, Reggie reached over and touched her thigh."

"Oh, Lord, I've gone to heaven."

"Come closer." Gladys obliged. Reggie whispered in her ear. "This is our secret. I could get into a whole lot of trouble."

"You don't have to worry about me," Gladys whispered back. "It's therapy."

Gladys took the thermometer from his mouth and then bent over and kissed Reggie on the lips. He had enough strength to pull Gladys to him. He felt for her behind and squeezed."

"Oh my goodness." Gladys closed her eyes and squeezed her hands together. "Please do that again."

Reggie squeezed her behind and she in turn moved closer to take his member that stood at attention and squeezed it.

"Please do that again," Reggie said, mimicking Gladys. "That felt good."

❧ 68 ❧

BOILING POINT

P ersenia couldn't turn off the faucet. Her tears were genuine and it hurt like hell to hear Reggie utter those words that were so final. *"I want a divorce,"* he said so nonchalantly, as if he read it off of a teleprompter. Well, she was going to give him his divorce, and he could kiss her black ass while she did it.

And then she remembered the pictures she'd taken...pictures that she took pains to conceal from Reggie—pictures of him with Major General Neal, as they entered a hotel for a so-called meeting with the Joint Chiefs of Staff. She needed to secure them for easy access. Without a doubt, she would be using them during the course of their divorce proceedings, pushing for alienation of affection that had become a reliable tool in the state of North Carolina when it came down to settlement time, although she wasn't sure that it would work in D. C.

Sitting on the crowded Beltway rattled her nerves even more. It was a crying shame that traffic had to always move at a snail's pace every time she got on the damn thing. If she knew how to navigate around the Beltway and not get lost, there wouldn't be a problem. The problem was she didn't trust her navigation system totally, although it was probably her incompetence at not knowing how to work it.

She reached over to the passenger seat and retrieved her cell phone from her purse. It didn't take long to pull up Remy's number. She hit the icon with his name on it and waited for the phone to dial with hopes of hearing a familiar voice.

"Hey, I didn't expect to hear from you. How's your husband?"

"Hey, Remy. It's so good to hear your voice. As for Reggie, who gives a damn?"

"Did something happen? Is Jacoby and Carlitta still in D. C.?"

"Oh, you should've seen Brigadier General Reginald Charleston today. He sat up in his bed looking like the picture of health when suddenly he blurted out some cold, calculated words without any prelim."

Remy remained quiet and let Persenia do all of the talking.

"He asked me to sit down and then he told me he wanted a divorce." Persenia snapped her fingers. "Yep, just like that. No music to accompany his announcement like they do on the Soaps. But he made it plain that it was the end of the road for us. I accepted his announcement graciously and got the hell out." Persenia began to sob.

"But I'm correct in that this is what you wanted? You said to me that your marriage was over."

"You don't understand, Remy. I was with this man practically my whole adult life. I loved him with my whole heart, sacrificed so much to enhance his career. I couldn't give him the one thing he wanted, though, which was a child, but I'll be damned if I wasn't the best wife a man could've ever had. I did everything right—almost by the book, but maybe that's where I went wrong."

"Don't beat yourself up about it, Persenia. Reggie has been disrespecting your marriage vows for a long time."

"And am I any better, Remy? Am I any better?" Persenia shouted into the phone. "I slept with you."

"Yes, you did, but you'll agree that it was the first time in your eighteen, nineteen, or twenty-year history with Reggie that you slept with another man."

Sniffling and blowing air from her mouth, Persenia couldn't bring herself to say anything. She could hear Remy calling her name through the phone, begging her to talk to him. After a minute or two, she brought the phone back to her face. "Remy, I loved my husband and while I confessed my love for you, my heart was still hoping and praying that my marriage would stay intact, no matter how raggedy it was on the surface. I enjoyed being with you and I'm sure that I do love you, but I loved Reggie more."

"You don't know what you're saying. I love you and you love me."

"That sounds good, but am I being fair to you?"

"Look, you're confused right now. Reggie hurt your heart by telling you he wanted a divorce before you could tell him that you wanted one. He's not going to change, Persenia. He's set in his ways. I'm sure I sound like a beggar hustling for a nickel, but I meant every word when I told you I love you."

"Remy, my heart knows you do. Why, you were the first person I called after leaving the hospital. As for Carlitta, she and I got into a nasty, verbal altercation about my knowledge of Jacoby and Kimiko's affair. Although I was trying to protect her fat ass, she was so mad that she caught a flight back to California. Everyone seems to be disappointing me all the way around."

"Where's Jacoby?"

"He went to the airport to see Carlitta off. I guess he'll be staying with me until he leaves. I'm not sure what our interaction will be once Reggie tells him that he asked me for a divorce. And if Jacoby thinks that I'm going to run him back and forth to the hospital, he's got it wrong."

"Jacoby has enough money to buy Enterprise. Let him rent a car."

"Good idea."

"And I want you to be careful around him...I mean with you being in the house with him and there being no other distractions."

"You're not making any sense, Remy. Jacoby knows better and I don't think he'd try and take advantage of his best friend's wife."

"Let's say that I warned you."

"Don't sweat it, but I hear you." Persenia sighed. "I was at my boiling point minutes ago, but I'll be all right."

"What about us?"

"Remy, I can't answer that right now. I do love you, though."

"But not as much as you do your husband, although he's a snake-in-the-grass mother…"

"The traffic is picking up and I better give the road my full attention."

"So, you hit me up with good news and are now dropping me off by the side of the road."

Persenia laughed. "You're funny. Don't forget me, Remy. I won't be far away. I've got to deal with some things right now and I'd appreciate your patience. When I left the hospital, I was poised to give him his divorce, while dragging his good name through the mud. But I'm not that kind of person."

"Whatever you decide, I'm here for you. I'm disappointed that I can't come there and help you through your anguish. I'm a good listener, a good friend, and a…"

"And a good lover. Yes, you are that and a bag of chips."

"I've never been compared to a bag of chips before, but I'll take it. Call me if you need me no matter when it is—night or day."

"Thank you, Remy. You've been a rock." Persenia hit the OFF button and drove home.

❧ 69 ❧

FOR THE CAUSE

Crawling through a dark, dank tunnel was all for the cause, although Rasheed wasn't so sure that he was ready to die for it. As he continued to crawl, a sudden image of Rebecca flashed before him, her body falling to the pavement like a rag doll. Although he couldn't see his hands in the dark, he remembered what his hand looked like as he pulled the trigger, releasing the bullet that killed his cousin.

It was no secret that Rasheed had made his parents' lives a living hell growing up. Smoking weed and graduating to coke in his latter teens kept his parents at odds with each other. His father was a disciplinarian and his mother the peacemaker, trying to shield her son from a father that had zero tolerance for what he was doing. Without warning, his father left them penniless, almost vanishing without a trace. And Rasheed had become hard, mean, and uncaring. His mother would occasionally get monetary help and wisdom to deal with Rasheed from her brother, who was a big man in the military. But their struggle was real.

Unable to detach himself from the drugs that became his key to survival, Rasheed began to steal money from his mother, his friends, from the parents of his friends until he was eventually caught and did a short stint in jail. But it was during that time his life took on a new direction.

Working in the laundry room one day, an inmate Rasheed had made an acquaintance with when he first arrived at his new dorm room called jail began to share some propaganda with him about a movement that would shake up the world. Rasheed was immediately drawn into this movement talk that would have the world recognize this organization as a power to be reckoned with. And he soaked up all the information he could get each time he had the opportunity to meet up with his friend. After all, he was a rebel, and when he got out of jail, he was going to join forces for the cause—something that for the first time he could say he was proud to be a part of.

Looking up into the black hole, Rasheed suddenly saw the rope that was being let down for him. Amon's head appeared above as he pushed the rope further into the dark cavern. "Let's go."

Rasheed put a foot through a loop at the end of the rope and grabbed some of the extended rope with his hands. He climbed up the rope at the same time feeling a pull on it. Amon must've connected it to something above and was using his strength to pull Rasheed up. It was a struggle, but after fifteen or so minutes, Rasheed was able to brace and pull himself up through the opening. Finally, he saw Amon struggling to keep the rope taunt enough for him to get safely through the passage. His breathing was heavy but happy to be in a place that would provide safety until he and Amon were rescued by the head of their group.

RASHEED AND AMON WAITED AND WAITED. THE STREET OUTSIDE was eerily quiet. They dared not go to a window and peek out of the dwelling they found themselves for fear of looking into the eye of the enemy, although the enemy had no idea that they'd long since left the residence they had entered.

Amon sat up and looked at his cell phone. A message had come in and he was anxious to read it. Pulling it up on his smartphone, Amon's eyes traveled over the text and breathed a sigh of relief upon finishing.

"So, what did the text say?" Rasheed wanted to know, while sweat crawled down the length of his face from his brow.

Our contact is in the vicinity. He and another are performing surveillance, checking to see how many and where the feds are lurking. Amon began to type.

"What are you saying?"

"Letting the contact know that you have the package. It won't be long now before we execute our next major offensive."

"What about the General who's still alive?"

"You're going to take him out. He may be able to identify you. We can't take any chances—that's if he's still alive."

"I'll do it. We can't leave any stone unturned."

Amon slapped Rasheed on the back. "For the cause."

"Yes, for the cause," Rasheed repeated.

❧ 70 ❧

MAN WHORE

Jacoby was frustrated! Fighting with Carlitta had left his brain exhausted. All the way to the airport and then inside the airport they fought with words. Jacoby was tired of it, although he wasn't oblivious to the fact that he'd created the monster that Carlitta had become.

He loved Carlitta, but Kimiko had offered him something that he couldn't taste at home. Carlitta was an old-fashioned girl and wasn't into hard and rough sex that he really enjoyed. And now with three children to look after, Carlitta was a deadbeat wife at the end of the day when Jacoby wanted some loving. And he loved the feel of a woman next to his body...a body he could torture and penetrate with his lewd kind of sex.

Seething in the back seat of the taxi, he balled up his fist and hit the palm of his other hand. He was wrong; he'd broken the rules...his vows to his wife. And worse than that, he'd slept with Carlitta's favorite cousin, who was probably on her way to being ejected from the family tree—if Carlitta had her way. But Jacoby didn't care; the deed had been done and he needed for Carlitta to forgive him. He breathed a sigh of relief once he reached Persenia and Reggie's house.

Jacoby jumped out of the cab and paid his fare, grateful that the fight was over and that Carlitta would soon be somewhere in the friendly skies.

⚜

WITH OVERCAST SKIES HANGING IN THE BALANCE, JACOBY WAITED on the porch for Persenia to let him in the house. He rang it three more times before the door opened and Persenia appeared behind the screen door with a book clutched to her chest.

Jacoby slithered into the house thankful that there would be some semblance of peace. However, for the first time, he really paid attention to Persenia, who was dressed in a pair of skin-tight jeans and a silky, sleeveless tee that was tucked in her jeans that hugged and framed the top half of her body well. When she turned to walk away from the door, Jacoby couldn't keep his eyes off of her booty. "Hey, P, you look relaxed."

Persenia turned around and looked at Jacoby with a different set of eyes. Remy's warning suddenly came rushing back to her, although she wasn't sure why. "Yep, I'm going to read awhile. Did your wife get off okay?"

Jacoby shook Persenia's image from his head. "Yeah, screaming and cussing the whole, damn way."

"What did you expect? The moment Carlitta found out that I was privy to your escapades and hadn't shared it with her was grounds for fireworks. I hate that she left feeling the way she did, but I tried to explain why I kept it from her."

"That's Carlitta. When she's pissed, she won't listen to reason."

"But you do realize your responsibility in all of this. If you hadn't flaunted your affair with Kimiko in my face, I'd be none the wiser and wouldn't have had to keep a secret."

"That doesn't excuse the fact that she was mad at you."

Persenia put her hands on her hips. "Get over yourself, Jacoby. You and Reggie belong in a rehab facility for men with sex addictions."

"We're not different than any other male."

"You don't get it do you? And I thought you were smart."

"Okay, P. I'd just left a howling dog; don't you start throwing darts at me."

Persenia threw her hand out to dismiss Jacoby. "Conversation over; I'm not the one who has to live with you."

Jacoby looked at Persenia and sighed. He wasn't in the mood for any one-on-one verbal assault on his character, regardless of how good she looked. "What time are you going to see Reggie?"

"I'm not."

There was a puzzled look on Jacoby's face. He rocked back on his legs and looked up at Persenia. His eyes began to shift from left to right. "So...so, what's up with that?"

"Speak English."

"Okay, P, I can see that you're in a funk about something. Your fight with Carlitta was hours ago and hope you're not taking it out on me."

"To the contrary; I've already been to see your boy today, and he told me point blank that he wanted a divorce. So, the hell with him. If you want to see Reggie, you're going to have to rent a car and drive there yourself."

"But..."

"I'm not a taxi service. In fact, you probably have enough money to buy Enterprise or Hertz Rental Car Service." Persenia couldn't help borrowing that little tidbit from Remy. This was the appropriate time to use it, and it fit the bill.

Jacoby began to laugh. He dropped his neck and began to howl. "You women are something else." He threw his hands out. "No problem, sis. I'm a big boy. I'll call and have one delivered."

"Do that." And Persenia walked toward the kitchen.

"Reggie is a fool," Jacoby said as Persenia moved away.

Persenia stopped in her tracks, turned around and stared at Jacoby. "I know that. So, what's your point?"

Jacoby watched Persenia twitch her mouth, as he stared at her, possibly making her a little uncomfortable. "If I had a woman as fine as you by my side, I'd be a fool to let her go."

"I'm sure that's what Carlitta is counting on," Persenia said with sarcasm in her voice.

Jacoby lost himself and moved to within an inch of Persenia. He was now up close and personal and pushed himself to do the unthinkable. He grabbed Persenia around the waist and tried to cover her lips with his.

She pushed him back. *Slap, slap!* With a scowl on her face, Persenia drew her hand back and slapped Jacoby once more. "Don't ever touch me again, you man whore." With tears in her eyes, Persenia raised her hand and pointed her finger in his face and gritted her teeth. "Get your stuff and your sorry ass out of my house. I don't ever want to see you again."

Jacoby clutched his cheek and stood defiant. And then as if sense and sensibility had struck him, he turned and headed for the bedroom that he'd shared with Carlitta the night before. He closed his eyes, wishing he could take that one moment back, but it was too late.

He gathered up his things as fast as he could and placed them in his suitcase. Then he stopped, closed his eyes, and shook his head. Why did he have to let his penis rule his thoughts? He took a deep breath. Maybe he should've been on the plane with Carlitta. He'd be better off. If Persenia breathed one hint of what happened in the living room only minutes ago, he was a dead man.

71

DOWN AND DIRTY

Nearly two hours had passed without a word from Rasheed and Amon's contact. Cooped up in the vacant house without food or water was the least of their worries, although the pair seemed agitated due to the lull in communications.

Amon got up, walked around in circles, and sat down, repeating the cycle more times than Rasheed could count. Not only had Amon worn a trail on the discolored linoleum-tiled floor, his actions pissed Rasheed off, as it illuminated the plight they were in. He was used to fast results—ready to move on to the next step too, but the situation wasn't going to change until the time was right.

In their third hour and sitting on the floor with his back against the wall, Rasheed continued to watch Amon pace back and forth. Suddenly, Amon raised his cellphone, pushed a few buttons, and began to read silently.

"At last," Amon began, "our contact says we won't have to wait long. They had to be assured that the feds hadn't penetrated the area... hadn't put a dragnet over the area that would keep them from rescuing us. This is good news. He said that they will hit us up in about fifteen to twenty minutes with further instructions.

Rasheed got up from his position on the floor. "That is definitely good news. I was a little irritated that it was taking so long."

Amon looked at Rasheed for a long time. "Brother, in this war, you've got to learn to be patient. There's a timing...a precision to everything that we do. It's like a well-oiled machine that you sometimes have to work the kinks out of when it gets stubborn. We have the documents our leaders want. Now, it'll only be a matter of time before we implement the plans that our arm of ISIS wants to carry out. We're about to get down and dirty. Boom, boom." Amon laughed as he pulled a loaded revolver from his backpack, pointed it toward the ceiling, and pretended to shoot at it.

Rasheed shook his head, went to where Amon stood, and gave him a fist bump. "Don't give me that crap that you weren't pissed off about having to sit in this place for hours. But it's all irrelevant now. I'm in all the way."

❧ 72 ❧

BOOM, BOOM, BOOM

The Feds had waited patiently for more than three hours for Jarod Biscolli aka Rasheed Ali Rashamrandon to reappear. They had surrounded the immediate area and deployed several SWAT teams to take position. Even their bullhorns hadn't produced a face in the window or any type of response to get this mess over with. Time was up and there would be no more waiting for Jarod Biscolli aka Rasheed Ali Rashamrandon to make an appearance. For all the Feds knew, he had slipped through their fingers again.

FBI investigator Rocky Davenport stood gap legged with a walkie-talkie in his hands. He and Detective Milo Harper from the Montgomery County Police Department were in heavy conversation. "He's been in there way too long without resurfacing. I'm afraid that if we wait any longer we'll regret it.

"I agree," Detective Harper said. He balled up his fists and blew air into it. "We need to act now. I'll give the word to the SWAT team to commence operations. We will proceed first by using the boulder to knock the door in."

"Remember, we want this imbecile alive before we chop him up into three-thousand pieces after interrogation."

Detective Harper lightly slapped Rocky Davenport on the chest with the backside of his hand. "Got you. Let's do this; it's now or never."

"Alright."

Rocky Davenport pulled his walkie-talkie to his mouth and barked some information to several agents. Likewise, Detective Harper radioed commencement orders to the SWAT team. Like ants filing out of their ant hills, eight to ten SWAT team members swiftly came from their hiding places, crossed the street, and took their positions on the front porch of the house that they were watching.

"On three," the team member in charge said, "we knock the door down."

All was quiet on the block except for the team leader's count. "One, two, three."

A loud crash could be heard as two members of the team in tandem took the boulder and slammed it into the door. The door didn't immediately come down, but when there wasn't any immediate response, they drove the boulder in again, and this time the door came crashing down to the floor.

The ten members that were assembled on the porch rushed in, looking left and right as they forced themselves into the interior of the house, their assault rifles drawn and ready. They crept slowly at first, looking behind doors and in crevices where the target could easily hide.

"Look at all of this ammo," one of the team members said, as the group continued to move throughout the house, up and down."

"Clear."

"Clear."

"Clear."

Detective Harper ran into the house when advised that the house was empty except for the Fort Knox size bounty of ammo that was stored there.

"He didn't disappear into thin air under our noses," Harper

shouted. "Check every crevice, every corner, and underneath all rugs and carpets."

The SWAT team moved on orders. Five minutes later, Harper stopped what he was doing when the announcement was made.

"In here."

Harper and other members of the SWAT team moved to the room in question. Right under their noses, underneath a thick rug with a coffee table sitting on top, was a trap door. When it was pulled back, Harper looked down into a deep, black hole and shouted an obscenity.

"That cockroach is way ahead of us. We've got to find him. I'm sure he had help. I need for several of you to drop in and investigate."

"I'm in."

"I'm in."

"I'm in."

There was no hesitation on the team's part. All ten men went in to be a support to the first.

Detective Harper went back outside and summoned FBI investigator Rocky Davenport.

"What did you all find?" Davenport asked.

"A big hole in the floor that possibly connects to a tunnel. We should've known the son-of-a-bitch would have some type of escape route. Why else would he have picked this particular location, in this neighborhood to run to?

"All ten men that entered the house are navigating the terrain now. We'll have the remainder to move into the back yards of every house that is in close proximity to this one. If there's a tunnel, it has to lead somewhere and a nearby house sounds like a sure bet from my vantage point."

"I want details every minute on the minute," Davenport said, slinging his walkie-talkie up to his mouth.

"Alright," Harper said with disgust in his voice. "We've got to catch this cockroach. We can't have the city in a panic."

Fifteen more members of the SWAT scrambled from their perches and moved swiftly into the yards of adjoining neighbors. Many in the neighborhood were elderly folks, and now they'd come to the door to inquire about the police presence in their vicinity. For many years, the neighborhood was quiet, as the middle-aged AARP card carrying adults became totally silver-haired invalids, watching television all day long. Now, the most recreation they had was stepping out on the front porch to see what was going on.

"Hey," a snag-a-toothed woman shouted at Harper. "What y'all doing in my yard?"

"Ma'am, go back in the house," Harper said, shooing his hand at her for emphasis. "We're conducting police business and we don't want you to be in the line of fire."

"Fire? Where's the fire? Where's the fire? Herbert, wake up. There's a fire. We got to get out of here."

"Ma'am simmer down. There's no real fire."

Boom, boom, boom.

❧ 73 ❧

ANGUISH

I t felt like an earthquake had demolished the city. Detective Harper almost lost his footing at the rumble that took him for a loop. FBI Investigator Davenport ran in the direction where Harper stood, along with Chief of Police Murphy of the Montgomery County Police Department. Armed policeman and SWAT team members swarmed the area, waiting for a directive.

Taking the walkie-talkie from Harper and pushing it to his face, the Chief of Police mashed a button and began to speak. "What happened, Harper?"

"Chief," Harper stuttered, "we lost all but three men in the tunnel. "The target threw a grenade in the hole at the end of the tunnel that led into another house somewhere in this neighborhood. We didn't stand a chance."

"Damn," Chief Murphy said out loud, throwing his fist in the air. "What is your status?"

"Those team members who survived are heading back to the point of origin."

Davenport ran up to Chief Murphy. "Ground crews have

approached the house which the alleged target was believed to be in. There's not much left and it appears our target may have escaped. The fire department is on their way, and the team is going in to check and sift through the remains once they've been given the okay by the fire department. I'm on my way to the scene now."

Moments later, a car whizzed by with FBI Investigator Davenport in it.

"I want that damn target apprehended," Chief Murphy screamed. "No one will sleep until that son-of-a-bitch is caught."

"Right, Chief."

"This is a sad day for us. Seven of our highly trained men bit the dust because of one man...who may or may not be tied to ISIS."

"The target must have had help." Harper pointed toward the house. "There's an arsenal of weapons in there and the target didn't bring them here. This is much bigger than we think."

"You're right, Harper, it is. And I believe our military are still in great danger. Two highly decorated Generals were killed with an attempted assassination of a third. We need round-the-clock surveillance and security at the hospital where the wounded General is recouping."

"Right, Chief. I'm on it."

"Good. Now, I'm going to the house to assess the casualty myself. Stay close."

"Will do."

🏵 74 🏵

DAMN SHAME

There was no sign of life where once stood an older home in an old community. Everything that remained was either burning or pretty much charred. Chief Police Murphy arrived behind the ambulances, whose EMS teams waited for the fire chief to give them access. It was a waiting game, as the task at hand, removing the bodies of the seven SWAT team members would be a grueling one once the fire was put completely out.

The main source of contention had eluded them and was now swallowed up in the bowels of the city. Three hours of wasted time had gone up in smoke with casualties. The police assumed the target was still holed up in the house they'd first saw him enter but hadn't figured on there being a way out, although it appeared that he'd been trapped far too long without surfacing.

Murphy walked to where FBI investigator Davenport stood and shook his head. A tear trickled down his face and he abruptly wiped it away before anyone noticed.

"A damn shame," Davenport said to Murphy. "I didn't see this coming. He ran into a house, for goodness sakes...in an old neighborhood. Who'd figure that an elaborate tunnel had been concocted to serve as a getaway?"

Chief Murphy shook his head from side to side and sighed. "This is a damn, dark day in the neighborhood, the city. Tongues are going to wag about our inability to capture this scrub. If you'd ask me this morning what I'd look forward to today, this certainly wouldn't have been on the list. In fact, at briefing this morning, no one knew that we would suffer this kind of casualty today, although we always have to expect the worse in our line of duty."

Davenport slapped Murphy on the shoulder. "Chief, you win some and you lose some, but we're going to get that sorry ass son-of-bitch and he's going to be sorry that he messed with anyone in this town."

"The sad thing, Rocky, is that this thing is bigger than any one person...than any two people. We have a crisis on our hand and we better get prepared for it."

"Yeah, you're right."

"I sent Harper to secure the hospital where that General is recuperating. There may be another attempt on his life."

"Damn shame," Rocky Davenport said, turning to watch the fire fighters put out the smoldering embers.

"Yes, but with everything I have within me, we're going to stump this enemy into the ground."

Davenport and Murphy bumped fists.

75

A COLD DAY IN HELL

Hearing the blast of a horn, Jacoby left the comfort of the bedroom, moved into the living room, and looked out of the front window. The taxi had arrived and he was ready to get as far away as possible from that house and Persenia Charleston. The house was quiet and still after he and Persenia had words and she'd announced that he was to leave right then and there. He'd made a mess of his life and his heart told him things might get worse.

Jacoby hurried to the front door, opened it, and waved to the taxi driver. He rushed back to the bedroom and got his suitcase before proceeding to exit. As he crossed the length of the living room, Persenia appeared in the foyer with her hands on her hips and stared at him. He gently put his suitcase on the floor.

"Jacoby, I hate that our friendship has come to this. You've been a part of my life...Reggie's life for over twenty years. Carlitta and I have been best friends for most of our lives, and now we're like an estranged couple whose hate for one another is so strong that there seems no way in hell to repair the damage. That goes not only for Carlitta and I but you and Reggie as well. I can't believe the ride and die friendship we've had over the years is dead."

Honk, honk. Jacoby looked toward the door. "That's my taxi." He paused then looked at Persenia with regretful eyes. "I'm sorry for what happened earlier. You're probably right about the need for counseling. I'm a messed-up individual, Persenia, but I can say with all assurance that I love my wife."

"Do you really mean to form your lips and say that you're in love with your wife? I've been a witness to your prowess with another woman to include you coming on to me. The man I once knew no longer exists, Jacoby."

Jacoby picked up his suitcase and stared at Persenia with sorrowful eyes. "Look, my taxi is here and I've got to go. All I can say is I'm sorry. I'm not happy with what our friendship has become but at the moment I can't do anything about it. Have a good life." Jacoby turned and began to walk out of the door.

"Pitiful is what you are and it will be a cold day in hell before I'll forgive you for what you've done." And Persenia turned and walked the other way.

Jacoby closed the door behind him, walked to the taxi and got in. "To Bethesda Medical Center."

⚜

SITTING BACK IN THE TAXI, HE HAD A LOT OF TIME TO THINK ABOUT his actions. He was wrong; no doubt about it, but in his own conscious mind, all males went through this. It didn't mean that he loved Carlitta less. Carlitta was comfortable raising their family and being a housewife. He still had his wild ways about him, and since Carlitta didn't want to indulge in the 21st century's mode and variety of sexual explicitness, he found someone who'd rumble with him. Well, there had been several attentive females, but they were only for his pleasure.

Jacoby shook the thought from his head. He had to remain calm when he saw Reggie, so as not to give away his nervousness about what had happened with him and Persenia. Anyway, he'd gotten a flight on a redeye that night, and all that had happened in D. C. would soon be behind him. Facing the music with Carlitta would be a piece of cake; he knew how to finesse and break her down. She'd be putty in his hands.

He arrived at the hospital, paid his fare, and proceeded to Reggie's room. As Jacoby approached, he noticed that there was an excessive amount of police presence at the hospital. He dragged his suitcase behind him and after entering the elevator and getting out on the floor where Reggie was being cared for, he was suddenly surrounded by police.

"We're checking all visitors to the floor. We need to inspect your suitcase."

"Why?"

A tall, stoic, white police officer, whose face held no love for him stared back. Then the policeman's lips began to move robotically. "We'll ask the questions."

Jacoby arched his eyebrows in frustration and allowed the police to frisk him. There wasn't much he could do with loaded guns sitting in the policemen's holsters.

"Your suitcase is awfully big for a hospital stay. Open it up please."

Jacoby hastily opened up his suitcase, not pleased by any of it. He kept quiet while one officer rambled through his things and another read some inked material he'd stashed away, making a mess of Jacoby's neatly packed suitcase. They performed a thorough search. Finding nothing, the officers stood up and told Jacoby he could close the suitcase. Anger streamed from Jacoby's pores.

"Where were you going with this suitcase?" one of the policemen asked, giving Jacoby a side-ways glance to indicate that he'd better tell the truth.

"I was on my way to see my friend, General Reginald Charleston," Jacoby said, proud to be associated with one of the military's finest.

"Why the suitcase?" the other policeman asked accusingly.

"I will be taking a flight back to California tonight once I leave here. Reggie and I go way back. We used to play football at Cal Berkeley together."

The tension in the police officers' faces seemed to ease with Jacoby's last statement.

"You must've been a receiver back in the day."

Jacoby began to laugh, although softly. He was happy for the temporary reprieve. "Yes, I was meaner and leaner, although I still have some of my handsomeness on me. I made the record books. My name is Jacoby Morgan."

Both officers shook Jacoby's hand. Sorry for the inconvenience. A dragnet has been placed over the city for the person or persons who may have made the attempt on General Charleston's life. We've got the hospital heavily guarded."

"Damn, this is worse than I thought. If I didn't need to get back home, I'd stay."

"Probably the best thing for you is to get on that plane and stay out of harm's way."

Jacoby didn't respond. He picked up his suitcase and headed for Reggie's room. He stopped midway and turned back to get the police officers' attention. "Thank you." The officers nodded.

Reaching Reggie's room, Jacoby took a deep breath before going in. He hated to tell Reggie that he'd be going home tonight, but it was for the best. Although, Persenia seemed to be of the mindset that she and Reggie were through, he didn't want to have to run into her, in the event she decided to pay Reggie a visit.

He pushed the door open with the palm of his hand, dragging his suitcase behind him. Reggie was sitting up, which was a good sign. A full-figured nurse was assisting him with his food and he seemed to be teasing her. Jacoby cleared his throat.

"Reggie, my boy," Jacoby said, interrupting the patient's playtime.

"Jacoby, my man, meet Gladys. She's attending to all of my needs."

Jacoby gave a weak smile. "You better watch out for him, Gladys. The General can sometimes be a bad boy."

Gladys blushed and then gave Reggie the eye. It didn't get past Jacoby.

"What's with the suitcase? I thought you were staying awhile."

"I've got to get home. There are some problems with a couple of the accounts I've been working on that need my undivided attention."

"Don't you have some underlings who handle that kind of stuff for you?"

"Probably, however, some executive decisions have to be made and I need to be present in order to act. Sorry about that, bro, but duty calls."

"Understandable." Reggie turned toward Gladys. "Sweetie, I need to talk in private with my boy here. I'm not going anywhere. You can come back and play later."

"Okay." With a smile on her face, Gladys left the room.

"You aren't trying to mess with that?" Jacoby asked, his face bunched up in a frown.

"Jacoby, Jacoby, Jacoby...relax. I'm in no shape to mess with anyone. She's a distraction. I gave Persenia the word this morning."

"What word?" Jacoby asked, as if he didn't already know.

"I told her that I wanted a divorce."

Jacoby stood still, watching Reggie talk animatedly about his marriage, as if he'd been exonerated for a murder he hadn't committed and was now being released from prison. Reggie's yakkity-yak soon fell on deaf ears, as Jacoby's mind strayed to the incident earlier in the day. Why did he touch Persenia? Why did he try and kiss her, knowing good and well things would end up badly? Now guilt was stabbing him in the heart as he unplugged his ears to hear what else Reggie spewed from his mouth.

Snap, snap, snap went Reggie's fingers. Man, you didn't hear a word I said.

"I heard every word. It makes me sad; you and P have been connected at the hip for so long. She loves you man."

"I'm not in love with her any more. The woman that had my heart is lying six feet under. She was my everything; we were true soul mates who were connected from the crown of our heads to the soles of our feet."

"Well, it's a damn shame, but only you can say how you feel."

"Jacoby, I've toiled with this. It'll be a cold day in hell before I'd even contemplate changing my mind."

"I hate to be the bearer of more bad news, but there's a heavy police presence on hospital grounds and outside your door."

Reggie hesitated, frowned, and then looked up at Jacoby. "Police presence? Why?"

"It's obvious to me that whoever did this to you might attempt to do it again. One of the officers said that something went down earlier this afternoon."

"Have one of them come in and report to me what happened."

"Okay."

✲ 76 ✲

TWO DOWN

R asheed and Amon lay flat in the bowels of the SUV. They were now safe but had narrowly escaped the emergence of the SWAT team that had finally sniffed out their path. Their contact had texted that he was sitting on the corner in a dark blue Ford Highlander and they had only two to three minutes to make it to the car before he would leave, not wanting to risk being detected. They were lucky to be alive, although the grenade that Amon threw in the hole leading to the tunnel left behind a slew of casualties.

Lots of time, energy, and money would be lost now that the FBI would seize the stockpile of ammunition that had been placed in the first house in ready for their group's homegrown war on the United States government. At present, they were thirty members strong, although, Rasheed wasn't privy to that number. However, the organization wouldn't be deterred from its mission, as provisions at another safe location had been made in the event a situation such as what they'd experienced occurred.

"I'm going to drive you to one of our safe houses out-of-town," the driver said. "You do have the documents."

"Yeah," Rasheed said, now that his anxiety level had plummeted. But he wasn't totally onboard with the group, as nothing seemed to be going the way he'd envisioned. He'd hold onto the documents for insurance. "When are we going to make things happen? That's why I joined," he found himself saying out loud.

Amon pushed back on Rasheed's chest and motioned for him to be silent. "A war takes skill and careful planning. Be patient, my friend. It's all about to go down soon. There's one little matter we've got to take care of...that you've got to handle."

"Yeah, two down; one to go."

✺ 77 ✺

PLAN OF ACTION

L ife as she knew it had readjusted itself without Persenia having a say so. She hadn't been poised for the moment when it happened, but without a doubt it had become reality.

Persenia began looking through her belongings, taking mental notes of what she had—what she'd keep and what she would destroy. She'd make a special pile for those things that she'd put in a folder marked DIVORCE and keep it separate from her other personal belongings that she planned to have shipped to a location still yet to be determined.

Sitting on the edge of the bed, Persenia reached over and picked up her cell phone. Toying with it for several moments, she took a deep breath and found Remy's number. She took several breaths, bowed her head, and selected his name from the list. And then with her magic finger, she hit the green telephone icon and waited for it to connect with her savior on the West Coast.

"Hi," said the voice at the other end of the line.

Persenia couldn't tell if Remy was happy to hear from her. She'd been very indecisive as of late about ending her marriage—how she felt about him, jerking his feelings and emotions around as if it were a scripted scene on a reality TV show. Remy was the only common denominator that made her life worth living, and although she might appear to be wishy-washy again, she needed her anchor...she needed Remy. "Hey, Remy."

"So, what do I owe the pleasure of this phone call? Are you alright? Jacoby hasn't been a jerk has he?"

"No, I'm not alright."

"What happened?" Remy asked, the agitation in his voice as clear as bell. "Is Reggie okay?"

"Reggie's okay as far as I know. You were right about Jacoby, though."

"Persenia, I want you to take your time and tell me the truth; all of it. What did Jacoby do?"

"He grabbed me around the waist and tried to kiss me. No, he actually touched my lips with his. I gave him what he deserved, though; I slapped the hell out of him."

Persenia didn't expect to hear quiet. When he spoke, she knew Remy was madder than hell. "That was more than enough cause to get a bullet in his gut, but please tell me he didn't violate you further."

"Remy, he didn't do anything else. I ordered him out of my house. Please don't do anything crazy. I need you."

"I've watched him abuse women, knowing good and well he had a good woman at home. I tried to talk to him, but anything I ever said fell on deaf ears. But he took this too far, and he's going to pay for it."

"He's gone, Remy. He packed his suitcase and caught a cab to wherever."

"I'm going to catch a flight as soon as I can."

"Okay, but I can't have you stay at my house and I won't be able to stay with you at the hotel. I'm not sure when Reggie will be released, but I don't want to put either you or I in danger. I don't trust him. I'm sure Reggie has someone who'd do his bidding for him."

"I want you to get away from that place as soon as possible."

"I'm sorting through my things now. I can't leave Reggie while he's in the hospital though, but I'm going to start shipping some of my things; I'll need some place to store them. Honestly, you can better serve me by staying where you are at the moment. If you can get a storage unit for me, I'll ship my things to you."

"Your wish is my command."

"It may mean that I'll have to stay in Washington for a while."

"Why, Persenia? Why do you want to do that?"

"I've got a plan. I'm going to see a lawyer, as soon as I can make that happen. I'm going to file for divorce and hopefully he'll still be in the hospital when they serve the papers. I have enough incriminating evidence on Reggie to make him pay and be done with his ass. I deserve to be compensated for the last years of hell he's put me through. As for my plan, I don't want to jeopardize my being able to come away clean on this."

"Okay, I'm with you. You've really thought this out."

"Not as well as I should, but I'm working on it. Every minute that I spend in this hell hole makes me more determined to get out—without a scratch. I'm not going to falter this time, Remy. And I want you to be there when I come running."

"Are you cognizant of what you're saying? I'm not the perfect guy, but I do love and want to be with you. Whatever you need from me, I'm there for you. If you can get someone to pack up as much of your stuff as possible and send it to me, that'll be half the battle."

Persenia sighed. "That's going to take some doing. At the moment, all I want to ship are my private things—clothes, books, collectibles, and some electronic stuff. I don't want Reggie to get suspicious."

"If he gets served in the hospital as you plan, he will already be suspicious. But I agree, we can't give him any ammunition to make your life more of a living hell while you're going through this."

"Truthfully, I'm scared, Remy. I've never gone through anything like this before and it seems easier talking about it than actually doing it. My whole body is shaking right now. But I've got to do this and there won't be any turning back."

"As much as I hate to say this out loud, Reggie is the one who wanted a divorce. He may be happy that you 'finally got it' and have decided to move on."

There was quiet for more than a few moments. Persenia stood up with the phone clamped to her ear. "Yeah, you're right; he probably doesn't give a damn what I do, as long as I'm out of his sight." Tears fell from her eyes and she began to stutter.

"Don't cry, Persenia. We'll get through this. I'm going to be with you through the whole ordeal. Lean on me for whatever you need."

Sighing, Persenia wiped her face of tears with one hand. "Putting this whole scenario into perspective, I have no choice but to get up off of my ass and move forward." Persenia began walking in circles and then stopped. "No more wasting time. And thank you for being the level head that I need. I've got to do what I've got to do, but the great thing about all of this, you'll be there waiting for me."

"Yeah, girl. I'll be here with open arms. And when you get off that plane, I want you to be wearing nothing but a man's long-sleeve, white dress shirt and a five-inch pair of ruby-red pumps."

Persenia broke out in laughter. "Are you serious, man? Can I at least have on a pair of ruby-red thongs?"

Remy laughed louder than Persenia. "Yeah...I guess so."

The two of them laughed and laughed until they became serious again. Remy cut in first.

"I'm so happy that we're going to be together. I want you to know that I'd never intentionally try to come between a man and his wife. Your life with Reggie seemed so broken...a Humpty Dumpty story—when he fell down all the king's men couldn't put him back together again."

Persenia smiled. "You are a man of integrity. I recognized it the first time I met you."

"As I said earlier, I'm not perfect by any means, but I'll be the best man to you. I'll love you with all I've got. We'll not have any secrets. But I'm looking forward to our love growing and I hope to make you my wife one day."

Persenia smiled on her end but didn't say anything. She ingested his words and thanked God for putting Remy in her path. "Thanks, Remy. I'm ready to do this—now."

"It's done."

"Let's rock 'n' roll."

"Look, I've got a good friend I used to play football with who lives in Virginia. I'll call him and see if he can take care of getting those things moved for you. I'll give you a call back."

"Alright. I'll talk to you later."

"Later won't be long." And the line was dead.

❧ 78 ❧

THE PRICE OF SERVICE

Rasheed and Amon arrived at the safe house on the outskirts of town. Once the driver determined that all was clear, Rasheed and Amon jetted from the vehicle and entered the house. There were at least five or six other people in the house when they entered, and Rasheed was amazed at the stockpile of weapons that exceeded the amount that was housed at the other place.

A dark-skinned brother with a long, black beard and a white brother with a head full of curly, blond hair and shades hiding his eyes, sat at a table in one corner of what was once a living room, engaged in animated conversation. They both looked up when Rasheed and Amon entered the room.

"So, my brother," the dark-skinned brother whose name was Salamon called out, waving to the guys to come closer, "I see that you've brought the documents. I will retrieve those from you now so that we can move forward with our plan."

Rasheed looked at Salamon with a reluctant look in his eyes, while Amon stared at Rasheed as if he was crazy. Rasheed wasn't used to taking orders from any black man, regardless of who he claimed to be. "Before I hand over the documents, can you share your plan with me?"

Salamon quickly got to his feet and began to approach Rasheed until the white brother named David threw out his arm to stop him. Then David took off his shades and stood up, almost in slow motion, and looked at Rasheed.

"When you have a need to know, we will tell you," David said. "Now hand over the documents and all will return to normal. Amon, I trust that you'll instruct your charge to retreat and wait for the next set of orders, although, I understand that there is one piece of business that he still needs to attend to."

Without further hesitation, Rasheed handed David the package. David reminded Rasheed of a prophet he'd read about in the bible when he was younger—the wispy hair and the loose fitting, washed-out-colored clothing. Rasheed purposely didn't look him in the eyes, as fire was in his. But he had no choice but to do what he was told.

Amon didn't seem happy about the rebuke. "We will take care of it, David." He looked at Rasheed and waved his hand to follow.

As soon as they were out of earshot, Amon whispered to Rasheed. "What's up with you man? These cats are serious about their mission and they will kill you if you in any way compromise it."

"All I asked was for a simple explanation. That's how I roll. I want to be a part of this organization, but I have rights, too. I have a need to know what I'm getting in to."

"It's like this. You're not in the "I need to know" category. Those guys in there are the captains and we're the worker bees and we help lay the foundation for what's getting ready to happen. You're already aware that we're an establishment against the government...an on-U.S.-soil agent of ISIS. That should be explanation enough."

"Whatever. Let's take care of the General."

"Do you have a plan?" Amon asked. "I'm surprised the dude hasn't identified you yet."

"Maybe he didn't get a good look at me; I did surprise his ass. He probably went into shock as soon as he felt the bullet rip his skin."

"Well, we can't take that chance. If the General marks you, it'll lead to the rest of us before we execute our plan, which is only days in the making."

"I'm probably already marked. We've spent most of the day running from these dudes. They must have some kind of intel. I have a question, though. Do you know what 'the plan' is, Amon? You seem to have a lot of answers."

"If I do or I don't, Rasheed, you heard what David said. You're to wait for your orders. I'm warning you. Double-cross these dudes; you might as well be wearing a suicide vest."

Rasheed didn't bother to respond. He turned and walked away. He was confused. His head was spinning. He was pissed off to high heaven. He hadn't done all that he'd done, to include killing his cousin, Rebecca, to be pushed aside and up against the wall. He was all for taking orders, but he wasn't going to be pushed around and treated as if his usefulness was no longer necessary. "Hmph," Rasheed said under his breath as he passed through a room and saw Salamon and David examining the documents he'd given them. "Somebody is going to tell me something."

❧ 79 ❧

OUT OF TIME

Agitated wasn't the word. Reggie was hyperventilating and stressed to the max at the thought that the person who'd made an attempt on his life was still at large and possibly after him. He'd been briefed by his office on what had occurred earlier in the day—the number of officers that were killed and that the suspect had gotten away.

Reggie was a trained officer in the United States Army with numerous accommodations and medals for bravery. But to realize that he was a marked man off the combat field scared the hell out of him. And to think that Rebecca may have had a hand it. He was glad that her ass was dead.

"I'm ready to go home," Reggie said out loud, addressing no one in particular, although Jacoby was in the room.

"That's probably not a good idea, man. The hospital has armed guards stationed around the perimeter twenty-four seven. You're probably as safe as Fort Knox."

"A squadron of elite soldiers...police officers was killed this afternoon. They were members of a SWAT team for goodness sakes, trained to take out the enemy."

"They were ambushed and didn't have a hooker's chance in hell to be saved."

Reggie pulled the covers from his body. "Well, I'm not going to stay here and wait for them to kill me. I'm going home."

"If you're not here, don't you think the next place they'd go looking for you would be at your house?"

"There's truth in what you say, but it's a much smaller dwelling than this big ole hospital. I can control what happens at my home. And I'll have twenty-four hour security placed around the house and you'll be there with me."

"I'm not sure that I'll be welcomed at your home."

Reggie took a good look at Jacoby. "What the hell are you talking about? You're my boy and if I say that you're going home with me, that's exactly what I mean. I pay the damn rent where I live."

"Well, the blow-up this morning between Persenia, Carlitta and I was too much. We all said things to each other that were hurtful, and I'm not sure Persenia will forgive me."

"It's not her damn house. Call a cab and let's go."

"Reggie, this is probably a mistake. You may not be well enough to go. What if you require medical assistance?"

"I'll call the doctor; I'm getting out of here today—now."

Jacoby sighed. He understood Reggie's frustration but getting him to understand that it would be in his best interest to stay put was another thing. But there was no way in hell that he was going to be under the same roof with Persenia. She'd become the wicked witch of D.C., and he wasn't about to test his friendship with Reggie by placing his feet on either side of their doorway. It would be definite suicide. "Let's think about it."

"What's wrong with you, Jacoby? My decision isn't up for debate. This is about my life and I'm running out of time."

"Alright, since I can't convince you otherwise, I'll call a cab and get you ready for travel."

"That's more like it."

❧ 80 ❧

ALLEGIANCE TO THE CAUSE

A rmed with the pistol he used to kill Rebecca, Rasheed left the safety of the safe house with orders to kill General Reginald Charleston. He was given one of the four small sedans that was at the disposal of the organization and was to go it alone. Rasheed wasn't satisfied with being left in the dark when he played a major role in moving the organization forward, however, he'd go ahead and do the deed he'd been tasked with. After that, he'd demand answers to his questions.

❦

AMON WAS SUMMONED INTO THE ROOM WHERE SALAMON AND DAVID sat, still huddled over the table they'd been sitting at when he first arrived. David spoke first.

"Sit down, brother. You've done well. Brother Salamon and I are concerned with Brother Rasheed, though. He seems to be for the cause, however, his volatile, impulsive nature gives me pause. Brother

Salamon and I believe he may be a detriment to the organization because of his blatant need to know what he doesn't need to know. We're afraid that he might jeopardize all that we've spent months putting together.

Sighing, Amon cleared his throat and looked at the two advisors. "Rasheed is down for the cause. That I'm sure of. I was somewhat surprised with his forwardness, also."

"Likewise, we were taken aback. We can't have disloyalty among the ranks. Having said that, we want you to follow Rasheed and ice him after he's taken care of the General."

Sweat instantly began to slither across Amon's face. The short time that he'd been with Rasheed, he'd come to like him; he grew on him. In fact, he had some of the same questions as Rasheed, only he dared not ask them. Amon was critical of the government and he was down with making them pay for some of the ills and injustices he felt his family had suffered at their hands.

As a Syrian native, who was also Muslim, he and his family had been subjected to a number of prejudices since entering the United States fifteen years earlier. The mosque where they'd worshipped was twice firebombed and they'd been discriminated against when trying to secure housing for their family. Amon's family had some money but weren't rich like his mother's brother who gave them access to the United States in the first place. His parents settled for life as it had become, as it provided a better life than the one they'd left in Syria. But Amon wasn't buying into it.

Now he was asked to kill a man who'd come into the brotherhood, although he barely knew Rasheed. But if he wanted to achieve what he'd set out to do, it was allegiance to the cause, with no questions asked. In the end, it would be a benefit to the organization and their survival.

"Whatever you need me to do for the organization," Amon said.

"Good," David said, looking to Salamon for approval.

Salamon nodded his head up and down. "Be careful, comrade. What you're doing for the organization is necessary. We appreciate your allegiance."

With his face void of expression, Amon nodded in agreement. He picked up his backpack that contained the necessary ammunition to do the deed and walked cautiously toward the front door. He turned around to face David and Salamon. "For the cause." And Amon walked out of the door.

❦ 81 ❦

A DATE WITH DESTINY

Sneaking out of the hospital was one thing, but getting past all the guards who were there to protect Reggie was another. Jacoby peaked out of the doorway to Reggie's room, pulled his head back in, and shook his head.

"Reggie, you've got sterile strips all over your neck. Who's going to dress your wound? And God knows you're going to need medical attention when you get home. There's no way we can get past all of those guards without an explanation."

"You'll think of one. Anyway, I feel fine and I'm tube free. Any meds I need to take can be done orally. I'll have Persenia come back to the hospital and pick them up."

Jacoby sighed. "Whatever you say, General, although I haven't come up with anything in the last four seconds."

"You wouldn't make it in this man's Army." Reggie pointed his finger at Jacoby. "Decision making is high on the qualification list. You can't be indecisive when it comes to saving a life or negotiating a hostage release."

"Well, I'm not doing either one. However, what *I* do in my real life is very decisive. As one of the few blacks in Silicon Valley, decision making is a top priority in my camp, too."

"Didn't mean to offend, brother, I'm just anxious to get the hell out of this place for the comfort of my home."

Jacoby was more than sure that Reggie's statement was a false one, although, he didn't know it to be true. Persenia was not a happy camper when he left that comfortable place Reggie was trying to get to, and now he wanted to put everyone in danger. For a General, Reggie's decision making needed a lot of tweaking. "Okay, no problem, but I've come up with an idea."

"Speak, brother, speak. I'm worked up and in a hurry."

"Why don't you get one of your nurse friends to bring in a wheel-chair? I'll say that you want to get some fresh air and I'll wheel you right out of the hospital. Once we secure the wheelchair, I'll call a cab."

"Since we don't have another plan, that one will have to work. I'll ring the buzzer for Gladys. She won't mind doing anything for me."

"Let's get to buzzing."

Reggie called for Gladys who came to his beck and call as soon as the buzzer stopped. She said it would take her no more than fifteen minutes to get a wheelchair.

"Call the cab company now, Jacoby, so we won't have to wait too long and cause the guards to become suspicious."

"Alright." Jacoby called and smiled. "The dispatcher said he could have one at the hospital in twenty minutes."

"That will work in our favor. God is good."

Jacoby raised his eyebrows. None of this felt good. "All the time," he responded.

Right on time, Gladys swooped into the room pushing a wheel-chair. "Want me to help you into it," she asked Reggie.

"Yeah, I'll feel safe with you assisting me." Reggie looked at Jacoby and smiled. Jacoby's face was expressionless.

Reggie slid off the bed and walked the couple of inches to the wheelchair with Gladys' assistance.

"You did that well, big boy," Gladys said with a smile, bending over him to make sure he was tucked in the wheelchair while also giving him a great view of her ample breasts. "You're almost ready to go home."

"That's what I aim to do." He kissed the top of Gladys' breasts, where the V on the collar of her uniform met. Then he placed his hands on her buttocks and squeezed.

Gladys loved every minute of it. She started to say something but saw Jacoby's face with his turned up lips of disapproval. Gladys shrugged and dismissed Jacoby. "You can do that again, baby. It felt so good."

Reggie rubbed and squeezed her left and right buttocks, while Jacoby rolled his eyes. "Alright, Jacoby, wheel me out so I can get some fresh air."

"Remember, you can only go as far as..."

Jacoby cut Gladys off at the quick. "I'm well aware of my perimeters. I'll take care of him." And then Jacoby rolled out of the room.

Explanations were given to the guards as Jacoby tried to roll by them. Reggie was playful and entertaining and assuredly let them know he was okay and would be back in an hour.

"Sir, our orders are to stay with you at all times," one of the guards said.

"Relax," Reggie said. "I'm not going far. I only need a few minutes out of my room. Whoever is after me won't be able to get through your team."

"Sir, again, we have strict orders and I'll have to adhere to it or risk being reprimanded."

Reggie put on a big fake smile. "I appreciate your being here; I'll be right back. Just need a little air and a bit of privacy. If anyone asks why you allowed me to go against the wishes of your command, tell them General Charleston insisted and wasn't taking no for an answer. Your partner is your witness."

Neither guard acknowledged Reggie. They turned their heads and let them pass. Jacoby pushed the wheelchair by before they changed their minds.

Once in the elevator, Reggie's voice changed from jovial to serious. "We've got to move as fast as we can. I don't want to give these guys any reason to retain me...keep me from getting to that cab."

"I've got you," Jacoby said in disgust, looking straight ahead until the elevator opened. He pushed right past the guards, who'd paid them little attention.

Right on cue, a yellow cab drove up in front of the hospital. With Jacoby's assistance, Reggie got out of the wheelchair and into the cab.

"I've got to take the wheelchair back," Jacoby said.

"Leave it; we've got to go." For the first time in a long while, Reggie let out a genuine smile.

☙❧

RASHEED WATCHED AS REGGIE WAS TRANSFERRED FROM THE wheelchair into the cab. He was puzzled but stayed far enough behind so that he wouldn't be tagged. Another car pulled up behind him as he pulled to the curb, pretending to be waiting on someone. And as soon as the cab Reggie was riding in had taken its passengers and moved down the street, Rasheed followed in steady pursuit.

"I'm going to get you, bastard," Rasheed said, pointing his fingers in the direction of the cab, as if they were a gun. "Boom, boom. Today will be your last day on earth, General."

✤ 8 2 ✤

THE INCONVENIENT TRUTH

Wasting no time, Persenia busied herself with sorting out things she wanted to box up and send to storage from those things she'd keep until it was time for her to make her final stance in her marriage that had crumbled at the seams. Obtaining boxes in order to pack things away would be on her agenda for tomorrow.

It wasn't her imagination; the doorbell rang. Persenia pulled herself away from her task and headed for the front door. She wasn't expecting anyone—Jacoby certainly wouldn't have been a fool to block her doorway anytime soon—but curiosity made her move faster.

When she reached the door, and looked through the peephole, she saw an attractive cocoa-complexioned brother with a nice bushy moustache standing on her porch. He was dressed in the standard uniform worn by the Federal Express people. Again, it could've been her imagination, but it seemed that every FedEx delivery guy that ever graced her doorway was fine as hell—black, white, red, yellow (well, she hadn't seen any Asian delivery guys). She opened the door with a smile.

The tall handsome specimen smiled back as he handed Persenia the package. "Please sign here ma'am," the carrier said, indicating the place with his finger.

Persenia noticed that a ring was wrapped tightly around the ring finger on his left hand. She signed on the space indicated, gave the guy a nice smile, took the package and went inside.

Curiosity got the best of her as she stared at the addressee's name on the package. It was a medium-size box addressed to Brigadier General Reginald Charleston. Persenia quickly looked at the return address and noticed that it was from Virginia. She started to set it aside, but looked at the box again and took it to the kitchen with her.

She sat in on the kitchen table and looked at it, as if it might possess some magical powers. Persenia's brain was in overdrive, her persuasive powers of the mind willing her to open Pandora's Box. What if it contained something that she wasn't supposed to see—a classified document that was the property of the Army? Curiosity caused her to pick up the box again and stare at the return address. This wasn't Government issue; it came from a private residence.

Without giving it another thought, Persenia went to her cutlery holder and pulled out a sharp butcher knife. Immediately, she took the knife and sliced open the box where strong packaging tape was affixed to it. She ripped at the box so hard that the contents spilled out of its guts when it fell on its side.

Persenia's hands went to her mouth. Inside the box was another smaller wooden box, an envelope with both Kaleah and Reggie's name on it, and a black leather day planner with Kaleah's full name embossed in gold on the bottom. The sight of these items caused Persenia to frown and get worked up. She threw her fists in the air and blew air from her mouth.

Not waiting another moment, Persenia tore into the box, oblivious of what she might find. Tears began to flow and her breathing became erratic as she tore open the envelope that contained airline ticket stubs to Dubai. Reggie's name was on each stub as the principal.

The nerve of Reggie to suggest that they go to Dubai after he and Kaleah had already been there as a couple—not long before Kaleah had come to Washington State—the night Persenia had taken those photos of the two of them going into the hotel. Persenia wrung her hands together and cursed to high heaven.

Unable to deny herself the right to proceed, Persenia opened up the wooden box. Inside were thirty, forty, fifty or more pictures of Kaleah and Reggie taken at various venues, even in hotel rooms with little to nothing on. "I hate you, Reggie," Persenia shouted to the rafters.

Her tear-stained blouse caught hell but Persenia continued on. There was no stopping her now that her soul had been ripped apart. She browsed Kaleah's planner/diary, noting dates and times of her and Reggie's rendezvous. Some of the dates came back to Persenia, dates that Reggie claimed his military presence was needed. Maybe that was true, but he and the tramp made sure they were in the same place at the same time. It was all there, documented in black ink. If Persenia needed additional ammunition to take Reggie down, the evidence was neatly gathered in that nice FedEx package that'd been delivered.

Something caught Persenia's eye. There was a note tucked in the back of the planner that had somehow slipped beyond the edge of the last calendar page. Curious, Persenia lifted it from its hiding place, unfolded the piece of paper, and read the contents.

Persenia's eyes nearly flew from their sockets. In Kaleah's own handwriting were written the words, *ISIS...find a way to extract files from Reggie and Michael. Their lives depend on it. Deal with Rebecca—overstepping her boundaries.*

"I'll be damned." Was Kaleah funneling military secrets to ISIS? Was she responsible for Michael's death...the near attempt on Reggie's life, and even her own demise, which must've somehow backfired on her?

Persenia's hands began to tremble. She had to get a hold of Reggie right away. His own tramp of a General girlfriend had sold him down the river. But why? "That's what you get for playing with fire." Persenia laughed out loud.

Not wasting another minute, Persenia rushed to the bedroom and retrieved her cell phone. She quickly dialed Reggie's room at the hospital, and when there wasn't an answer, she dialed his cell phone; still no answer. Puzzled, she tried again; but still there wasn't an answer. She didn't want to alarm him by leaving a message; however, the only other choice was to wait until Reggie called. Given his state of being where it concerned them, he might not even bother. Persenia couldn't wait to rub this bit of information into Reggie's smug face.

❧ 83 ☙

YOU'RE GOING DOWN

Nervous energy kept Persenia moving from one room to another. She walked back into the kitchen and looked at the FedEx box that still sat on the table. As if she'd been given some sign, she quickly put everything back in the box, picked it up, and rushed to her bedroom. Once there, she scratched her head and took the box back into the kitchen and sat it in a corner on the marble countertop. Unable to make up her mind, she once again picked up the box and sat it on a shelf in the utility closet.

Just as she returned to the kitchen, the doorbell rang. Her hand flew to her mouth and then down to her chest, wondering why her doorbell was ringing a second time today. Could it be another package with another ominous message?

As if she had wings, she flew to the front door and opened it, surprised to see her bandaged husband walk in with Jacoby at his side.

"What are you doing out of the hospital? And why is he with you?"

"Hell, don't start in on me with that shit, Persenia. In fact, you can get to packing and take your raggedy ass out of here. Jacoby will always be welcomed wherever I am."

Persenia put her hands on her hips. Her eyes widened as she stared Jacoby down.

Jacoby helped Reggie sit down in one of the chairs in the living room. But he dared not look at Persenia.

"Well, I say that Jacoby isn't welcome here. I live here too and that's my final word on the subject."

"The bitch is crazy," Reggie said to Jacoby. "Put your suitcase in the spare bedroom."

"Don't move, Jacoby, unless you want me to tell your best friend what happened earlier today."

Reggie's face was full of rage. "He already told me about the argument and I'm sure you're the one who started it. You're so unhappy with yourself that you have to make others miserable."

With clenched fists, Persenia went and stood over Reggie.

"Don't do it, P. I'll leave right now," Jacoby said, waving his hands in the air.

Reggie tried to jump up from his sitting position, but Persenia lightly pushed him back into his seat. "On second thought, I want you to stay, Jacoby. I need for you to hear what I've got to say."

"Damn bitch," Reggie shouted, his face twisted in rage while staring straight ahead.

"I'm your damn bitch alright. But your dead girlfriend was a bigger bitch."

Reggie rose up in his seat and pointed his finger at Persenia. "Don't you ever say anything about Kaleah. She was more of a woman than you'll ever be."

"Yeah? Well she fooled all of us." Kaleah rushed to the kitchen and came back with the FedEx box.

"What's that?" Reggie hissed. Jacoby looked on, afraid of what was to come and not daring to open his mouth.

Persenia poured the contents on Reggie's lap but kept the piece of paper that was most incriminating.

"What the hell is this?" Reggie screamed, as he began to pour over the items in his lap.

Persenia picked up the small wooden box, took the lid off, and turned it upside down. Out flew pictures of Reggie and Kaleah.

Reggie's face went blank, as his eyes roved over the collection of pictures.

"Where did you get this?" Reggie's eyes were red and his nostrils flaring.

Without answering him, Persenia picked up the leather day planner with Kaleah's name on the front and threw it on Reggie's lap. "Don't play me dumb, Reggie." Persenia kneeled down in front of him. "The only thing you need to know is that your house of cards is about to tumble and fall. Further, the woman you called your girlfriend was using you."

"Shut up and get out of my face. You're jacking at the jaws just to hear yourself speak."

"Persenia, please don't do this," Jacoby pleaded.

Persenia let her head bounce to the side and gave Jacoby a sly smile. "Really, Jacoby? You're only a minute from getting busted yourself."

Jacoby clamped his lips, turned in the opposite direction, and sat in a vacant chair.

"What's she talking about, Jacoby?" Jacoby didn't respond. "Damn, didn't you hear me? What is this damn bitch talking about?"

"Call me a bitch one more time, and I'm going to punch you in your neck and make the wound much bigger than it is. Now, shut the hell up. I'm the one doing the talking." Persenia paused then broke out in a fake smile. She unfolded the piece of paper she held in her hand.

"I have a piece of paper in my hand that you're going to find offensive and heart wrenching. Myself, I found it entertaining. Your dear Kaleah had you and Michael penned as marked men." Persenia rustled the piece of paper in her hand and began to read the contents. "What I'm about to share with you is something that Kaleah wrote down in her own handwriting."

"You're a sick bitch, Persenia. Just because she's a better woman..."

Persenia kicked Reggie in his shin. Jacoby jumped up from his seat.

"Damn crazy woman," Reggie shouted.

"I'm leaving," Jacoby announced. "I don't need to be here for any of this."

"Sit your ass down, Jacoby," Persenia said, pointing her finger at him for emphasis. Without wasting another moment, Persenia began to read. "*ISIS...find a way to extract files from Reggie and Michael. Their lives depend on it. Deal with Rebecca—overstepping her boundaries.*"

Persenia looked up from the piece of paper.

"Let me see that," Reggie yelled. "Give me that piece of paper."

Persenia turned it around for Reggie to see although she didn't allow him to touch it. "This is evidence. You see, while you were cavorting with your girlfriend, she was using you to steal secrets for ISIS. Why she did it, is a mystery to me. I guess your Homeland Security folks will have to figure it out. But you see, fool, you meant absolutely nothing to her but a link to what she really wanted. I'm sure she hadn't planned on being a casualty herself—only two down—you and Michael. You should feel blessed to be able to sit in that chair and breathe air."

"So, this is what you've been doing while I've been in the hospital. Conjuring up ways to hurt me, but I'll have you to know, Persenia Charleston, I don't believe one damn thing you said."

"You don't have to. The proof is in the package that arrived from Kaleah's relatives today by FedEx. Don't worry; I have every intention of leaving you. I no longer want your sorry ass hand in marriage; I deserve so much better than the pitiful man sitting in front of me. But you're going down, and that star you wear so proudly on your shoulder won't be able to help you."

Jacoby jumped to his feet. "Look, I have a flight that I'm going to catch tonight. I wish you both well, and I'm sorry for all the stink that Carlitta and I caused, Persenia."

"Not so fast, my former friend. Aren't you going to tell Reggie how you came on to me this afternoon? Are you going to leave here without telling him that you grabbed me and tried your best to tongue-kiss me before I slapped you in the face? No honor among men. Trifling asses; that's what you both are."

Calm as a cucumber, Reggie turned in his seat and looked at Jacoby. "Is it true?"

Jacoby turned his head away, lifted his suitcase from the floor and proceeded to the door. "Yes, it's true."

"You're going to burn in hell!" Reggie shouted. "You're going to burn in hell you sorry mother..."

Jacoby opened the door. *Pop, pop, pop.* And Jacoby fell to the floor.

✻ 84 ✻

TWO DOWN

Blood gushed from Jacoby's body like a geyser.

"Oh, hell to the no," Reggie said, his voice ten decibels higher than a moment ago. "What in the hell is going on?"

Persenia stood transfixed in the foyer with her hands crossed over her breasts. And out of nowhere came a blood-curdling scream that lasted for almost a minute. And when she stopped, she dropped her hands to her sides and then back up to her breasts, holding her chest while trying to catch her breath. Otherwise, her body wouldn't move no matter how much she willed it to do so.

And then there were the sounds of additional gunfire and the screeching of a car as it moved away from the curb in a hurry. Was the gunman still outside or had he or she driven away in the vehicle that made the loud noise?

Persenia was afraid to go outside. Not knowing what else to do, she peeked through the curtains of a nearby window and saw the body of a man lying on the sidewalk with a gun in his hand.

"Call the ambulance," Reggie shouted. "What are you waiting on? Call the ambulance, now."

"Yeah, yeah," she said, scooting back from the window and halfway running to her room to get her cell phone, forgetting that there was a land line only a few feet from where Reggie sat. She dialed 911.

"Nine-one-one, what's your emergency?"

"Two down. Two bodies on the ground, one was shot."

"Are they both alive?" the 911 dispatcher asked.

"I have no idea. Please hurry. My address is..."

"Yes, we have it. We've been called to this number before. But, ma'am..."

"Please hurry. One of the wounded is losing a lot of blood and we have to save him."

"Stay on the line. I'm dispatching someone to your residence as we speak."

"Just hurry."

⊗⊗⊗

IT SEEMED AS IF HOURS HAD PASSED BEFORE THE PARAMEDICS arrived. There was a lot of activity upon the arrival of the paramedics and the police—to Persenia, it seemed like utter chaos.

The paramedics checked Jacoby's wrist and neck for a pulse. And when Persenia saw the look on one the paramedic's face, she knew her call to save Jacoby's life was in vain. And they gently placed a white sheet over his body and asked that no one approach it until after the police and forensics had come in and completed their work.

Reggie wept.

Persenia looked out of the living room window. It was apparent that the man who was lying prone on the sidewalk in front of their house had met with the same fate. A sheet covered the body. Who was he...or she? Had they come to finish the task that Kaleah alluded to?

Persenia turned around when she heard her name.

"I'm sorry," Reggie said. "I'm sorry; I need you."

"We've got to call, Carlitta."

❦ 85 ❦

BEHIND EVERY DARK CLOUD IS A SILVER LINING

Jacoby's remains were flown to California. The hardest task of all was calling Carlitta to tell her that her husband had been killed by a bullet probably marked for Reggie. Both Reggie and Persenia flew home to be with Carlitta.

There were no words that would bring Jacoby back. You live by the sword; you die by the sword, Persenia had heard her mother say on many occasions. Although, Jacoby may have taken the bullet for her husband, Persenia couldn't shake the thought that maybe Jacoby got what he deserved.

The service for Jacoby was a somber affair, although the sun and heat outside was prime beach weather and begged for fun. Reggie was dressed in his formal military attire, while Persenia stood tall in a wide-brimmed, lacy, black hat; a sleeveless black Channel dress that hit right at the knees; and a pair of four-inch Louboutin heels, with its red soles the only color in her wardrobe. Persenia looked longingly at the doting wife Jacoby left behind, all dressed in black, and her three young children, as they stood at the gravesite all dressed in their Sunday best— lavender taffeta dresses, white Mary Janes, and white lacy socks with lavender embroidery around the top. She and Carlitta had an opportunity to get it right between each other, but their friendship would never be the same. Absent from the funeral was Carlitta's cousin, Kimiko, and Remy.

Persenia was glad that she was able to visit with her family. It helped remove her from the awkwardness she found herself and Carlitta in. Maybe one day, they'd be able to overcome the elephant that clouded their friendship, although Carlitta had another enormous thing to blame she and Reggie for—the death of Jacoby.

"I'm going back to D. C. tomorrow," Reggie announced, looking forlorn. "Homeland Security was able to access Kaleah's accounts and found that she had deposited several hundred thousand of dollars into it in recent months. I've been a fool."

"Well, it's hard to say what I'm feeling at this moment, but right now, I don't want to rehash sour memories of our marriage with this being such a sad day."

"I agree."

Persenia moved closer to Reggie and brushed the collar on his Class A uniform. "I want you to move forward with your life; I want to move forward with my life. Most of all, I want you to be happy."

The preacher began to administer the last rites over Jacoby's casket before releasing it into the ground. All was quiet.

When the minister finished, family and friends began to toss white rose petals onto the casket. Reggie turned to Persenia. "I want you to come home with me, P." Silence and tears began to flow from Reggie's eyes. He wiped the tears, although his face was puckered up from being so overcome. When he got a hold of himself, he continued. "I've not been a good husband, P, but I want to make it right. We can fix this thing...our marriage. It's not over."

"The fat lady has sung, Reggie. It's much too late for us to try again. I'm through. You're feeling some kind of way now. Before long, it'll be someone else, and I'll have to sit on the sidelines and watch as my husband continues to disrespect me. But no, it's not going to happen again."

Reggie gently grabbed Persenia's arms. "What about the time we've invested in this marriage? Doesn't it count for something?"

"It's been like a no-interest baring account, Reggie. You didn't put anything into the marriage for the past five, six or seven years. It hasn't yielded any fruit, only heartache. I want to live; I want to have a life. I'm going to stay in Oakland with my family for a week or so and hopefully make total amends with Carlitta, and then I'll decide what my next move will be."

As an afterthought, Persenia turned to Reggie and sighed. "Carlitta says we're alright, but I know better. Jacoby wouldn't have been in D.C. if it weren't for us."

Reggie dropped his head and then turned toward the car that some of his family members were waiting for them in. "Please, Persenia, not now. I need you."

"You've never needed me, Reggie. I can't do it anymore. I'm going to be with Carlitta...and...and, I'm going to go through with the divorce."

Reggie stared at Persenia, then turned and walked away. Persenia watched as he got into the car and was driven away. A tear streamed down her face.

FOLLOWED BY HER GIRLS, CARLITTA MOVED TO WHERE PERSENIA now stood. Carlitta seemed to have a hard time expressing herself. "Thank you for coming, P. I appreciate you being here. Maybe, just maybe if I hadn't gotten so angry, I wouldn't be burying my husband today."

"It's not your fault, sweetie. It was a case of being in the wrong place at the wrong time. If Reggie had stayed in the hospital, the outcome might have been different. I..."

Carlitta threw her hand up. "Let's take it one day at a time. I'm not mad at you; I've come to terms as to why you didn't tell me about Jacoby and Kimiko. But today isn't the day I want to discuss it. Maybe later when my nerves have settled and I can make further sense of all that's happened. My life is about to change, P. I won't have a husband to ride shotgun when I need someone else to be with the kids. The principal breadwinner in my home won't be making deposits at the bank, paying private school tuition or even my college expenses. No more expensive trips and who knows, I may have to move out of my lavish house with all of its expensive trappings. But that doesn't matter to me. The warm body that I used to cuddle up to, whether good or bad, has been lost to me forever. I wish I could lean on your shoulder, but not now. We'll talk later."

Persenia reached over and patted Carlitta on the shoulder. "I'm here for you whenever you need me."

"Thanks friend." Carlitta turned away and grabbed the second youngest by the hand. "Let's go, babies. We've got to leave your daddy and go home."

Watching in silence, Persenia looked on as Carlitta and her family plopped into the waiting limousines and drove off.

It was at that moment that Persenia realized she didn't have a ride. She'd let Reggie go with every intention of catching a ride with Carlitta. Frustrated she walked in her four-inch heels to the edge of the cemetery and looked through the bars of the gate that held the dead inside. She looked toward heaven and sighed.

As she reached inside her purse to get her cell phone, it rang. Surprise sprang into her eyes.

"Hey," she said. "I was expecting you to come to the funeral but was disappointed when I didn't see you."

"For whatever reason, I thought it best for me not to come—partly because of you. I couldn't be sure how I'd react to seeing you with Reggie. I couldn't afford to take that chance."

"Well, it's good to hear your voice. Where are you?"

"I'm at a hotel in town."

"You're in town, Remy?" Excitement rose in Persenia's voice.

"Yes. But where is Reggie?"

"Gone. He's flying out to D. C. tomorrow. I told him we were through."

"Persenia, don't tease me. Do you mean it?"

"Remy, I couldn't be more certain about how I feel. I'm probably jumping out of the frying pan and into the fire, but I've got to take my chances."

"I hope you mean that, although, I'm not going to let you get burned."

"I mean it with every ounce of my being."

"I'm staying at the Courtyard at the San Jose Airport."

Persenia began to giggle. "Okay. But first, I'm going to run home after I call my brother to pick me. Then I'm going to take his car and drive back to San Jose so we won't be stranded."

Remy and Persenia laughed. "Promise you won't be long."

"Not a minute longer than necessary."

❧ 86 ❧

A NEW PAGE... A NEW CHAPTER

As soon as Persenia reached her mother's house, she stripped out of her mourning clothes, jumped in the shower, sprayed herself generously with her favorite cologne, and adorned her body in more appropriate clothing for her meet up with Remy. Excitement oozed from every pore on her body, as the anticipation of seeing him again made her temperature rise. She blew fake smoke from her lips, exhaled, and went into the bathroom to apply a dab of lipstick to show off one of her sexy assets.

Before leaving the room, she put on a lightweight trench coat and took another look at herself in the mirror. Satisfied, she headed for the door.

"Persenia?" her mother called, as she walked into the living room, wiping her hands on a dish towel.

"Yes, Mama?"

Even at age seventy, Persenia's mother looked like a mature, young woman about to hit the half-century mark. Her curly, black hair streaked with large strands of silver was pinned on top of her head, and she wore a red and white apron that tied around the waist that looped over her head. "Where are you going all bundled up in that coat? You've been outside so you're aware that you don't need it."

"Yes, Mama, I'm quite aware of the temperature. But it'll probably be cold when I return home. The Bay Area still gets cold at night, surrounded by all this water."

"Well, okay. Will you be back in time for dinner? I'm roasting some chicken and making smothered potatoes the way you and your brothers like them."

"I may be late, but save me a plate. Tell Woody and Alvin I'll spend time with them later."

"Alright, baby. You be safe out there in those streets. How are Carlitta and the children holding up?"

"As well as can be expected."

"Give them a hug for me. Tell her I'm sorry that I wasn't able to go to Jacoby's services. I do need to give her mother a call."

Persenia hesitated and then thought better of it. "I'll do that, Mama." But it wasn't going to be this evening that she'd give her the message.

Nearly skipping to the car, Persenia set it in motion. She'd already set up her phone's navigator to take her the fastest route to her man. And in less than forty-five minutes she was pulling up into the parking lot of the hotel.

Persenia sat outside and dialed Remy's number. He answered on the first ring...almost as if he'd been sitting by the phone waiting on the call.

"I'm downstairs," she purred.

"Room two thirty-nine—one king bed, sofa bed, with a courtyard view."

Persenia laughed. "I'm not sleeping on the sofa bed."

"Neither am I." It was Remy's turn to laugh.

"Come on in."

Persenia had gathered the few things she could get into her large Prada tote. She had no plans to return to mama's house that evening, especially if the loving was going to be as good as she'd imagined. Not wanting to waste another minute and with a smile on her face, she headed inside to her man—the new page, the new chapter in her life.

Softly, she knocked on the door. A broad grin went from east to west across her face. When the door opened, Persenia's heart began to palpitate faster than Little Richard's fingers streaking across the piano keys, playing a fast rendition of "Tuttu Frutti." There he stood in all of his glory—the bare-chested, muscular, cocoa-brown brother, with the short, curly black hair she remembered from her first meeting. She sniffed. His body was bathed in a tropical oil that smelled like coconut with a mango mix. She sniffed again.

Remy raised his index finger and curled it up toward Persenia. "Why are you standing out there in the hallway?"

With the smile still wrapped around her face, Persenia slung her hips from side to side, her shoulder-length hair swinging with it, and slid into the room. Still wrapped in her trench coat, she hunched her shoulders and pulled back on it with her fingers. The coat dropped to the floor and underneath, Persenia was draped in a long-sleeved white shirt that came to the middle of her thighs and buttoned only at the top. Underneath the shirt, Persenia wore a sheer pair of red thongs that accentuated the only other thing she had on her body—a pair of red, four-inch high-heeled shoes.

Remy's lip dropped to the floor. There wasn't too much left to the imagination but he didn't care. Her body he craved, but the rest of her —Persenia's intellect, smile, compassion, and free heart—he wanted to keep safe for a lifetime.

"Hmmm, I'm going to hurt myself this evening," Remy said, making no apologies for what he was about to do.

Unbuttoning her shirt, Persenia slipped seductively out of it and let it fall to the floor. Remy watched her with baited breath, letting his eyes roam up and down her body. She went to him and sucked his lips like a vacuum cleaner. Remy pulled and held Persenia close; and the fire between them became combustible fuel.

Their bodies were like hot, molten lava—so entwined with each other, it appeared they were one. Their lips hummed a tune only they understood, and the constant twisting and turning of their bodies said they were in full exploration mode. Remy caressed the full length of Persenia's flesh, teasing and sucking along the way until the foreplay was almost too much to endure. And she stroked the embers of his desire, giving all of her loving to the man she adored.

And when their passion had escalated to the point of no return, Remy rode his golden chariot to the edge of heaven and back. Wrapped in each other's arms, Remy and Persenia stayed in the clouds —the clouds of lust, love, and a new beginning. And the heavens burst opened as the lovers filled the room with loud rants of pleasure.

He kissed her nose. "You were perfect in every way," Remy said. "Making love to you every night..."

"Every night?" Persenia laughed softly. "I'm game; I'm in. I've been waiting for my knight in shining armor to come and rescue me from the evil castle."

"You don't need Reggie. I've got everything you'll ever need. As soon as you're divorced, we're going to get married."

"You mean I won't get to experience what it'd be like to be a single lady?"

Remy kissed her nose again and then pulled her to him. Moving down to her lips, he kissed them, lightly at first. Then he parted them and began to assault her lips like a savage beast. They both committed to the frenzy they found themselves in and let their bodies do the verbalizing.

And when they'd both been satisfied, they once again fell onto their backs and tried to catch their breaths.

"This is a new page and a new chapter in my life," Persenia said looking up at the ceiling. And then she turned to him. "I love you so much, Remy. I didn't believe that this day would ever come for me. And to think Carlitta buried Jacoby today; he was the one who'd innocently brought you into my life."

"It was an inconvenient moment for you, but the truth is, it was our destiny."

"You're right, Remy. And I'm so thankful that in all that was wrong that day, we found each other. I hate that I've got to go home and face Reggie. He probably has my things boxed up already." Persenia and Remy laughed.

"Besides after what he's been through, there's still the matter of his assassination attempt and all that ISIS stuff he's got to deal with."

"Reggie's a big boy, at least that's what he told me on a daily basis. He's part of the big brass thinking machine. The man can take care of himself. The military and the feds will handle the ISIS situation and he'd only be gloomy until the next female THOT throws her red, white, and blue panties at him; he can't help it. If he'd taken better care of me, I'd still be with him. But he'll find out soon enough that I'm the one who had his back all along."

Remy looked thoughtfully at Persenia. "I hope you don't return home and Reggie persuades you to stay with him. He's lonely now and thinks he's lost his best friend."

"Oh, no, there's no way in hell that will ever happen. I'm putting my life in order so I can get back to my *man*."

Remy reached over and hugged Persenia. "I love you, P and I'm going to do everything within my power to make sure that you'll always be happy."

Tears sprang from out of nowhere. "I'm ready, baby. I'm ready to start over again."

❧ 87 ☙

TWO DOWN

Reggie sifted through paperwork that had been strewn across his desk. Then he picked up the contents of the box that Kaleah's family had sent that contained the pictures of Kaleah and him together and her diary that incriminated him in so many ways. But he couldn't find the letter that Persenia had waved in his face with Kaleah's handwritten words of betrayal written on it.

Picking up the FedEx box, Reggie threw it across the room. "Bitch. You sneaking, conniving bitch. I sold my soul to you."

Not a soul answered back. The house was quiet, almost too quiet for Reggie's liking. He paced back and forth in his office until he finally dropped into the leather chair that sat in front of his laptop.

Resting his head on the palm of his hand, his mind wandered to all the times he and Kaleah had been together—trips across the continent, across the Continental United States meeting at various resorts, hotel rooms, restaurants and other secret rendezvous points, confessing their love for one another. But it was all a lie; she was doing this for ISIS. "I hate you bitch," his voice rang out in the quiet.

He'd lost Persenia for sure. Although, Kaleah wasn't the first woman he'd been with during his eighteen…nineteen years of marriage to his wife, he'd always been in love with Persenia—that is until Kaleah came along. Kaleah may have been high up in the military ranks, but she was a whore in bed and he loved her generosity when she gave all of herself to him. And her intellectual mind was above the stars. Reggie had never seen such a quick, calculating, decisive mind when it came to problem solving or providing input that would put Homeland Security way above the mark, or so he thought. But Homeland Security couldn't save her; her ISIS affiliates used her brain against her.

Now, he'd come to a crossroad in his life. Persenia wanted out, and he was going to give it to her. He'd be the first to admit that she'd suffered severely with all of his wrong doings and she deserved better. But in his heart, he really didn't want her to go. Even with almost twenty years gone by, she still looked like that varsity cheerleader who stepped onto the field at Cal Berkeley and nearly knocked him off his feet. Those pretty brown legs were to die for. Reggie wandered if she would get up with the guy that Jacoby introduced her to.

Sighing, he looked up when the telephone rang. It was the Pentagon.

"General Charleston here."

"Reggie, this is Wallace Elston. I've got some news for you."

"Hey, Wallace, I need some good news about now."

"The Feds made a major find today. They found the control center of the homemade ISIS stronghold, operating right here in the area. And you'd never guess who had their tentacles deep in this organization."

"Major General Kaleah Neal."

There was a moment of silence. "How in the hell did you know?"

Reggie held the phone tight in his hand. His mind roamed the corridors of his brain as he recalled the moments he and Kaleah shared. "An unlucky guess. I was blindsided like everyone else. I didn't have a clue."

"It seems that quite a few people knew that you were romantically linked to her."

Reggie remained quiet longer than he'd intended. "It wasn't hard to figure out I guess," he finally said.

"Well, the Pentagon...the Joint Chiefs are none too happy about your liaison with her. The military tribunal and the FBI are going to be conducting a full investigation into the matter. Reggie, I hope you're listening to me. This could be detrimental to your military career. You have a long, upstanding service that could be wiped away with this investigation. Do you have anything you'd like to say on your behalf that will at least help me lend you support?"

"I can't believe I've been such a fool. Nothing she said or did gave me any indication that she was in bed with the enemy, Wallace. Fortunately for me, we were in the same circles, and she knew as much as I did, if not more. The only thing I can conclude is I was lucky; there was supposed to be two down—Michael Forbes and myself. I'm sure she hadn't any inkling that she'd been tagged too."

"This is far from over, and the Feds are looking at other streams that may be attached to this one. They're still trying to determine the group's true motive for targeting the Pentagon. Their arsenal stockpile was massive and there were at least eight or nine operatives. Their goal, for sure, was to do real damage to the military and the country. The guy that was killed in front of your house was Rebecca's cousin. We believe that Rebecca and Kaleah were probably in cahoots."

"I never discussed business outside of the office. The only thing they got from me were my files."

Wallace sighed. "I hope for your sake, Reggie, that you're telling the truth. The weeks ahead aren't going to be easy. Well get some rest and try and take it easy."

"Okay." Reggie ended the call, resignedly, put the phone down and picked it up again. Without hesitation he hit the icon to begin dialing Persenia. One ring; he was hopeful. Two rings; he wasn't giving up. By the fifth ring he hung up without leaving a message. He needed her and wanted his wife to come home.

Made in the USA
Columbia, SC
10 July 2018